# BRASH ENDEAVOR
## A STAN TURNER MYSTERY

# BRASH ENDEAVOR

## a Stan Turner Mystery

## WILLIAM MANCHEE

Top Publications, Ltd. Co.
Dallas, Texas

# BRASH ENDEAVOR

A Top Publications Paperback

SECOND PRINTING

*TO MY MOTHER*
*WILMA MARY MANCHEE*

# Acknowledgments

For over thirty years I tossed around in my mind a couple of ideas for a book. It was a busy time building a law practice and raising four children so nothing ever became of my ideas. But when the kids grew up and left home, it became more and more difficult to come up with excuses not to write. Finally, one night after being inspired by a viewing of the movie, *The Shawshank Redemption*, I sat down in front of the computer and began *Twice Tempted*. I didn't tell anyone what I was doing for fear of having witnesses to my failure. Midway through the book I realized I didn't know what I was doing so I started reading every book on fiction writing I could get my hands on. I learned enough to finish the book, although it was only after ten or twelve revisions that it was finally published. What was most enjoyable about this experience was seeing the complete and utter shock of my wife, family and friends when I advised them I had written a novel.

After I completed each of my novels, I would make a dozen or so copies and pass them around to my family and friends. I want to thank my wife, Janet, and children, Jim, Jeff, Michael and Maryanna, for suffering through those awful first drafts and offering me so much encouragement and support. I want to thank my mother, Wilma Manchee, and my mother-in-law, Lee Mello, for their relentless enthusiasm for my work. Then there is my sister-in-law, Patricia Mello, who bought and sold more of my first two books than Barnes and Noble.

To my staff and friends outside the family, who so graciously read my works, I am most grateful. The constant flow of positive comments helped build my confidence and inspired me to improve myself as a writer. I particularly want to thank George Lodge who believed in me from the start and spent countless hours trying to help me find a publisher, as well as Bob Leraas, my unofficial editor, who read everything I wrote and gave me excellent feedback. Then there were those on my staff who were particularly supportive such as Corina Petersen, Jennifer Ouellet, Marilyn Altamira, Tom Hogle and David Santillan. There were many others, too numerous to name, who helped keep me on course, and for all of them I am most grateful.

Finally, I want to thank Mary Klaasen for sharing with me her wealth of knowledge about the publishing business and for being such a good friend. And I want to express my thanks to my fellow writers, Paris Afton Bonds, Laura Castoro and Sylvia Dunnavant, for the inspiration they provided me and for all their sound advice about getting a literary career off the ground.

# BRASH ENDEAVOR
## A Stan Turner Mystery

# PROLOGUE

**September 1979**

THE LIGHT OF FIRST dawn inundated our bedroom, waking me from a troubled slumber. In all the turmoil of the previous evening I had neglected to set the alarm. For some strange reason, neither the boys nor the baby had yet awakened. They must have sensed Rebekah's need to sleep. I looked at the digital display and saw it was 8:15, so I rolled out of bed and started doing some stretching exercises. From the other room I heard Reggie talking to his younger brothers, Peter and Mark. After a minute, they must've heard me moving around as they came running into our bedroom.

"Good morning, Daddy," Reggie said.

"Hi, bums. You guys sure slept late. . . . You must be hungry?"

"Uh huh," Peter replied.

Rebekah sat up and looked at us curiously. "What time is it?"

"Eight-twenty."

"Oh jeez, it's so late, why did you let me sleep so long? The kids must be starving."

"Why don't you just stay in bed, I'll fix breakfast. Maybe I'll even give you breakfast in bed. How would you like that?"

"Oh no, Stan, you've got to go to work."

"Somehow, I don't think I'll be meeting with Bird and Tomlinson this morning. Not after Sheila died."

Rebekah looked at me and said, "Oh my God. That wasn't a dream, was it?"

"No, honey. I'm afraid it wasn't."

Rebekah fell back onto the bed, put her hands over her face and began to cry. I went over to her, sat on the bed next to her and took her limp hand in mine.

"Why don't you kids go play?" I said. "Mom's not feeling so good. I'll call you when breakfast is ready."

"What's wrong?" Reggie said.

"Nothing, just take your brothers and go play!"

"Okay, okay," he said, and ran off with Peter and Mark close behind.

"Maybe you should get up. It's probably not a good idea for you to lie around worrying about what happened last night. Come on, I'll help you get dressed."

Getting no response, I took her hand and gently pulled her to her feet. I looked into her dispirited eyes and wondered if she'd ever recover from the horror of the previous night. After pulling off her nightgown, I managed to get some shorts and a T-shirt on her. Then I brought her into the kitchen and made her and the kids breakfast. After Rebekah had consumed a couple of cups of coffee, she seemed more alert.

"You look like you're feeling better, honey," I said.

"I'm fine, don't worry about me," she said, trying to force a smile.

"I'll take Reggie and Mark to school. I don't think you should drive today."

"That's okay, I can take them."

"No, you stay home. You'll have your hands full with Peter and Marcia."

As I yelled for Reggie and Mark to get ready for school, the doorbell rang. I looked at Rebekah and said, "Who could that be?"

I went to the door, opened it and there stood two uniformed policemen and a man in a suit.

"Stan Turner?" the man in the suit asked.

"Yes."

"I'm Detective Small of the Dallas Police Department. Is your wife home?"

"Yes. What's going on?"

"We'll need to see her now please," Detective Small said.

"What do you want with her?"

"We have a warrant for her arrest."

"What? You can't be serious."

"We're quite serious. Now step aside and let us do our job."

The two uniformed officers pushed their way into the house, slamming me into the doorjamb. They immediately started searching the house for Rebekah. Reggie and Mark stared in shock as they ran by. One of the policemen, having spotted Rebekah sitting at the kitchen table, ran over to her, yanked her up and pushed her up against the wall. She winced in pain as he cuffed her and then jerked her around to face Detective Small who had just entered the kitchen.

"Mrs. Turner, you're under arrest for the murder of Sheila Logan. We're going to have to take you downtown."

"But I didn't kill her! I was downstairs in the ER when it happened. . . . Stan, don't let them do this!"

Anger swelled within me as I watched the officer manhandle Rebekah. "You can't treat her like that!" I said, rushing over to defend her. The other officer drew his gun and pointed it at my head.

Rebekah screamed, "Don't shoot him!"

Detective Small glared at the officer and yelled, "Put that gun away!" He then turned to me and said, "Mr. Turner, you're an attorney, you know you can't obstruct this arrest. Now back off!"

"Do what he says, Stan," Rebekah said.

By this time Marcia had been awakened by the ruckus and was wailing from her crib in the next room. Mark and Peter were standing up against the wall in shock, tears streaming from their eyes. I went over to them and held them as we watched Rebekah being taken away. As they were escorting Rebekah to the squad car, Reggie suddenly darted after them screaming, "You can't take my mommy! Leave her alone. Leave my mommy alone."

One of the officers intercepted Reggie and restrained him until I got there to get him. I pulled him back to the house, yelling and kicking. Then I rushed into the nursery to get Marcia who had been screaming so loud that she was starting to turn blue. I picked her up, held her tightly and then gazed out the window. Tears swelled in my eyes as I watched the squad car disappear around the corner. Why hadn't I listened to Father Henry?

# HANGING OUT THE SHINGLE

**Six Months Earlier**

WHAT IS IT THAT makes a seemingly rational man set out on a perilous journey knowing full well that the odds of success are quite remote and the consequences of failure are likely to be devastating? Is it pride, stubbornness, a yearning for adventure or just a reckless disregard of reality?

Not being a psychologist, I wouldn't presume to suggest why my personality developed the way it did, nor does it matter, but by age fourteen, I had a fixation on becoming an attorney, and any casual observer at the time could've easily predicted that my legal career would be anything but conventional. It had been six long, trying years since I first started law school at the University of San Diego. Many times I had almost given up on ever making it through. It seemed like every obstacle imaginable had been cast before me, and I couldn't possibly overcome them all. But somehow, by the grace of God, I had made it and actually taken the bar exam just two months earlier.

Assuming I passed the bar, which by no stretch of the imagination was a sure thing, the question became, what do I do now? While I was waiting for the results of my bar exam, I took a job with the Helms Insurance Agency doing estate planning.

I had learned a lot about estate planning while peddling insurance to earn my way through law school, so it was an easy transition to my new position. Unfortunately, several weeks after joining the firm, I found out it was in a precarious financial condition and likely wouldn't make it to summer. I broke the news to Rebekah one night at dinner.

"Put Marcia in the high chair, would you honey?" Rebekah said.

"Sure," I said, and then lifted Marcia up and dropped her into the high chair.

"Use your fork, Peter," I said.

"Hey Dad, will you play soccer with us after dinner?" Mark asked.

"Sure, for a little while."

"What happened today at work?" Rebekah asked.

"You don't want to know," I said.

"What's wrong?"

"I was looking for the production reports for the agency today. I wanted to figure out what commissions I was going to get next month. Well, while digging through the files, I ran across the agency contracts with all our insurance underwriters."

"Yeah."

"Well, I started to read one of them, and discovered that Mr. Helms had talked the insurance company into advancing commissions on projected sales for the upcoming year."

"Really?"

"Uh huh, so I started comparing the projected sales against actual sales, and we're not even close to meeting projections."

"So what does that mean?"

"It means by summer Mr. Helms will owe his insurance carriers nearly a quarter of a million dollars. The bottom line is Mr. Helms will be out of business and I'll be out of a job."

"Can't anything be done?"

"It's too late. Even if the next two months were spectacular, by the time you submit all the applications, go through underwriting and place all of the policies, it'll be fall."

"Dad are you ready to play soccer?" Mark asked.

"Not yet, hotshot. I haven't finished my supper yet and I'm trying to talk to your mother. Go outside with Reggie and start kicking the ball around. I'll be there in a minute."

"What're you going to do?" Rebekah said.

"I don't know. I've been kind of thinking about starting my own practice."

"With what money? If you hadn't noticed, we're broke."

"Well, I'd have to start out slowly and keep my overhead low."

"We've got to have a regular income. What if you don't get any clients?"

"I've talked to some of the guys at Cosmopolitan Life and they say they'll send me lots of business."

"What kind of clients would they send you?"

"Wills, trusts and corporation work mostly. They want to send their clients to an attorney who won't torpedo their insurance sales."

"That's nice, but do think you could get enough business for us to survive?"

"I don't know, I think so. I'll have to borrow some money to set up an office."

"How much will you need?"

"I was thinking fifteen to twenty thousand."

"Who would loan you that kind of money?"

"The bank I suppose. Next week I think I'm going to go by our bank and see if they'll lend me the money."

"I don't know honey, it seems pretty risky."

"Well, I have a gut feeling it'll work out okay, and I'm kind of excited about starting my own law practice."

"I guess I could work at the hospital for a few months until you got things going. That would bring us in a hundred and fifty dollars a week."

"Oh, I hate for you to have to do that, babe."

"I guess I don't have much choice," Rebekah replied.

"Well, you don't have to do it, we'll manage."

"No, it'll make it a lot easier for you to get started, so I don't mind for a few months," Rebekah said.

The following Monday I went to Canyon Valley National Bank to see about a loan. I had never borrowed money before, except student loans, so I wasn't sure what to expect. I didn't know anybody at the bank, so I went up to the new accounts desk and asked whom I should talk to about a loan. I was directed to a gray-haired loan officer named Martin Campbell.

"Mr. Campbell, hi, I'm Stan Turner."

Mr. Campbell peered up at me through his glasses without smiling. "Have a seat, I'll be with you in a minute," he replied, and then returned to the paperwork in front of him.

"Okay," I said, and sat down in one of the two leather side chairs in front of his desk. When he was done he put the papers in a folder and dropped the folder in his out box. Then he sat back in his chair and looked me in the eye.

"So, what can I do for you?" he said.

"I'd like to talk to you about a loan."

"A loan. Sure, what kind of loan do you need?

"Well, I just graduated from law school and I want to start my own practice."

"Your own law practice? Really?" Campbell said.

"Yeah, it's something I've always wanted to do."

"That seems like a rather brash endeavor, don't you think?"

"What do you mean?" I asked.

"Starting a law practice wouldn't be easy. It would require substantial capitalization. Do you have any clients lined up yet?"

"No, but I've got friends who'll send me business."

"Friends. . . . Right, we all have friends, and friends will tell you what you want to hear, but will they deliver on their promises?" Campbell asked. "Not that they wouldn't want to, but how many opportunities are they going to realistically have to send you business?"

"They're mainly insurance salesmen, so probably quite often."

"I hope you're right," Campbell said, as he reached into his drawer and pulled out a loan application. "Okay, before I get started I need to ask you one question."

"What's that?"

"Do you have any collateral?"

"Collateral?"

"Yeah, . . . you know, like stocks, bonds or real estate?"

"No, like I said, I just graduated from law school, I haven't accumulated any assets yet."

"Well, I'm sorry but we don't give unsecured loans."

"But I'm a lawyer. I'll pay it back."

"Lawyers are notoriously bad businessmen."

"Is that right?"

"Yes, that's a fairly well-known fact."

"You don't even want me to fill out an application?"

"No, without collateral the only thing we could give you would be a Gold American Express Card with a $2,000 line of credit?"

"I'm supposed to start a law practice with $2,000?"

"Well, that's the best we can do. Why don't you go work for a law firm for a while?"

"Oh, I've heard about that, working eighty hours a week for peanuts and having to kiss everyone's ass, hoping they'll make you a partner. No thanks."

"Okay then, go get one of those fat juicy government jobs where they pay you lots of money to sit around and occupy desk space," he said.

"All the good government jobs are in Washington, D.C. I want to stay here in Dallas. I applied for the DEA and they would've hired me, but my wife failed her interview."

"Your wife failed *her* interview?"

"Uh huh, they asked her what she would do if I was doing undercover work and came home with lipstick on my collar and smelling like perfume. She said she'd divorce me."

"Then get a job with a major corporation, being an attorney will give you a great advantage," Mr. Campbell persisted.

"I didn't go to law school to become a businessman. I want to practice law, and one way or another I'm going to do just that."

"Well, I'm afraid I can't help you."

"Fine!" I said, and rose to my feet. "Thanks anyway."

I left the bank upset and discouraged by the cold shoulder that had been thrust before me. To think of all the time, effort and agony I had put into becoming an attorney and all it got me was a $2,000 line of credit. It occurred to me that maybe other banks might have a different attitude, so I visited several others. Unfortunately, the reaction at each bank was pretty much the same—no collateral, no loan.

Although I was disappointed at not being able to get a loan, I was not deterred from my resolve to start my own practice. Call it stubbornness, pride or stupidity, but whenever someone told me I couldn't or shouldn't do something, it just intensified my desire to do it. That night at Mark's soccer game I broke the bad news to Rebekah. I explained the banks' policy about collateral and their offer to give us a Gold American Express card. She didn't seem upset.

The thought of starting my own law practice was dropped for a few weeks. But when Helms announced the firm was shutting down and gave us all two weeks notice, the issue again surfaced. We had just put the kids to bed and were sitting down to watch TV when I gave Rebekah the news.

"Mr. Helms called it quits today," I said.

Rebekah's faced dropped. "Oh no, already?"

"He gave us two weeks notice."

"Oh, crap, I thought we'd have another couple of months."

"He tried to get another advance from one of the underwriters, but they turned him down."

"Are you going to start looking for another job?"

"No, I think I'm going to take the plunge."

"You mean start practicing law by yourself?"

"Yeah, I really want to have my own law practice."

"Stan, come on, you don't have any clients."

"I really think the guys will send me quite a bit of business, and I'm already getting requests from friends and acquaintances for wills and stuff."

"What happens if you don't get enough business?"

"Then I'll go look for another job."

"I don't know."

"I was looking in the newspaper today and I found an ad for a furnished office with Burton Realty in the North Dallas Bank Building," I said. "You know, those towers near the LBJ Freeway and Preston Road. It would be perfect, and he only wants a hundred and fifty dollars per month."

"That couldn't be much of an office."

"Well, I only need a desk and a typewriter to get started. Anyway, when clients come in they'll think the whole office is mine."

"But you won't have a secretary."

"Well, it's a good thing I took typing in high school. Anyway, I'll just stay there six months or so, and then I'll get a real office with a live secretary."

"I guess we can go take a look at it."

"Good, get your mom to baby-sit tomorrow at lunch. I'll come pick you up and we'll go check it out."

"Okay, if you promise to feed me."

"We might arrange that."

The following day we visited the North Dallas Bank Building and met General Horace Burton. He was a retired army general who sold commercial real estate as a second career. He greeted us when we walked into his office.

"We've come about your ad for office space."

"Oh yes, it's over here."

General Burton pointed to a small room off to our right that appeared to be about eight by ten feet. It was furnished with a desk, a chair, a typing stand, typewriter and a few prints on the walls. Despite its small size it looked pretty impressive.

"What kind of work do you do?" General Burton asked.

"I'm a lawyer. I just graduated from law school and wanted to start up a law practice."

"A lawyer, huh? I may need your services."

"Oh really?"

"Yeah, I just got sued by some bastard who's trying to get out of paying a commission he owes me."

"You're kidding?" I said.

"Anyway, I don't like the way my attorney is handling it. I may want to switch," the general said.

"Well, I'd be happy to take a look at your case."

"Good, my patience is running out with this clown."

I smiled and held up the ad in front of the general. "Your ad said it was a hundred and fifty dollars a month, is that right?"

"Yes, that's including all the furniture. You'll have to get your own phone line though."

"No problem," I said. "What do you think, honey?"

"It's beautiful Stan," Rebekah replied.

"Then we'll take it."

Rebekah frowned. "I thought we were just looking?"

"I know, but we're not going to find anything better than this," I said.

Rebekah shook her head and frowned at me. I gave her an excited smile and said, "We'll take it."

"Great, it'll be good to have an attorney close at hand. What kind of law do you practice anyway?" the general asked.

"I don't know yet . . . probably estate planning and business law."

"Good, maybe I can send you some business."

"That would be super."

Needless to say I was ecstatic to find such a great place to start out my law practice. The office was attractive and the location was excellent. If General Burton did send me some business, that would be an added bonus. But with overhead of only a hundred and fifty dollars a month, I surely could survive long enough to get some business rolling in.

That night we took the whole family out to dinner to celebrate the beginning of my new venture as a sole practitioner. The kids didn't really understand what the celebration was about, but they loved the pizza. Rebekah was a little scared, but I assured her it would all work out for the best. I told her the important thing was that I was doing what I wanted to do and that usually was the ticket to success.

About ten days later I walked into my new office, placed a sign on my new desk that read "Stanley Turner, Attorney at Law" and waited for my first client. About an hour later General Burton came in from playing golf, which was his passion, and shot the breeze with me until it was almost noon.

"Do you have any lunch plans, Stan?" General Burton asked.

"Well, not really," I replied.

"How would you like to meet Rufus Green?"

"You mean THE Rufus Green of the Yankees?"

"The one and only," General Burton said.

"Wow, that would be fabulous."

"Well good, I'm having lunch with him today and you can join us."

"Why thank you General, that's very nice of you."

"No problem, I think Rufus will like you a lot, and God knows the way that guy wheels and deals he must use a lot of attorneys."

"Oh really?"

Just then the door swung open and a tall, muscular man walked in. I immediately recognized him as being Rufus Green. He had blond hair and blue eyes and looked like he wasn't a day over thirty-five, although I knew he was close to fifty. Although I lived in California at the time and was a Dodger fan, I always admired Rufus Green as a great center fielder and tremendous hitter. I couldn't believe he was standing in front of me.

"Rufus, you son of a gun, how are you?" General Burton said.

"Just fine, General, you ready for lunch," Rufus replied.

"I'm ready. Hey Rufus, I want you to meet my new tenant and friend, Stan Turner. He's an attorney."

"I won't hold that against him," Rufus said and then smiled. "Nice to meet you."

"It's a pleasure to meet you. This is such a surprise. I've been a fan of yours for years and I never dreamed I would ever see you in person."

"Well, I'm flesh and bone, just like everybody else."

"I invited Stan along for lunch. Is that all right Rufus?" General Burton asked.

"Sure, I may need a new attorney here pretty soon anyway," Rufus replied. "Can you believe my attorney was just appointed to the federal bench? He's been my attorney for years. I don't know what I'm going to do without him."

"Is that right? Well, let me know if I can do anything for you," I said.

After lunch I couldn't wait to call Rebekah and tell her I had just had lunch with Rufus Green. I knew she wasn't much of a baseball fan, but she would have to be impressed because everyone knew him. As it turned out, my afternoon wasn't too shabby either, as one of my old insurance buddies, Tex Weller, showed up unexpectedly to get a will for him and his wife. Not only had I eaten lunch with Rufus Green, but I also made seventy-five dollars to boot.

# THE PROMOTER

DURING MY FIRST WEEK in law practice I made $280, about as much as I had been making per week before I got out of law school. I went ahead and got the American Express Gold Card with the big line of credit, just in case I came up short during the month. Late Monday morning of my second week of practice, I got a phone call from Rufus Green.

"Listen a friend of mine needs an attorney and I thought maybe you and he ought to meet."

"Sure, that would be great. What kind of work does he need done?"

"He's a real estate investor. Do you handle real estate?"

"Oh yeah, of course."

"Well, he finds apartment houses and commercial buildings for sale and flips them."

"Flips them?"

"Yeah, you know, buys them and fixes them up a little and then sells them for a profit."

"Oh, . . . okay. What does he need me to do?"

"He needs you to do all of the documentation of the sales."

"Hmm. Great, that would be excellent," I said.

"I need to tell you a little about Kurt though."

"Kurt?"

"Harrison, Kurt Harrison."

"Right."

"Now, Kurt moves pretty fast and he needs someone to give him special attention."

"That shouldn't be a problem at this stage of my career."

"Hey, that's right. Will he be your first client?"

"Just about."

"Don't tell him that."

"No, of course not."

"Anyway, Kurt doesn't have time to come to your office. You'll need to go to his place, and he'll need his work done fast."

"Okay, where does he live?"

"In Arlington, about forty-five minutes from your office."

"Arlington? That's no problem. When can I meet him?"

"Can you go over right now?"

"Now?"

"I told you he moves fast."

"Okay, give me an address and I'm on my way."

"One thousand Lake View Trail."

"Okay, I'll be there in forty-five minutes."

I had mixed reactions to this sudden new business. In law school I had taken property law, but I had never had any practical experience in closing real estate transactions. Now suddenly I was expected to show up at Kurt Harrison's place as a real property expert. Obviously Kurt was going to know a lot about real estate and he would quickly spot my inexperience if I wasn't careful. As I jumped into my white, 1972 Ford Pinto hatchback, butterflies began swarming in my stomach.

I got out my Mapsco and found Lake View Trail. It was in a ritzy neighborhood about three miles southwest of downtown. When I arrived there, I was astonished to see a dozen or so waterfront mansions overlooking a small but scenic lake. The water was choppy as there was a strong wind from the south. Several sailboats were taking advantage of the strong wind. After passing Lake View Country Club, I approached 1000 Lake View Trail. I noticed a large concrete block fence around the perimeter of the property. There was a gate at the front entrance, which kept visitors out and required them to request permission to enter. Inside the gate were several Doberman pinchers patrolling the property.

I pulled up my car to the entrance, stuck my head out the window and pushed the intercom.

"Yes, who is it," a voice answered.

"Hi, I'm Stan Turner, I have an appointment with Mr. Harrison."

"Okay, drive on in," the voice answered.

The gate slowly opened. I drove down the circular driveway around a large fountain until I was in front of the mansion. There were several vehicles already parked out front, including a limousine, a Rolls-Royce and a Maserati. I felt humiliated getting out of my dirty old Ford Pinto in the midst of such opulence, but there was nothing I could do but swallow my pride and go on inside. I parked my car, walked over to the two large glass front doors and pushed the doorbell. After a minute, a pretty young brunette came to the door and opened it.

"Hi, I'm Stan Turner. I've got an appointment to see Kurt Harrison."

"Hello Stan, I'm Cynthia Carson, Kurt's personal secretary. Come on in and I'll take you to him."

"Thank you."

I was delighted to be greeted by such an attractive and friendly young woman. I walked inside and eagerly followed her through the magnificent living room with its spiral staircase leading up to what appeared to be second-floor bedrooms. Upon leaving the living room, we entered a large atrium area filled with tropical plants and assorted patio furniture. Cynthia continued on through a door that led into a large den. The room was decorated in an African motif, complete with zebra skins and elephant tusks. A slender, good-looking young man of no more than thirty years of age was sitting behind a large oak desk reading through some papers.

"Have a seat," Kurt said.

"Oh, thanks," I said and sat down in a Zebra-skin chair.

"Can I get you some coffee?"

"No, I'm fine. . . . Rufus Green tells me you're a real estate investor."

"That's right. We operate several apartment complexes and office buildings in Dallas, Fort Worth and Amarillo. What I need your services for right now is a rehab we're doing on an office building in Dallas on Turtle Creek."

"Oh really?"

"Yes, I've got some Canadian investors coming in tomorrow who are going to put up the capital to buy the building, and I need the paperwork done by morning."

"Tomorrow?"

"Yes, is that a problem?"

"Oh, no, . . . not at all. How's the deal going to work?"

"I'll have Cynthia and Dan fill you in on the details, I've got to go meet some people for lunch."

"Dan?"

"Yes, he's my partner and CPA. He should be here pretty soon. You can just hang around until he gets here."

"Okay, . . . well, it's been nice meeting you," I said.

"Likewise, I'll talk to you tomorrow."

Kurt got up, put on his coat and left the room. Cynthia followed him to the front door and then returned to the den, where I was admiring the full-size replica of an African Pygmy that adorned one corner of the room.

"Well, I think Kurt likes you," Cynthia said.

"Oh, . . . really? Well, I hope so."

"He's very particular about who he deals with. He seemed comfortable with you."

"That's good, he seems like a very nice guy."

"I think you'll like him once you get to know him?"

"How long have you been his secretary?"

"About two years now."

"Do you handle all his affairs?"

"I just work part time. I take care of his correspondence, paperwork and appointments. His partner, Dan, handles most of Kurt's financial affairs. I'm working on getting my brokerage license so I can represent Kurt when he buys and sells property."

"Well, I guess you better fill me in on what's going on since we have a lot of documents to prepare before morning."

"Sure, what do you need?"

"I'm going to need the names and addresses of all the buyers and what percentage each is buying, a copy of the previous deed to the property, the purchase price, the details of any financing and any other documentation you might think is relevant."

"Okay, I'll start rounding up all that stuff. Would you like a drink?"

"Sure, what are you having?"

"I'm going to have some wine?"

"I'll have the same."

"Fine, I'll be right back."

Cynthia left the room, and I sat down in a large stuffed chair. I didn't usually drink during the middle of the day, but it seemed like the right thing to do at that moment. After a few minutes, a maid came in with my drink and some cheese and crackers. I dug right in as it was after eleven and I was beginning to get hungry. Several minutes later Cynthia walked in with a glass of wine in her hand. She walked over to Kurt's desk and sat down in the large burgundy chair. She fumbled through some files, took out a stack of papers and copied some names off of a Rolodex. Then she stuffed everything into a file, placed it on the desk in front of her, then looked up and smiled.

"Dan ought to be here pretty soon to explain the transaction to you in greater detail and outline the financing."

"That'll be fine. How long have Dan and Kurt been partners?"

"About two years now. They met at a closing in Beverly Hills a couple of years ago and got along so well they decided to become partners. Dan commutes between Beverly Hills and Dallas once a week. He's got a lot of rich clients who are always looking for good real estate ventures."

As Cynthia was talking, the door to the den opened and a robust man with thin curly hair and a red complexion walked in carrying a large briefcase. He smiled at Cynthia who immediately got out of Ken's chair. She stepped aside as he headed straight for Kurt's desk and sat down.

"Mr. Kelley, this is Stan Turner our new attorney," Cynthia said.

"Oh, you're the one Rufus spoke so highly about."

"That's right," Cynthia replied.

"So did Kurt fill you in on what we're doing?" Mr. Kelley asked.

"No, not really, he just gave me a quick overview of what he wanted."

"Well, I'll go through it with you in detail after lunch. You haven't eaten yet have you?"

"No."

"Good, let's go get something to eat then."

"Sure, that would be fine."

"Cynthia, can you come along?"

"No, Kurt has some errands I've got to do. You guys go on without me."

"Okay, come on Stan, I know a place not too far from here with the best steak in Texas."

"Good."

Kurt's chauffeur took us to the Texas Cattle Co. where we were escorted past the long lunch line into a private dining area. Everyone seemed to know Dan and went out of their way to please him. After getting a couple of beers, Dan began to fill me in on what he and Kurt were doing.

"We deal mostly with foreign investors from Canada, Japan, Great Britain or wherever else we can find them. When they come into town, we wine and dine them of course, but they want to look at the properties and meet our accountants and attorneys before they make a decision. This is where you fit in. Not only do we need you to do our initial contracts and acquisition paperwork, but we need you to meet these people and make them feel at ease."

"Well, I don't see any problem with that, I get along with just about everybody."

"Good, now about your fee. What do you charge for your services?"

"My usual charge is ninety-five dollars per hour."

"Is that all? That's certainly no problem."

After lunch we went back to Kurt's place and Dan explained the deal in detail. Then I took the papers Cynthia had gathered for me and headed back to the office. I was excited to get such a great client, but I was nervous because I had never done a real estate contract before and this deal was rather complicated. General Burton had gone to play golf as he usually did in the afternoons so I had the place to myself. I called Rebekah to tell her about my good fortune.

"Is it a big job?"

"Yeah, it's pretty big. I'm going to have to spend most of the night at the library though."

"Why? Can't you do it tomorrow?"

"No, they want to close tomorrow."

"But you don't have a secretary."

"I'll just have to type the paperwork myself. Luckily I can go by the Dallas Association of Realtors and get most of the forms I'll need. Then I'll just have to fill in the blanks."

"I wish you didn't have to work tonight. I haven't seen you all day and the kids are missing you."

"I know but it's going to take me six or seven hours to do this job, so that means I'll make six or seven hundred dollars at ninety-five dollars per hour. And Dan says there's going to be a lot more deals like this coming up."

"That's good."

"I could kick myself though."

"Why?" Rebekah asked.

"I guess I should have charged a higher hourly rate."

"Oh really?"

"Yeah. Dan thought ninety-five dollars per hour was cheap."

Rebekah shook her head. "These guys must be rolling in the dough if they think that's cheap."

"Kurt does seem like he's doing well. He lives in a ten thousand square foot house, drives a Maserati and takes his clients around in a limousine."

"Wow! Is he married?"

"I don't know. Somehow I don't think so. . . . Well, I've got to get to work, babe. I'll be home pretty late tonight so kiss the kids good night for me and don't wait up."

"Wait a minute. Reggie wants to talk to you."

"Okay," I said.

"Daddy, when are you coming home?"

"Well, I've got some important work to do, hotshot, so I probably won't see you until tomorrow."

"What do you have to do?"

"Oh, it's a real estate transaction."

"What's real estate?"

"Well, you know, land and buildings like your Fisher-Price Gas Station. If it were real, that would be real estate."

"Oh."

Doing a complex real estate transaction in one night was not easy, particularly when I didn't have a secretary and had never done even a simple one before. Luckily, I had worked briefly one summer for an attorney who owned a title company, Ron Johnson, so I called him for some advice. He was helpful and even let me come by and use his real estate reference books to find some of the less common forms that the Dallas Board of Realtors didn't publish. By midnight I had completed the job and went home to bed. Rebekah was still up when I arrived.

"Stan, you're home. Did you get it all finished?"

"Yeah, it's all done and ready for tomorrow morning."

"Good. What'd you say your client's name was?"

"Kurt Harrison."

"Did you know he was on the news tonight?" Rebekah asked.

"No. What'd they say about him?"

"It was something about him refusing to make repairs on some apartments, and all his tenants being up in arms."

"What! You're kidding?"

"No. Apparently the city issued him one hundred and eleven separate citations, and the TV station was looking for him to get his comments."

"Oh shit! I can't believe this . . . Kurt's loaded. Why wouldn't he keep his properties up?"

"I just hope he pays you for all the work you did today."

"He will. Surely this must be some mistake."

# GENA

WHEN I GOT TO Kurt's place the following day for the closing, I was escorted into the den and it was apparent everyone was talking about the TV report of the previous evening. I was very interested in this topic so I paid particularly close attention.

"It's just another case of the press making wild accusations without checking out the facts," Kurt said. "If they'd done their homework they'd have discovered that I didn't own the property anymore and wasn't responsible for the repairs. But, of course, they liked the story the way it was. They didn't want the truth to get in the way of a good headline."

"Why didn't the new owner make the repairs?" I asked.

"When I buy property, I usually fix it up and then resell it. In this case there were some investors who wanted to buy the property from me immediately. They were trying to qualify as a like-kind exchange. They had to move quickly or they would have to pay taxes on some property they'd just sold. They bought it 'as is.' They're in the process of getting the repairs made right now. Anyway, enough history, it's time to get down to the business at hand. Stan, do you have the paperwork ready?"

"Yes sir, it's all right here. I've got a packet for everyone," I said, as I began passing around several large envelopes.

The closing went well and Kurt seemed pleased. After all the papers had been signed, Kurt rode in the limousine with the investors to the airport, and I went back to my office.

Although everything was going well with my new law practice, I hadn't actually seen any money come in except the seventy-five dollars from Tex. Accordingly, I had to draw down another three hundred dollars on my American Express card to pay bills. After paying General Burton three hundred dollars for first and last month's rent and buying two hundred dollars worth of supplies, I had already depleted my line of credit by eight hundred dollars, leaving only $1,200 of precious capital. Unless some money came in soon, I would be in serious trouble. While I was assessing my financial situation the phone rang. It was Tex.

"Hey, I met a guy today you need to talk to. He's got an oil company, I think he calls it Inca Oil Company, and he really needs an attorney."

"Oh good, that oil and gas class I took wasn't a total waste of time then," I said.

"You took oil and gas?"

"Yeah, it was the only thing that fit in my schedule my last semester. I never thought I would ever use it."

"Well, it's a good thing you took it Stanley my boy because this guy could be a good client for both of us."

"Great. When do I get to meet him?"

"Are you free in the morning to go over to his place?"

"He can't come here?"

"No, you know these high rollers with big egos, they think they're so good everybody has to come to them."

"Well, okay, but I never pictured law practiced like this. For some reason I thought my clients would come to me."

"Well, you know Stan, if you want to sit in your nice, slick office and wait for them to come to you, you can. But you may starve to death in the meantime."

"You're right, what time is our appointment?"

"Nine o'clock."

"Okay, I'll meet you there."

"Good. See you tomorrow."

Just as I hung up the phone, it rang again. It was Derek Donner. He was the casualty insurance agent I had become good friends with while I was briefly in the insurance business several years ago. He was one of the kindest men I knew, and I always referred anyone who needed car insurance to him.

"So how's the law practice going?" Derek said.

"It's going better than I expected, it's just that it takes so long for the cash to start coming in."

"Welcome to the wonderful world of business," Derek said.

"Thanks. . . . I hope I survive the first month."

"You know, I always used to worry a lot about surviving each month, but I found that worrying didn't help. Somehow it always works out. You just have to be patient and a say a few prayers so the good Lord doesn't forget about you."

"Actually, I've been praying a lot and Rebekah's been going to Mass every morning."

"Well, your prayers are already being answered as we speak."

"What do you mean?"

"I've got a client for you."

"Oh, great. Who is it?"

"Her name is Gena Lombardi. She came in for some insurance on her Corvette this morning. It seems her bank's trying to repossess her car for several reasons, one of which was not having it insured."

"Hmm."

"Anyway, it looks like she needs an attorney. I think she's several months behind on her payments and may need to file bankruptcy."

"Oh no," I said.

"Well it's bad for her I guess, but good for you, right?" Derek said.

"Well, the only problem is I didn't take bankruptcy in law school. I did take creditor's rights and bankruptcy did come up a few times," I said.

"Well, can you handle it?"

"Yeah, sure. I'll figure it out. Do you have her phone number?"

"Yes, I have her card right here, it's Pilgrimage Travel Agency, Gena Lombardi, Owner, 555-2277."

"A travel agent huh?" I said.

"Not just an ordinary travel agent to hear her talk."

"What do you mean?"

"Well I guess she really makes traveling as easy and exciting as possible."

"Oh really, how do you mean?"

"She plans every detail of your trip, including food, lodging, sightseeing, theater tickets and anything else your heart desires. She'll even arrange for an escort so you won't get lonely."

"That's what I call a full-service travel agency."

"Exactly. Anyway, give her a call."

"I will, thanks a lot, Derek."

Just as soon as I hung up, I immediately called Miss Lombardi at the number on the card. The phone rang several times before a male voice answered. I asked for Gena Lombardi and he put me through to her.

"I've got a problem I need to discuss with you. Derek says you're a nice guy and I can trust you."

"Absolutely," I said. "I'll do my best to help you in any way I can. What's your situation?"

"Well, it's too complicated to discuss over the phone. Can I come see you?"

"Sure, when would you like to come?"

"Well, how about today?"

"Today?"

"Uh huh."

"Okay, could you come at three o'clock?"

"Sure."

"Good, I'll see you then."

Immediately after hanging up, I rummaged around and found my creditor's rights book and scanned everything on bankruptcy. Then I ran over to the county law library and read everything I could find there on the subject. It was getting close to three o'clock so I returned to my office, arriving just before three. General Burton had gone to play golf, and I had the office to myself. I straightened up my desk and put away all my books. As I put the last one away, the door opened and a pretty young woman appeared. She was medium height, black hair and wore a very short skirt and halter-top. In her arms she was carrying a large packing box. She didn't smile when she saw me."

"Hello, is this Stan Turner's office?"

"Yes, I don't have a sign yet, but this is the right place. Can I help you with your box?"

"No, it's not that heavy."

"Did you have any trouble finding this place?"

"No, my dentist is in this building."

"Oh good. Have a seat."

"Thank you."

"Well, Derek told me a little bit about you, but he didn't really get into why you need an attorney."

"Well it's kind of a long story."

"That's okay, I need to know everything if I'm going to be of any help to you."

"My boyfriend and I were partners in the travel agency and we recently broke up. Of course, he took all the money when he left."

"Oh no, how much did he take?"

"Well, we had $25,000 in the checking account the day before he left and now we're $840 overdrawn and thirteen checks have bounced."

"Damn. He really cleaned you out, didn't he?"

"Yeah, you'd think the bastard would've at least left enough money in the account to cover the outstanding checks."

"Who signed the checks that bounced?"

"I did, and now there are warrants out for my arrest," Gena said.

"Oh really? How have you avoided being arrested so far?"

"I keep a good lookout for the constable."

"What was this I heard about a Corvette being repossessed?"

"Well, I drive a Corvette. I'm two months behind on the payments and my bank's looking for it to repossess."

"How much are your payments?"

"Six hundred and thirty dollars a month."

"Whoa! That's pretty steep."

"Not when you're making $150,000 a year like we were before Tony left me. That bastard, if I ever find him I'll kill him."

"Well, what's in the box?" I asked.

"All my bills," Gena said.

"What do they total up to? Do you know?"

"No, I have no idea. I meant to go through them and sort them out, but I've just been so upset I haven't been able to do anything."

"You obviously didn't have a bookkeeper?"

"No, Tony handled everything or at least I thought he was handling everything."

"Well, we can file bankruptcy for you, but that won't help you with those criminal warrants."

"I don't know what to do, Stan. I just need you to give me some advice."

"I guess we'd better start by sorting out all those bills so we can get a feel for the extent of your indebtedness."

"Okay," Gena said, as she carried the box to the middle of the floor and dumped it out. "I'm sorry I didn't get a chance to do this before, but I've just been too upset."

"It's all right. Let's see what you got."

Gena sat down on the floor and folded her long, nicely tanned legs in front of her as she began sorting out her bills. I felt a little uncomfortable watching her work half-naked in front of me. I wondered what General Burton would think if he walked in and saw Gena sitting there on the floor. After an awkward moment of silence, I said to her, "Can I get you a cold drink or something?"

"Yes, do you have a Coke?" she replied.

"Sure, I'll be right back."

I escaped from the office and headed for the vending machines, hoping she would be finished when I returned. I pondered what in the hell I was going to do to get her out of her predicament. I didn't know anything about criminal law, nor did I really want to learn about it. In my first year of law school, I barely survived my criminal law class and really didn't like it one bit. I seriously considered suggesting she find another lawyer. When I got back she was still on the floor, but in my absence she had managed to build quite a number of stacks of bills.

"Okay, here's your Coke."

"Oh, thank you. I think I've got these pretty well sorted out."

"Good, why don't you give me the latest statement for each account."

"Okay, here's American Express."

"Hmm, $12,301.47?"

"Yeah, we've been doing a lot of traveling lately."

"I guess so."

"Okay, what else you got?"

"Here's my Visa Gold."

"Okay, $9,327.36."

"You had some pretty high credit limits."

"Well, like I told you, Tony and I were doing damn good until he took off."

"Do you know why he left?"

"Bridgett."

"Bridgett?"

"He ran off with my best friend, Bridgett."

"Oh shit. How did that happen?"

"Bridgett worked in the office and I guess I was just too busy to see what was happening between them. Then, when I finally woke up and discovered what was going on, I confronted them and all hell broke loose."

"I can't believe a best friend would do something like that."

"Tony was handsome, and Bridgett had always been jealous. I can't say I'm surprised."

"Well, it looks like you owe about $50,000, not including the hot checks," I advised her. "I don't know if Derek told you or not, but I don't handle criminal cases."

"That's all right, I've already talked to a criminal attorney."

"Oh good, so you just need me to file a bankruptcy?"

"I just need you to save my Corvette."

"I can file a Chapter 13 which will allow you to keep the Corvette and pay it out through a plan, but I'm wondering if you really should keep the Corvette."

"What do you mean? I've got to have my Corvette. In my business you've got to look prosperous to be successful. If people saw me driving around in another car, they would know something was wrong and quit doing business with me."

"Oh really?"

"Yes, you have to save my Corvette, I'll die if I lose it."

"Okay then, if you can make the payments in the future, I can cure the default in your Chapter 13."

"Good."

"I guess we need to talk about my fee. A Chapter 13 cost nine hundred dollars plus the filing fee of sixty dollars."

"I'm eight hundred dollars overdrawn."

"I know, but if you want to file bankruptcy, I've got to get some money from you."

"My mom said she could send me five hundred dollars, and I'll give you the rest after I get my business going again."

"That'll be all right, but we can't file the bankruptcy until we have the five hundred dollars."

"My mom said to call her and she would send you the money."

"You want me to call your mother?"

"Yeah, here's her phone number," she said, as she handed me a piece of paper. "She won't send me the money direct, you know, she's afraid I'll spend it on something else."

"Oh really?"

"Yeah, you know how mothers are always suspicious."

"I'll call her, but I still can't file until I get the down payment, and you better keep your Corvette locked up until we get the bankruptcy filed and the automatic stay is in effect."

"Please file it now Mr. Turner. I can't lose my Corvette. You've got to file it now."

"Well, do you have the three hundred sixty dollars, three hundred for me and sixty for the filing fee at least?"

"Maybe I can get that together. I'll try to scrape it up and I'll call you later with it, okay."

"Well, I don't know, but I guess if your mother says she's mailing the five hundred dollars, and you give me the three hundred sixty dollars, then I can go ahead and file it."

"Oh, thank you Stan, you'll be glad you did this for me."

"Don't worry about it, that's my job."

"I know, but you've been so nice to me. All the other attorney's were nasty and yelled at me."

"What other attorneys?"

"The other ones I talked to about my problems before you."

"Oh. I didn't realize you had been shopping around."

"Well, I'm particular about whom I do business with and you're the first attorney who hasn't been condescending. I feel comfortable with you. When I get things back on track, we're going to do lots of business together."

"Oh, . . . well, . . . thank you. I'm looking forward to it."

Gena got up off the floor, walked over to me and extended her hand.

"Thanks a lot Stan, I can call you Stan can't I?"

"Sure."

After Gena left, I went to the stationery supply store to get a bankruptcy kit, and then went home early for soccer practice. After practice, I sat down to play with Marcia and watch TV. It was about 7:30 P.M. when the phone rang. It was Gena.

"Stan, I've got the money."

"Good, how did you get my home telephone number?" I asked.

"You're in the telephone book."

"Well, just bring the money by the office in the morning."

"I can't do that."

"Why not?"

"I've got to leave town tonight. I won't be back for about a week. I need to give you the money tonight. Can I meet you somewhere?"

"I don't know if that's such a good idea. Can't you just bring it by my house?"

"No, I'm sure I'd get lost. Can't you just meet me somewhere?"

"Okay, okay, I'll meet you at the Gulf station at Parker and Coit in fifteen minutes, but I wish you could just bring it to my office in the morning."

"I'm sorry, but like I said, I'm going to be out of town."

"All right, I'll see you in fifteen minutes," I said, and then hung up the phone.

"Shit!"

"What's wrong, honey?"

"I got this new client today, and I can already tell she's going to be a royal pain in the ass. She wants me to meet her at the gas station."

"What for?"

"To give me the retainer and filing fee for her bankruptcy."

"She wants you to go meet her right now?"

"Uh huh, she's leaving town, and we've got to file the bankruptcy right away. That reminds me, I better bring the petition with me for her to sign so I can file it in the morning."

"I hope she's paying you a lot of money for this."

"Well, . . . her mother's going to send me some money."

"You're going to file it without getting paid?"

"Well, worst case, I can put the entire fee in the plan. I'll eventually get paid. She's just really desperate."

"You're crazy Stan. I'd tell her to take a hike."

"Well, Derek referred her to me, and if I don't take good care of her, he won't refer any more clients to me. I'll be back in just a minute."

I jumped into the Pinto and took off towards the rendezvous point. When I got there, Gena was sitting on the hood of her yellow Corvette wearing a black crepe halter dress with a slit up the side. One knee was raised, exposing her long luscious legs. I felt a tinge of excitement as I approached her cautiously.

"Hi, Gena."

"Hi, Stan. Thanks for coming."

"It's okay, but in the future we need to conduct our business at my office and not in parking lots. And please don't call me at home."

"I'm sorry. Did I get the little lady of the house upset?"

"Well, as a matter of fact you did."

"Well, I thought maybe we could get a drink before I left town."

"A drink? . . . No, I don't think so. Just give me the money so I can get back to my family."

"Come on Stan, one little drink won't hurt anything."

"Gena, forget it. If you want me to file your bankruptcy then give me the money, otherwise I'm leaving and I'm going to return all your papers to you."

"I'm sorry. Here's your money," Gena said, as she handed me a plain white envelope. I opened it and counted eighteen twenty-dollar bills. "I'll call you when I get back," she said.

"Okay, have a good trip."

"Thanks."

Gena slid off her car hood, walked over to the door, smiled and winked at me. Then she got in and sped off down Parker Road. I shook my head in disbelief and was about to get into my car when a police car drove up with its lights flashing. A sick feeling suddenly overcame me as I would soon be facing two police officers with an envelope full of twenty-dollar bills. *What if they think I'm selling drugs?*

The big black-and-white squad car stood in front of me with its headlights glaring in my face. The officer riding shotgun opened his door and stood up beside his car cautiously. The blare of the police radio sent shivers down my spine. Finally the officer approached.

"What are you doing here sir?" he said.

"Just meeting a client."

"What kind of client?"

"Oh, I'm an attorney and I just met one of my clients. I'm filing bankruptcy for her in the morning."

"You're Gena's lawyer?"

"Yeah, you know her?"

"Every officer in the precinct knows Gena. She's been spending a lot of time down at the station lately."

"You're kidding?"

"No, I'm afraid not."

"What has she done wrong?"

"Heaters mainly."

"Heaters?"

"Hot checks, I don't think she knows how to balance a checkbook."

"Well, I have trouble with that sometimes myself."

"Isn't it a bit unusual to be conducting business in a parking lot?"

"It was her idea. I told her to come to my office, but she insisted I meet her here."

"What's in the envelope?"

"Oh that. Ah. That's her bankruptcy filing fee. I wouldn't file her case without it."

"Can I see some identification, please?"

I pulled out my wallet and handed the officer my driver's license and my bar card. The officer inspected them closely and then gave them back to me."

"Is this your car?"

"Uh huh."

"Hmm. You must've just got out of law school."

"That's right."

"Well, I'd conduct your business in your office if I were you. Someone might mistake you for a drug dealer or a pimp. Especially if you've got clients like Gena."

"I usually do work in my office, she just insisted on meeting me here."

"Well you best be careful, Gena's a wild one. Personally I like her, but there are a lot of people who'd like to nail her."

"Oh really? Well, thanks for the advice. I'll be careful."

# INCA OIL COMPANY

Rᴇʙᴇᴋᴀʜ ᴡᴀs ᴘʀᴇᴛᴛʏ ᴄᴏᴏʟ to me all night after my meeting with Gena. I didn't dare tell her about the encounter with the police. The next morning I filed Gena's bankruptcy and then headed to my appointment with Tex at Inca Oil Company. The meeting was in a small office building off the Dallas North Tollway on the third floor. When I walked in, Tex was sitting in the reception area reading a magazine.

"Good morning Stanley. How are you?"

"Okay, I guess."

"You guess? What's wrong, you get up too early this morning?"

"No. I just got through filing a bankruptcy and I don't feel too good about it."

"Well, at least it wasn't your own."

"Yeah, but I've got a real bad feeling about this case."

"Why'd you take it then?"

"Well, I didn't really know there was anything wrong until it was too late."

"Oh well, it probably won't turn out so bad."

"I hope not."

As we were talking, the receptionist advised us that Mr. Tomlinson was ready to see us. We got up and followed her into his office. As I entered the large corner office, I noticed a short, obese man of about forty-five chewing on a cigar and sitting behind a big oak desk. He was discussing something with a younger, dark-complexioned man seated to his right. When he saw us, he got up, walked toward us and said, "Come on in, gentlemen."

We all shook hands and then everyone sat down.

"I guess Tex has filled you in about our business, Stan," Mr. Tomlinson said.

"Well, he told me a little about it, but not in any great detail."

"Then let me fill you in. Inca Oil Co. was formed about five years ago to search for existing wells in proven fields that were shut in and abandoned because of low oil prices. With oil and gas prices as high as they are today, oftentimes, new productive wells can be developed near the old sites. By researching production records we can almost predict what a well will do in advance of drilling it. We've drilled about a dozen wells to date, and eight of them are currently in production."

"How do you find your prospects?"

"Well, we have a geologist who goes from courthouse to courthouse, to the Railroad Commission office, or to various oil companies and pours over old production records to find wells that have been plugged. When he finds one that fits a certain criteria, then we go take a look at it."

"I see."

"Recently we've run into a snag, however."

"What kind of snag?"

"Well, the abstract companies have been deluged with so much business lately it takes six weeks to three months to get a title report on a prospective lease."

"Huh. That *is* a long time."

"Well, we just can't afford that kind of a delay and that's why we need an attorney."

"I see, you need an attorney to check out the title to the land you want to put under lease?"

"Exactly."

"That shouldn't be too difficult. I'd just have to go to the county courthouse in each county where a prospective drilling site was situated and check out the deed records. The only problem is the travel time to each of these courthouses could make my work pretty expensive."

"Well, we just have to figure your fees into the cost of the project."

"Right."

"The way we raise our money is to solicit investors. We have a lot of doctors, corporate executives and others who invest in our wells. When we get a prospect ready to sell, our sales staff of about ten men and women start calling our old investors and new prospects to see if they want to invest in the well."

"How do you determine how much money you need to drill the well?" I asked.

"That's Bird's job. He's been in the oil business for over twenty years, and he can price out a well better than anyone," Tomlinson replied. "So what do you think, Stan?"

"I'd love to represent you. It sounds exciting."

"It is, there's nothing more exciting than seeing a well come in. All that black gold just pouring out of the ground like a gift from God. And when those royalty checks start coming in, it's like you've won the Irish Sweepstakes."

"So you've been successful eight out of twelve times?"

"That's right. Our success rate can be attributed to Bird's experience in picking out good wells, and the strategy I just outlined of exploiting proven wells that were abandoned for economic reasons. Many times when these wells were shut in, the technology wasn't advanced far enough to allow the full exploitation of the wells. Many times fifty to sixty percent of the oil was left in the ground. But with today's technology we can pull out ninety percent."

"Huh, that's quite an improvement."

"I should say so," Tex said. "Stan, I've watched these guys from when they drilled their first well. They know what they're doing, believe me."

"I do."

"So do you want to work with us on these projects Stan?" Tomlinson said.

The question gave me an uneasy feeling. Why the big sales pitch? I felt like I was buying a used car. Then I made eye contact with Bird. He was a mysterious-looking man with this long, silky black hair pulled back into a ponytail. Who was this guy?

"Stan. Wake up, boy," Tex said.

"Oh. Definitely, count me in."

"Good, welcome aboard," Tomlinson said.

"Thanks."

"Okay then, Bird has a well he needs checked out as soon as possible."

"Fine. Do we need to talk about fees?" I said.

"I suppose we better get that out of the way," Mr. Tomlinson replied.

"I charge a hundred and twenty-five an hour plus expenses."

"That's pretty reasonable. Our last attorney charged one-fifty," Tomlinson said.

"You might want to consider doing this on trade," Tex said. "That's what I'm doing."

"What do you mean?"

Tomlinson sat back and answered for Tex, "Well, for every dollar you charge us, we put that much money into one of our wells. Then if the well hits . . . hell, you may end up making nine hundred and fifty dollars an hour."

"Well, that's tempting, but I've just started a law practice and I need to get my cash flow going."

"I can understand that, Stan, but look how much cash flow you'll get if one of your wells come in."

"True, but I can't afford to gamble right now. Maybe later on, when I get my practice stabilized I'll consider it."

"Okay, but if you change your mind, just let me know."

"Sure, I'll do that."

"Now, go with Bird into his office and he'll show the prospect and give you your assignment. It's been a pleasure meeting you Stan and I'm looking forward to working with you."

"Thank you, sir."

"Now that you're on board you can call me Brice," Mr. Tomlinson said.

"Thank you, Brice," I said.

"Tex, you stay here, I need to talk to you about that policy you're working on. What's this about rating me just because I weigh two hundred and eight-five pounds?"

Bird took me into his office and immediately began asking some personal questions. I told him about Rebekah and the children and how I had just started practicing law. Then I asked him about himself.

"Are you married?" I asked.

"Yes, but Sheila and I don't have any children. We wouldn't have time for them. I travel a lot, and Sheila is heavy into the social scene down in Corpus."

"You live in Corpus Christi?"

"Uh huh, we've got a place on the bay."

"Do you have to spend a lot of time in Dallas?"

"I'm here during the week, but I'm back home on the weekends."

"Your wife must hate that?"

"She's gotten used it."

"My wife wouldn't tolerate that. She needs relief from the kids at night."

"I bet. Does she work at all?"

"Uh huh, she's an R.N. She works part time in the ER and ICU at Central Receiving Hospital."

"Really? That must be pretty exciting."

"She enjoys it most of the time, but it's pretty intense work. Some of the doctors can be pretty nasty, I guess."

"Central Receiving, that's off of Central Expressway near Walnut Hill Lane, isn't it?"

"That's right."

Bird picked up a file off of his desk, opened it up and said, "Well, we've been looking at a prospect out in west Texas, near Cisco. We need you to go out there as soon as possible and check it out."

"I've been through Cisco. It's about a two-hour drive, isn't it?"

"Right. When do you think you could get out there?"

"Probably in a couple of days."

As we were talking, the door to the reception area opened and a young woman appeared. She was wearing a crisp white blouse with a windowpane plaid skirt, mid-thigh length. Her legs were conversation stoppers. She gave Bird a concerned look and said, "Don't forget about tonight?"

Bird frowned and said, "Relax, I haven't forgotten."

"Good."

"Melissa, I want you to meet Stan Turner. He's our new attorney. . . . Stan, this is Melissa Madigan."

"Hi," I said.

Melissa smiled and replied, "Oh, it's nice to meet you."

"If Stan needs anything, get it for him, okay."

"Certainly," Melissa said and then left.

"Melissa's a pain at times, but she's got a body you wouldn't believe. I keep her around to keep up my morale."

"She'd definitely keep up my morale," I laughed.

"Okay, take this file and look it over. If you need anything else, let me know."

"Great, I will," I said, and then got up to leave. Bird escorted me out and I went back to my office. I was excited about the Inca Oil project. Pouring over deeds wasn't the most exciting thing I could think of doing, but it would pay well so I was happy. As I sat pondering my new project, the telephone rang.

"This is Gena. Did you get my bankruptcy filed?"

"Yes, I filed it this morning."

"Good. I think someone's been following me. I thought it might be someone from the bank."

"Well, the bank doesn't know the case has been filed yet, so you better be careful until we can get the word to them."

"You mean they can still take my Vette?"

"Well, they might take it by accident not knowing that a bankruptcy has been filed yet. I've been out of the office all day so I haven't had a chance to call and tell them you filed bankruptcy."

"Okay, well hurry up and call them. I just can't lose my car."

"I will. I thought you were going to be out of town today?"

"My plans changed."

"They did, huh. Well when you get your bankruptcy notice, be sure and note on your calendar when your creditor's meeting is scheduled. You've got to attend that meeting."

"Okay, I will."

I leaned back and took a deep breath. Maybe Gena's case would be okay. She seemed fine today. Before I could totally relax the phone rang again. It was Gena again.

"They took it!" Gena moaned. "They're hauling it down the street right now. You've got to do something, Stan! They can't take my Vette, you can't let them!"

"Shit! I'll call the bank immediately. Where are you?"

"I'm at Northpark . . . near Neiman Marcus."

"Do you have someone who can come pick you up?"

"No. . . . I don't have anyone."

"Well, can you call a cab?"

"I don't have any money."

I put my hand over the receiver and took a deep breath trying to contain my frustration, then I removed my hand and continued to talk.

"Okay. Just wait there and I'll come and get you. Don't cry, we'll get your car back."

I immediately drove to Northpark and picked up Gena. Then we went to a pay phone and I dialed Gena's bank and asked for her loan officer. After a few minutes a man came on the phone.

"Can I help you?"

"This is Stan Turner. I'm Gena Lombardi's attorney."

"You have my condolences."

"What? Never mind. You just repossessed her car, and she filed bankruptcy this morning."

"We didn't get any notice of a bankruptcy."

"I know. We just filed it this morning. You're under a court stay not to disturb her property."

"Well, I don't know anything about that. All I know is I've been trying to get that car back for three months and I'm not going to return it unless my attorney tells me I have to."

"Well, I suggest you get your attorney on the phone and advise him of the situation. I want that car returned today or I'll file a contempt motion."

"I'll call my attorney right now, but sometimes it takes days to get him to return my calls."

"Then I suggest you drive over to his office and camp at his door until he talks to you because I'm not waiting a couple of days!"

"Call me back in an hour. I'll see what I can do."

"All right. I'll call you back."

I turned around and Gena looked like she was in a trance.

"Are you all right?" I said.

"That was so great," Gena said.

"What are you talking about?"

"The way you chewed out that old bastard gave me goose bumps."

"What? Come on . . . give me a break."

"No one has ever stuck up for me like that before."

"I was just doing my job. It was no big deal. I'm sorry they took your car."

"Well, can we get that drink now since we have an hour to kill."

"It's a little early for drinking. How about a cup of coffee?"

"I'd rather have a martini."

"Let's stick to coffee. Come on, there's a coffee shop inside the mall."

After we killed an hour in the coffee shop, I got back on the phone and talked to Gena's bank officer. He had talked to the bank's attorney and had been instructed to give Gena her car back. He advised me where to go to pick it up."

"I've got good news for you, Gena."

"What did they say?"

"They're going to give you your Corvette back."

"Oh, thank God. I'm so happy. I hope they didn't damage it. When can we get it?"

"We can go right now, come on."

We drove to the bank and sure enough Gena's yellow Corvette was parked in the back. We went inside and asked for Gena's loan officer. He was busy, but his secretary brought over the keys to the car and gave them to her. Then we left the bank and walked over to the Corvette.

"This is a nice car," I said.

"It's fabulous. I love it."

"Well, I'm glad you've got it back."

"Stan, you were wonderful today. Thank you so much," Gena said, as she suddenly put her arms around my neck and gave me a big kiss. Gena jumped in the car and sped off down the street. I shook my head, wiped the lipstick off my lips and went back to my car. I had never met anyone like Gena. She was so confident yet so confused. She was determined to get what she wanted, but I doubt if she really knew what that was. She was wild, out of control and obviously dangerous. I wished I'd never met her, but I couldn't keep my mind on anything else.

I was happier than usual to see Rebekah and the kids that night. So much had happened during the day it seemed like I had been gone a week. It was nice to be around the people I loved. It's not that there was anything wrong with my new clients, but as I watched and listened to them, I wondered what was really going through their minds. What did they really

think of me? Were they impressed or were they laughing under their breath? Was I a pawn jumping at every command or
was I a knight charging off to defend each of them? I didn't
know the answer, but one thing I did know was that I didn't
like being in the dark. I wanted to know exactly what was
going on and how I fit into the game, otherwise I didn't want
to play.

# MELBA THORN

THE NEXT DAY I got a call from Dan Kelley. It seemed Kurt had another deal in the works and needed me to come by in the morning. I agreed, figuring I would take care of Kurt the next day, Thursday, and go to Cisco on Friday. Suddenly I had plenty of work to do, but I was still broke and it would be at least three more weeks until I could even bill my new clients. It was kind of depressing, but I didn't have time to feel sorry for myself. For now I had to dig out my oil and gas textbook and figure out the difference between a royalty interest and a working interest, and I had to figure out how to spot one from the other by the language of the deeds and oil and gas leases. It would be another long day of research and preparation for my next task.

While I was pouring over my oil and gas text, the phone rang. I was beginning to dislike the sound of the phone because of who and what might be waiting for me on the other end of the line. I let it ring three times and then I reluctantly answered it.

"Attorney's office."

"Hello, this is Melba Thorn. I need to talk to Stan Turner."

"This is Stan Turner."

"I'm so glad I found you! I've only a minute to talk. Someone is looking for me."

"Where are you?"

"They've already taken my property and now they want to lock me away in a sanitarium. You've got to help me!"

"How'd you get my name?"

"You know, I used to be a rich woman. I owned the Chronicle Building downtown. It was worth millions."

"I'm sorry, but you'll need to come in if you want a consultation."

"When they find me they're going to lock me up and I'll be a prisoner," she said. "You've got to help me."

"Where are you?"

"I never thought I'd see the day when my own flesh and blood would turn on me. After all the sacrifices I made for them, all they can think of now is how to get rid of me and steal my money."

"Ma'am, if I'm going to help you, I need to know where you are and what you'd like me to do."

"Oh no, here they come. You've got to help me. No, . . . no leave me alone. Please help me," she said, and then the phone went dead.

I looked at the phone and shook my head. About that time the door flung open and General Burton walked in.

"Stan, you're back. I haven't seen much of you lately."

"Yeah, I've been pretty busy. I never dreamed attorneys had to make house calls."

"You don't look so good. . . . What's wrong?"

"Some lady just called me and said she was being held prisoner and wanted me to help her."

"Who was she?"

"She said her name was Melba Thorn."

"Melba Thorn? I know a Melba Thorn."

"You do?"

"Yeah, I served with her husband, Howard Thorn, in the South Pacific during World War II. I stayed in the army after the war, but he went on to make a fortune in real estate."

"I wonder if it's the same person?"

"I don't know."

"When did you see her last?"

"We stayed in touch over the years and got together from time to time until Howard died a few years ago. I've kind of lost track of the family since then."

"Did he own the Chronicle Building?"

"It wouldn't surprise me if he did. . . . I wonder how she got your name?"

"I don't know."

"What are you going to do?"

"I don't have the foggiest idea. I probably should just forget she called, but what if she's been taken hostage by her children and is being held captive."

"That's pretty far-fetched," General Burton said. "She had two children as I recall, a boy and a girl. The son was a bit of a problem but nothing major and their daughter was an angel."

"Do you know where I can find them?"

"I don't know, but let me do some checking, perhaps I can come up with something."

"Great. Thanks a lot," I said.

"Well, I'm getting the hell out of here before that phone rings again."

"That's probably a wise idea. You look like you need a good night's sleep."

When I got home I immediately crashed on the sofa. Rebekah sat down next to me with a sympathetic look on her face, sensing I had a bad day.

"Are you okay, honey?" she said.

"Yeah, I'm going to survive."

"What happened?"

"I wouldn't know where to begin."

"Just start anywhere."

"Some lady just called me and said she was being held hostage by her children and wanted me to help her."

"Sounds like a loony."

"Well, I would tend to agree, but some of the things she said checked out according to General Burton."

"Really?"

"Yeah, she was from an old wealthy family that owned a lot of real estate, and she described some of that property to me."

"What're you going to do?"

"Nothing I guess, I don't know where she is, and she hasn't really retained me to do anything."

"Well, you can just forget it then."

"I wish it were that easy. She just seemed so desperate. She asked me to help her, but I don't know how I can."

"Don't worry about it honey, there's nothing you can do."

Rebekah snuggled up next to me and laid her head on my shoulder. Suddenly she began sniffing my shirt.

"You smell like perfume."

"What?"

"You heard me. Oh, . . . that. You remember Gena don't you?"

"Gena? You mean the girl who met you in the parking lot?"

"Yeah, well I filed her bankruptcy today, but I didn't have time to call the bank and advise them about it. Unfortunately they decided to repossess her Corvette today."

"So what does that have to do with you smelling like a perfume factory?"

I told her everything that had happened and then said, "I guess her perfume was so strong my clothes absorbed some of it."

"Are you done now with that little slut?"

"Well, almost. I still have to go to her creditor's meeting."

"You better stay clear of her Stan Turner. I can't believe this. That little piece of shit better leave you alone."

"Don't worry, honey, I wish I had never taken her case."

"What does she look like anyway?"

"Oh, she's not that great looking."

"Is she fat?"

"Well, no."

"She's good looking isn't she? Come on, admit it. I can tell by the look on your face that she's gorgeous."

"Come on, honey, you're getting ridiculous now."

From the back bedroom I could hear our arguing had awakened Marcia. She was crying.

"Go take care of your daughter," Rebekah said.

"Okay," I replied.

Rebekah didn't talk to me the rest of the night. I guess she had a right to be upset, but I didn't feel like I had done anything wrong. I wished there were some way I could get rid of Gena because somehow I was afraid the worst was yet to come.

That night I didn't sleep well. My mind played over the events of the day and the week. Finally I faded off into a shallow sleep and began to dream.

*I was sitting in my office alone working on something when the door opened. It was Gena. She walked into my office, took off her sunglasses and sat down. She was wearing a little fit-and-flare dress with wide flaps and buttons down the front. She crossed her legs and gave me a seductive smile.*

*"What's going on Gena? Why are you here?"*

*"I just got off the phone with my mother."*

*"Yeah, how is she?"*

*"We had a big fight, and now she won't send me the money for your fee."*

*"Oh no, . . . you've got to be kidding!"*

*"I wish I were, believe me."*

*"What about your business? Haven't you been able to generate any income yet?"*

*"Tony has called all my customers and told them I filed bankruptcy. None of the regulars will do business with me anymore."*

*"What an asshole!"*

*"I am so embarrassed."*

*"Embarrassed? . . . Why?"*

*"That I can't pay you."*

*"Oh well, I'll just have to put the entire fee in your plan? I'll get paid eventually."*

*"No, I promised you I would pay you."*

*Gena stood up and tossed her long black hair from side to other. "No, a promise is a promise," she said as she began unbuttoning her dress.*

*"What are you doing?"*

*"Giving you your down payment," she said as she slipped off one strap exposing a succulent breast. "I think you'll find this much better than money."*

*"Gena, you can't do this. Come on. Button up you dress."*

*Gena gave a little wiggle and her dress fell to the floor. My pulse quickened as my eyes devoured her splendid body. Then she casually began to climb up on my desk beckoning me to take her. I struggled to keep my distance, but I was drawn toward her by a force so strong I couldn't resist. Our lips were about to touch when, suddenly, the door opened. Startled I looked up and was horrified to see General Burton. He glanced over at Gena, crawling naked on the desk and blinked like he was looking at a mirage. Then he took a look at me, shook his head and continued into his office. Gena began to laugh hysterically and . . . ring . . . ring . . . ring.*

Rebekah leaned over and grabbed the phone. "It's for you Stan." I looked over at the alarm clock and saw that it was 2:03 A.M.

"Who in the hell is calling me now?" I said, as I grabbed the phone from Rebekah. "Hello."

"I only have a minute?" a voice said.

"They haven't missed me yet, but they will soon. They have someone watching me twenty-four hours a day."

"Who is this?"

"Melba Thorn."

"How did you get this number?"

"Please help me Mr. Turner. . . . You've got to help me!"

"Where are you?"

"I don't know."

"How in the hell can I help you if I don't even know where you are?"

"Stop it you bastards . . . leave me alone . . . help me . . . no . . . no!" The phone went dead. I shook my head, handed the phone back to Rebekah and fell back onto the bed.

"What was that all about?" Rebekah asked.

"It was that woman again, Melba Thorn."

"How did she get your number?"

"We're in the phone book."

"Do you think she's crazy?"

"Maybe, but I really can't tell. She seems genuine enough."

"Well, since you don't know where she is, there's nothing you can do."

"I guess not. I'm sorry she woke you up. I never dreamed practicing law would be like this. The responsibility that's suddenly thrust upon you is unrelenting. All of a sudden you're expected to be some kind of God. Perfect strangers walk into your life and tell you their most intimate secrets. They expect you to be an expert on everything, not just the law, but business, politics, religion, psychology . . . and they just dump their problems on you and expect you to somehow miraculously solve them overnight."

Rebekah rolled over on her side and put her arm around me.

"I know it's been hard on you, honey. I'm sorry I yelled at you earlier. I know you would never cheat on me. After all we've been through together, the one thing I'm sure of is that I can trust you."

I grabbed Rebekah, pulled her on top of me and began to caress her lips with mine.

"Maybe it's a good thing the phone rang," I said as I caught my breath.

"You'd think you'd let a poor girl sleep at night," Rebekah said, as she sat up, unbuttoned the top to her apricot satin pajamas and tossed it onto the ground. I rolled her over and pulled off her bottoms.

"Sleep? Who needs sleep?"

"You better find some protection or you'll have another kid to put through college," Rebekah said.

I leaned over and fumbled through the nightstand drawer.

"Oh God, please let there be one more Trojan left," I said. "Ah, . . . Eureka!"

# MISS DOVE

GENERAL BURTON WAS SITTING at his desk drinking coffee when I walked in. He was an early riser, I guess from all those years in the army. I felt kind of embarrassed after my dream the previous night or was it a dream? *Everything* the past few weeks seemed like a dream. I went into his office and told him about Melba Thorn's call.

"Did you happen to find out anything on her?" I asked.

"Yes, I did find her son's name and address for you."

"Good. Maybe I need to give him a call."

General Burton handed me a piece of paper with the number. I thanked him and went into my office. After I had two cups of coffee and was almost fully awake, I gathered my things together and went over to Kurt's place. As I approached the front gate, I saw that it was open so I drove in all the way to the front door. All of the expensive vehicles that usually were parked in front of the mansion were gone. The place seemed deserted. I went up to the front door and pushed the doorbell. The sound of magnificent chimes resounded through the house, but no one stirred. I stood in front of the door nervously wondering where everyone went. Then I pushed the doorbell one more time, but there still was no answer. Becoming impatient, I went around to the side yard, but I saw no one. I returned to the front door and rang the bell one more time.

As I turned to leave, I saw the most beautiful woman I had ever seen, wearing a white knit sleep chemise and clutching a short matching wrap, descending the spiral staircases. She had long golden blond hair, a perfect figure and deep blue eyes. She walked nonchalantly toward me, pulled the wrap up onto her shoulders and opened the door.

"Can I help you?"

"Yes, I'm Stan Turner. I have a 9:30 appointment with Mr. Harrison."

"Gee, I don't know where everyone is. I was asleep upstairs. Come on in. You can wait for Kurt in the den."

"Thank you."

"I'm Gwendolyn Dove."

"Oh, pleasure to meet you."

She pointed the way to the den and then went back upstairs. I strolled casually toward it, taking in as much of the place as I could along the way. I noticed to the left swinging doors that led into an enormous kitchen. I heard a noise in the backyard so I went to the window. Workmen were building a gazebo behind the Olympic-size pool. The yard had a European flare with Italian marble statues, fountains and a formal garden.

Miss Dove came up from behind me silently and said, "Did Kurt ever show you around the place?"

Startled, I jumped slightly as I turned toward her. "Oh, I'm sorry, you startled me Miss Dove. . . . No, he didn't. Cynthia was going to, but she never got around to it."

She had changed into white denim shorts and a lavender scoop-neck stretch top. Her skin was lightly tanned and smooth as silk. I couldn't help but smile.

"You can call me Gwen."

"Okay, Gwen."

"Come on then, I'll show you around."

"Thank you."

She led me into the kitchen, out into the six-car garage, through the living and dining rooms, then through the library and finally to a small movie theater and TV room.

"This is pretty neat to have your own theater," I said.

"Yes, we invite people over to watch movies or sporting events. The room seats twenty-seven."

"Well you certainly have a wonderful home."

"Kurt and I enjoy it a lot," Gwen said. "Gee, I don't know where everyone went. Would you like some coffee while we wait?"

"If you have some made."

"Go sit down at the kitchen table. I'll be right back."

After a minute Gwen returned with two mugs of coffee. "Here you go," she said. "So what do you do for Kurt?"

"I'm an attorney."

"An attorney. Good, it's about time Kurt got his own attorney. He needs someone to keep him out of trouble."

"Oh really?"

"Well, he just moves so fast sometimes he forgets details that come back to haunt him. I hope you can help him be more thorough."

"I'll do my best."

As we talked we could hear the sound of the garage door going up. "Well, that's either Kurt or Edward, the driver. Just then Kurt walked into the kitchen and smiled when he saw us drinking coffee.

"Well, I'm glad Gwen is taking care of you. I'm sorry I'm late, but I had to go make some arrangements for our visitors coming in tomorrow from Montreal."

"All the way from Montreal?"

"That's right. They're due in just before noon so I had to make all their arrangements," Kurt said. "Let's go into the den so I can fill you in on what I need for tomorrow."

"Okay."

I followed Kurt into the den and to his desk, which had a neat little stack of folders on it. Kurt pointed to the pile and said, "There's all the information I believe you'll need. This is just a simple apartment complex that I'm going to pick up and then sell to the Canadians for a condo conversion."

"I'm buying it for just $24,000 a unit and selling it a week later for $28,000," Kurt said.

I pulled out my calculator and asked, "How many units?"

"One hundred sixty-seven."

"Damn, that's $668,000 profit."

"Not a bad week's work is it?"

"No, but if the Canadians buy it for such a high price, how will they make any money?"

"Oh, don't worry. After they buy it, I'm going to convert it to condominium use for them and then each unit will sell for $38,000. I'll get a nice profit for the conversion, and Cynthia will sell the units, once she gets her real estate license, so she'll also make a six-percent commission."

"Pretty slick," I replied. "But how do find your investors for that kind of deal?"

"My family is from Montreal. My parents were very wealthy. They didn't have much time for me, and I didn't like them much, but one thing I did learn was how to wine and dine the rich and powerful and how to gain their confidence."

"So you have a lot of connections in Canada?"

"Not connections as such, but I've developed a reputation for putting together first-class real estate deals in Texas and making people lots of money. With the rich it's just a matter of perception."

"Perception?"

"It's not what you are that counts, but what people perceive you to be."

"Oh, I see," I said.

I didn't see and I was a little afraid to gain a complete understanding of what Kurt was saying, so I changed the subject.

"So, what's the game plan tomorrow?"

"We want to close at 9:00 A.M., so bring all the papers over about 8:00, okay?"

"Sure, where will you be this afternoon if I have any questions?"

"Just call over here to the house, and someone will know how to track me down. You can call Dan in California if you can't find me."

This second job for Kurt was much harder than the first one. After several hours of trying to figure out exactly how to do it, I finally gave up and called Ron Johnson at Big D Title Company. Ron got me back on the right track and then wanted to know when I was going to send some title work his way. I assured him that at the first opportunity I would do just that.

The following day I handled the closing at Kurt's place and then hit the road for Cisco, Texas. It was a three-hour drive so I sat back and relaxed. I got there at 12:30 P.M. and headed for the courthouse only to find it closed for lunch. Rather than hang around waiting for the clerk's office to open, I walked across the street to a cafe to get something to eat. Next to the cafe was an abstract company, and as I walked across the street, I noticed a thin gray-haired man had just walked out of it and into the cafe. The man was wearing a loose-fitting gray shirt and khaki pants. He went to the counter and opened a menu. I decided to sit next to him, hoping to strike up a conversation and maybe get some tips on doing title searches in Cisco.

"Hi, I couldn't help but see you come out of West Texas Title Company," I said. "My name is Stan Turner and I came up here to do some title work myself."

"Howdy, I'm Roscoe Wilder, I own the title company."

"Well, I'm glad I met you, I may need your services one day."

"What kind of title work are you doing?

Well I'm doing a job for Inca Oil Company. They've targeted an old plugged well to reopen and get back into production."

"What wells are they looking at?"

"Oh, . . . they're looking at the old Parker #3 if you've ever heard of it."

"Yeah, I've heard of it. I think I did some title work on the Parker wells many years ago."

"If you have any suggestions on how to expedite a search of that property, I'd be most obliged."

"If you'd like, you can come over to my shop after we're done here, and maybe I can find the work I did. If so, that will give you a big head start."

"That would be fabulous. I was worried about getting this done today. I didn't want to have to come back Monday."

After lunch I followed Mr. Wilder over to his shop. He led me into a back room filled with hundreds of books, plats and maps of all sorts. After putting on his glasses, he opened a big book and ran his finger down several columns of entries.

"I think it was 1963. Let me see, here it is. The Parker Prospects—2914. Okay, let's see if we still have 2914."

I smiled in hopeful anticipation and followed Mr. Wilder through a maze of dusty shelves filled with large brown file jackets.

"Here it is . . . 2914. Parker prospects. Let's take it to an examination table."

"Yes, please."

"Gee, we even have some production reports in here."

"Oh, really?"

"Yeah, let's see, this baby was pumping two hundred and twenty-five barrels a day when they shut her down."

I pulled out my calculator and began to figure out what the annual production of the well should bring.

"Damn, at forty dollars a barrel that would bring in over three million dollars a year after expenses."

"Well, back then I think oil was four dollars a barrel so it wasn't such a great well. Anyway, here's a report showing the ownership of the property as of the date the well was drilled."

"Boy this is going to save me a lot of time. Thanks."

After spending all afternoon updating the abstract on the property, I headed back to Dallas. All the way home I couldn't think of anything except the production report on Parker #3. Tomlinson had offered to give me a three-percent interest in the well in exchange for my legal services. Three percent of three million dollars would be ninety thousand, and that's every year the well is in production. Since the most I had ever made prior to becoming a lawyer was twelve thousand dollars a year, the thought of making ninety thousand dollars extra money every year was overwhelming. By 9:00 P.M., when I finally got home, I couldn't wait to tell Rebekah what I had learned. When I walked in the door Rebekah was watching TV. She was wearing her black silk nightgown that I got her for her birthday, which further intensified my excitement. She looked up at me so I said, "Hi, babe."

"Hi, honey, you finally made it home."

"It's a hell of a drive to Cisco, let me tell you," I replied, and then walked over to the sofa and sat down next to her. The sweet aroma of her body began to distract me. I began gently stroking her smooth, soft leg.

"I just put the kids to bed. They were terrible tonight. Whenever you don't come home on time they get really rowdy."

"I'm sorry, honey. I know it's hard on you when I come home late. I really missed you."

Rebekah smiled at me and replied, "I missed you too."

"You won't believe what I found out today."

"What?"

"You know that new well Inca's going to drill, Parker #3?"

"Yeah, I remember you telling me about it."

"Well, I met this old abstractor in Cisco and he found an old file where he had done some work on this property in the past. In the file was a production report that showed that the well was pumping two hundred barrels of oil a day when it was shut down and plugged."

"So?"

"So at forty dollars a barrel that would bring in almost three million dollars a year after operating expenses."

"Sounds like it's going to be a nice well."

"Do you know what three percent of that is?" I asked and waited for her to respond. She shrugged her shoulders so I said, "Ninety thousand dollars a year."

"You're not thinking what I think you're thinking, are you?"

"Baby, Tomlinson offered me three percent for the legal work on the well. I told him no, but he said I could change my mind."

"Stan, what if the well is dry?"

"Rebekah, it was pumping over two hundred barrels a day when they plugged it. I don't think even Tomlinson knows how good a well it is. He was only projecting seventy-five to one hundred barrels a day in his prospectus."

"Stan, we can't afford to gamble. We need every cent we can get just to survive. I'm glad you told him no."

"But if we make it big on this well, can you imagine how that would impact our lives? We could hire a maid so you wouldn't have to work so hard. We could get a bigger house and start putting money away for the kids' educations. Hell, it's only a few thousand dollars, which I don't have yet anyway. It's not like I'm taking money out of the bank."

"It won't happen! Nothing comes easy for us. Besides, I've already got a call from American Express. You're forty-five days late on your payment to them."

"When did they call you?"

"This morning?"

"Damn."

"So, I think you ought to just take your fee and forget the well. We need the cash now to pay bills."

"Maybe you're right, but I have a feeling this well is going to be a gusher, and we're going to regret not getting a piece of it."

"That's all right, I'll risk it," Rebekah said.

"Doesn't the thought of having an extra ninety thousand dollars a year tempt you at all?"

"No."

"No? Okay, whatever. How about a little backrub then for a tired traveler."

"I might manage that, but if that gleam in your eye means you're looking for what I think you're looking for, then your luck just ran out."

"Why? . . . Are you mad at me over Parker #3?"

"No, but your children have worn me out and I'm too exhausted to enjoy sex right now."

"Then why did you wear that nightgown?"

"I don't know, it was the only thing clean."

"Hmm. . . . All right, go to bed then . . . I'll be there later. I'm too keyed up to go to sleep now."

The next day I telephoned Bird Logan to advise him of the results of my work in Cisco. He asked me to come by the office around five and deliver my report. I spent the day neatly typing my notes and organizing the material I had gathered. At five I walked through the front door at Inca Oil. No one was in the reception room so I began to wander around looking for Bird or his secretary. My recollection was that Bird's office was the last one down the main hall on the left. As I made my way in that direction, I could hear faint voices in the distance.

When I got to Bird's door I knocked vigorously. There was a commotion inside and then suddenly the door opened and Melissa walked out. She didn't smile as she quickly passed me. I peered inside, and Bird was sitting on his blue leather sofa with a big grin on his face.

"You caught us," Bird laughed. "I forgot I told you to come by at five. Come on in."

"I'm sorry. I can come back another time."

"Nonsense, we were just getting a head start on happy hour. Don't mind Melissa. She'll get over it."

"Are you two serious?" I asked.

"No, strictly recreation," Bird replied. "It gets lonely up here in Dallas during the week. Sheila's my first and only love."

"Don't you worry about getting caught?"

Bird smiled. "No, you're not going to tell her are you?"

"Of course not, but women have a way of figuring things out. Rebekah would know I'd been unfaithful the first moment she saw me after it happened."

"Sheila's too caught up in her social life to give my fidelity a second thought. Besides, I'm not so naive to think that she's been totally faithful. I'm quite a bit older than Sheila."

"You think she's cheating on you?" I said. "Oh God! I can't believe we're having this conversation. I'm sorry, it's none of my business."

Bird laughed, "It's okay. But you're right. We have strayed a bit. So, do you have a report for me?"

"Yes."

After giving Bird the report on Parker #3, I drove home. While I was sitting in heavy traffic on the LBJ Freeway, I decided not to mention what had happened at Inca Oil to Rebekah, as she wouldn't want me to work for someone who cheated on his wife. Although she would never say it, she would be afraid Bird might corrupt me. It would drive her nuts. Since I only had three living clients, I couldn't afford to lose one of them at this critical stage of my practice. With that issue decided my thoughts turned to Melissa. Did she know her relationship with Bird was strictly recreational? Somehow I didn't think so judging by the look she had given me in the hallway.

# PAYDAY

THREE WEEKS LATER WE still had not received any material cash from the law practice. At the beginning of the month, we had sent out over $6,000 in billing, but since that time no one had paid us. The situation was desperate as we had exhausted our American Express line of credit and were nearly sixty days past due on that account. It was Saturday morning and we were getting ready to go to our first of two soccer games that day. We were not looking forward to Marcia attaining the age of five since that would mean we would have four soccer games every Saturday. I had just made pancakes for breakfast and was cleaning up. Rebekah was reading the paper.

"When is Kurt going to get off his butt and pay you?"

"I don't know, I can't understand why he hasn't paid me already. He's making an ungodly amount of money on these deals I'm doing for him."

"Have you said anything to him?"

"Well no, I hate to do that. I shouldn't have to do that."

"Well, what are we going to do for money?"

"If I don't get a check on Monday, I'll go visit him on Tuesday and ask him to pay me."

"What about Inca? Did you tell Tomlinson you wanted in on the well?"

"No, I told you that already."

"I hope not. Lone Star Gas is threatening to cut off our gas."

"When did they threaten to do that?"

"We got a disconnection notice in the mail today."

"That's why it would be so great to get in on Parker #3. If it came in, we'd never have to worry about disconnection notices again."

"You're a dreamer, Stan. Where did I find you anyway?"

"It was your lucky day when you found me. I've already given you more excitement in your life than you ever dared to imagine."

"Your kind of excitement I can do without."

"Well, we've got thirty minutes until we have to leave for the soccer game if you want some real excitement."

"That kind of excitement I can definitely do without." Rebekah laughed.

"Thanks a lot. I'll remember that the next time some voluptuous woman throws herself at me."

"What do you mean?"

"Nothing, just kidding."

"You better not ever cheat on me, Stanley Turner. I would never forgive you. Trust me."

"Relax, I wouldn't dream of betraying you. I love you too much."

"You better not."

On Monday there was no money in the mail, so I put a call in to Kurt to ask him about my bill. When I talked to him he seemed genuinely surprised that I hadn't been paid and suggested I stop by in the morning to get that situation rectified. I advised him I would be there at nine.

The next morning I arrived at Kurt's house promptly at nine. As I made my way into the den, I felt embarrassed coming to see Kurt to get paid. I wondered what he thought of me coming in, almost begging for money. It was awkward and I hoped he would just write me a check next time and drop it in the mail. Kurt was in a red velvet robe sitting at his desk when I entered the room. He looked up and smiled.

"Good morning, Stan. Come on in and sit down."

"Thanks. I'm sorry you had to come by today, but I guess we must have misplaced your bill. Do you have a copy of it?"

I pulled a copy of the bill out of my coat pocket, handed it to him and said, "Yes, right here."

"Let me see, three thousand one hundred dollars. That's a lot of money."

"Well, you've been working me pretty hard."

"And you've done a good job," Kurt said, as he leaned over and pulled up the corner of the rug next to his desk, revealing a floor safe. He spun the dial right, left and then right again until there was a distinct *click*. He opened the door and then pulled out a briefcase. He placed it on his desk and opened it in front of me, exposing a multitude of neatly wrapped one-hundred-dollar bills. He picked one up and carefully counted out thirty-one of them and handed them to me. "Just initial your statement so I'll know I've paid you."

"Sure."

I put my initials on the statement, smiled and then got up to make my retreat. "Thanks a lot. I guess I'll let you get back to bed. I heard you had a late night."

"I'm not going back to bed, I've got too much to do."

"Well, let me know if I can do anything else for you."

"I will."

I was excited to have thirty-one one-hundred-dollar bills in my pocket, but my excitement was blunted by a strange feeling that pervaded the Harrison mansion that day. There was something going on that I didn't know about, but I figured it wasn't any of my business so I soon forgot about it. I went immediately home to show Rebekah the money. I opened the door and ran into the house."

"Rebekah! Where are you?"

"In the baby's room," she yelled.

I ran into Marcia's room where Rebekah was changing a diaper. Mark heard the ruckus and came running in to see what was going on.

"What are you doing home?" Rebekah asked.

"Guess what?"

"What?"

I pulled out the thirty-one one-hundred-dollar bills and waved them in Rebekah's face. Rebekah's eyes lit up.

"Where did you get that?"

"Kurt paid me."

"Thank God," Rebekah said. "Did he pay all of it."

"Yeah, and there's lots more where that came from."

"What do you mean?"

"Kurt has a briefcase in his house that must have a hundred grand in it."

"You're kidding?"

"No, I've seen it for myself."

"Good, then maybe he can pay you on time next month."

"I would hope so."

In the weeks to come Kurt gave me more and more work to do and began to consult with me rather than just giving me orders. The more work I did for him the more I came to realize all was not well with his affairs. One of the projects he put me on was obtaining financing for a rehabilitation of a downtown Amarillo office building called the Panhandle Building. He was negotiating with a Houston S&L, Worldwide Savings and Loan, and they were demanding all kinds of documentation before they would consider doing the deal.

Unlike most of his other projects, the investors on this one were local people, a dentist, a small businessman and an executive at Frito Lay. Each of them had agreed to not only put up about $100,000 each, but also to sign a note on the property to Worldwide Savings and Loan for over a million dollars. Because the Panhandle Building had been designated a historical building and was over one hundred years old, it qualified for some attractive tax credits. My assignment was to meet with each of these investors and to form a limited partnership between them. Then the partnership would buy the building from Kurt after he acquired it. I invited the investors to my office to discuss the deal. All three of them, Tom Tower, Pete Hall and George Sanders, showed up and we met in General Burton's conference room.

"Good afternoon, Kurt Harrison asked me to meet with all of you to get started on putting together a limited partnership to rehab the Panhandle Building in Amarillo, Texas. Now, before we begin, I want to advise you that Kurt Harrison is my client, and therefore I have a conflict of interest in putting this partnership together for you. I must recommend that you obtain your own independent counsel to advise you on this venture. If you decide to obtain an independent attorney, I will be happy to provide your attorney with whatever information he or she might require to evaluate this venture," I said.

"We don't want to have to go find another attorney. Can't you just do it for us? You already know what the project is all about," Tom said.

"I can if you all sign a waiver of conflict of interest," I replied.

"Yeah, let's just get on with it. You're not going to screw us are you?"

"Well no, but that's not the point," I said.

"Kurt's already given us the numbers on the project so we just need to get it wrapped up as soon as possible so we can start taking advantage of the tax benefits in the deal."

"I also need to caution you that you should consult an accountant as to these tax benefits, as neither Kurt nor I have any special expertise in income taxes. We rely on accountants just like you do," I said.

"What about Dan Kelley, he's a CPA?" Tower said.

"That's true, but again he can't represent each of you, so you may want an independent opinion as to the tax benefits of this deal."

"Don knows more about tax shelters than anyone in Dallas. We don't have time to get anyone else involved this late in the game. . . . Let's just put the deal together right now and move on," Mr. Hall said.

"All right, then you all have a packet of documents in front of you which I want to go over with you. Basically there is the partnership agreement, a contract of sale, the waiver and a proposed closing statement. Let's go through these documents one by one, and then if you have any questions, I'll be happy to answer them," I said.

We spent about a half-hour going through the contracts and discussing the basic structure of the deal. When we were done everyone signed the documents and left, except Tom Tower who stayed to discuss another matter. Tom was a man of about fifty years of age and very laid-back and likeable.

"So what can I help you with, Tom?"

"My wife and I need to get some wills done. We don't have any and if something were to happen to either of us, it would be a mess."

"We can take care of that. Can you and your wife come in next week so we can discuss it?"

"Sure, I'll check with her and call you."

"Great."

"Tell me Stan, . . . do you think this a good deal?" Tom asked.

"Well, I really haven't analyzed it from a business stand-point, that's not really my job. My role is just to make sure the legal documentation is correct and adequate," I replied.

"I know, but what do really think? . . . What's your gut feeling?"

"It looks good on paper. The tax benefits are definitely there, but I have no idea if the price you are paying is fair. That would be the real estate appraiser's job and, of course, you can have a dozen appraisers appraise the property and they would all come up with different values."

"I don't have a lot of money you know, this $100,000 is all of my savings. I make a good salary with Frito Lay, but with three kids in college I don't end up saving much money each month," Tom said.

"The only thing I can promise you is that the partnership will own the property when the transaction is complete. Whether you got a good deal or not is anybody's guess. Like I said, you may want to get your own independent representation."

"That's all right. I trust Kurt, I've known him since he was a teenager. His dad and I go way back."

"Oh really?"

"Yes. Kurt's a good boy."

That night I began to worry a little bit about the Panhandle Building project. Although it looked good on paper, there was a lot about the project only Kurt knew about. I had tried to be as honest and straightforward with the investors as I could. One thing that made me feel better about the situation was that Kurt had never once told me what to tell the investors or what not to tell the investors. If he were trying to hide something, I would think he would give me instructions on what to say and what not to say. Since he didn't do that I felt like everything was on the up and up. It also gave me comfort that a big Houston savings and loan like Worldwide Savings was involved in the project. Surely they would check the deal out pretty closely before they lent any money on it. Despite all of my rationalization, I still had lingering doubts, which I expressed to Rebekah that night at the dinner table.

"I met the nicest guy today, Tom Tower," I said.

"Is he related to John Tower?" Rebekah replied.

"I don't think so. He's an executive with Frito Lay and he's investing in Kurt's Panhandle Building project."

"Oh really?"

"I'm kind of worried about him and the other investors."

"Why?"

"None of them have really checked this deal out. They're totally relying on Kurt and now me to protect them. I told them they needed to get their own attorney, but they didn't want to bother."

"Well, they're grown men, right?"

"I know, but I sure hope Kurt isn't taking advantage of them. I'm going to feel like shit if this deal turns out bad."

"Well, what else could you do?"

"I don't know. I have to believe my client unless I learn something that's inconsistent with what he's told me. So far, everything has checked out, but I still can't get rid of this lingering feeling that something's wrong, dead wrong."

"It's probably nothing. You're just not used to these big transactions yet."

"I hope that's all it is."

That night I couldn't sleep very well. I tossed and turned but couldn't get comfortable. My mind wouldn't slow down enough to allow by body to fall asleep. Then when I finally did fall asleep, the phone rang.

"Hello," Rebekah said. "Just a minute."

"Stan. It's for you."

"What?" I said as I struggled to wake up.

"The telephone. It's for you."

"Telephone?"

"Wake up, the telephone is for you."

"Oh okay," I said, as I reached up and grabbed the phone away from Rebekah. "Hello."

"Stan, I'm sorry to bother you, but I need your help."

"Who is this?"

"This is Ron Johnson."

"Ron? What in the hell's going on?"

"I'm in jail."

"In jail, why?"

"They're charging me with driving while intoxicated."

"Oh no. You've got to be kidding."

"I wish I were. Anyway, I need you to come get me out of jail."

"What time is it?" I asked.

"2:40 A.M."

"Oh, okay. Right now?"

"Yeah, I don't want to stay in this shit hole any longer than I have to."

"Okay. What jail are you in?"

"Dallas City Jail."

"Okay, I'll be right there."

"Good, thanks."

"Oh. . . . What do I do? I've never gotten anyone out of jail before."

"Jesus Christ, Stan! Didn't they teach you anything in law school?"

"Yes, but not how to get someone out of jail."

"Just come down here and tell them you want to run a writ."

"Run a writ?"

"Yeah, a writ of habeas corpus. Find a bondsman and get him to write you a bond to get me out. Then take the bond to the sheriff's office and fill out a writ, they have preprinted forms. Get the bond approved and bring it back to the jail and they'll let me out."

"Okay, I'm on my way."

"Thanks. See you in a few minutes."

I reluctantly climbed out of bed and wandered over to the chair where a pair of jeans, T-shirt and sneakers had been tossed before I went to bed. I put them on, grabbed a Windbreaker, jumped into my car and headed for city hall. With no traffic I made the twenty-mile journey in less than thirty minutes. The downtown area was deserted so I found a parking place right across the street from city hall. I was about to go inside to the jail when I remembered I needed to find a bondsman. I didn't know any bondsman so I cruised around downtown until I saw a neon light flashing that read *Alliance Bonding—Open 24 Hours.* Knowing downtown Dallas at night was not the safest place to be, I glanced up and down the street for any sign of trouble. The street seemed to be deserted so I dashed into the bonding company. Inside a young blond-headed man was sitting behind a desk busily working. His arms and chest were quite muscular, and for a minute I wondered if I had mistakenly wandered into a gym.

"Hello," I said.

The man didn't immediately respond, but finished what he was doing. Then he looked up and said, "Hi, what can I do for you?"

"I need to get a bond for a friend of mine in the city jail."

"What's the charge?"

"DWI."

"What relationship are you to him?"

"I guess I'm his lawyer."

"What do you mean, you guess?"

"Well, he's a lawyer too and I used to work for him . . . so it seems a little weird to say I'm his lawyer."

"Does he have any property?"

"Oh yeah, he owns Big D Title Company."

"Oh really? I've heard of it. Okay, I guess we can issue a bond for him. Have a seat and I'll start working on it."

The man pulled out a form from his drawer and began to fill it out.

"What's your name?"

"Stan Turner. What's yours?"

"Roger Rand," he replied. "Who usually handles your bonding for you?"

"Actually this is the first time I've needed anyone."

"Well, I hope you'll let us handle all your work in the future."

"Sure, give me one of your cards."

Roger pulled open his middle drawer and pulled out a few cards and handed them to me. Then he got on the phone and called the city jail to get all the necessary information on Ron Johnson's arrest. After about fifteen minutes, he handed me a completed bond and instructed me to go to the jail and get it signed and then take it to the county sheriff's office to get it approved. I looked at my watch and saw that it was 3:10 A.M. As I pulled up to city hall, a group of seven or eight shabbily dressed, angry-looking guys were coming out of the jail entrance. They were rather rowdy and gave me an unfriendly glance. I tried to ignore them as I entered the Dallas City Jail.

The jail was old, rundown and dirty. The waiting room was crowded with friends and relatives impatiently waiting to get their loved ones out of jail. I went up to the main desk and advised the desk sergeant that I had to get a bond signed. He took the bond and said he would go get it signed for me. I was instructed to take a seat and wait for him to return.

With considerable difficulty I found an empty spot on a bench and sat down. An old man with torn khaki pants and a badly stained shirt was fast asleep across from me. Every once in a while he would snore so loud he would wake himself up.

Several children were running around the waiting room play-ing tag. Their mother seemed to be oblivious to their disor-derly behavior. A well-dressed woman sat next to me engrossed in a book. I felt conspicuous and uncomfortable. What was I doing in a place like this? Now I knew why I didn't want to be a criminal attorney.

By the time I got out of the jail it was 3:45 A.M. I was getting tired so I drove quickly to the county courthouse and parked in front. I went up to the courthouse entrance, but was distressed to find it locked. How was I to get this bond approved if I couldn't get into the courthouse? I glanced around nervously wondering where the night entrance might be.

I heard a noise behind me and turned quickly to ascertain what it was. A slovenly looking man with a paper bag ap-proached me mumbling about something. I quickly extricated myself from his path and headed for the other side of the court-house hoping I would find an opened door. As I rounded the east side of the building, a car pulled up and a well-dressed man jumped out. It occurred to me that this man might be a lawyer, so I followed him and sure enough he led me to the night entrance to the sheriff's office.

Once inside I asked a deputy where I could find the pre-printed writs and the person who approved bonds. He pointed me to a large desk in the middle of the room. I got the appro-priate forms, filled them out and handed them to the officer in charge. After a few minutes he gave me back the approved bond and writ, and I returned to my car. It was now 4:15 A.M.

I never dreamed it was so difficult getting someone out of jail. When I got back to city hall I gave my paperwork to the desk sergeant and sat down to wait for Ron to be released. At 5:00 A.M. the large door to the cellblocks opened, and a steady stream of inmates were released. I asked one of the officers who were all the people they were letting go, and he advised me it was all the drunks that had been picked up the night before. I continued to wait until it was nearly 6:00 A.M.

Tired and becoming more and more disgusted by the minute, I went to the desk sergeant and complained that they hadn't released Ron yet. He apologized and explained that they had temporarily lost him. Somehow during transfer from one cellblock to another they had lost track of him and couldn't find him so he could be released. Finally at 6:45 Ron walked out of the cellblock entrance a free man, and I immediately escorted him out of the jail and to my car. We got in and drove off.

"Did you know they lost you in there?" I said.

"That doesn't surprise me as many inmates as there were."

"So you must have had quite a party last night?" I said.

"Yeah, and I've got a hangover to prove it."

"Where's your car?"

"Just take me home, I don't want to deal with that now."

"I hope you don't want me to defend you on this charge."

"Why, don't you do criminal law?"

"No way, I didn't enjoy this at all."

Ron laughed and said, "Well that's okay, I know a guy in McKinney that hasn't lost a DWI case in years. He'll take care of this for me."

"Good."

After I took Ron to his house, I went home to crash. Rebekah was up making breakfast when I walked in.

"I don't believe my husband is finally home," Rebekah said.

"It's a bitch getting people out of jail," I replied.

"I hope he's going to pay you a lot of money for spending the whole damn night away from home."

"I can't charge him."

"Why not?"

"Professional courtesy. He's been helping me out a lot on Kurt's real estate deals so I couldn't charge him for this."

"Damn it. You're out all night long and you're not going to get a red cent."

"I wouldn't have made any money sleeping so I didn't really lose anything."

"I know, but we're just so desperate for money."

"We're going to survive, don't worry."

"You want some breakfast?"

"No thanks, all I want is some sleep. Wake me up at noon okay?"

# THE GHOST

WITH EXTREME DIFFICULTY, REBEKAH got me up at noon and I went to the office. I wanted to follow up on the information General Burton had given me on Melba Thorn. I pulled out the piece of paper with her son's name and number on it and began to dial the telephone. It rang several times, and then a young man answered.

"Hello, this is Robert Thorn."

"Hi Mr. Thorn, this is Stan Turner, I'm an attorney and I'm calling about your mother."

"My mother?"

"Yes, Melba Thorn."

"My mother's been dead for over two years."

"Your mother is dead?"

"Yes, she is, so what's this all about?"

"Well, a woman has been calling me claiming to be your mother and asking me to help her."

There was a momentary silence on the line until Mr. Thorn finally said, "That's ridiculous. Who would do such a thing?"

"I don't know, but I'd sure like to find out. You don't have any ideas do you?"

"No, absolutely not, the whole thing is absurd," he said. "What did this woman say she wanted?" Thorn asked.

"She said she was being held against her will by members of her family, and she wanted me to help her regain her freedom."

"That's totally ludicrous. Aside from the fact that my mother's dead, no one in our family would have ever held her against her will."

"I don't doubt that Mr. Thorn, but I'm just telling you what the woman told me. What I don't understand is why this impostor called me."

"Who are you, anyway?" Thorn asked.

"Just an attorney here in north Dallas. I've just recently started a law practice."

"Is this some kind of a shakedown? Are you after something?"

"No," I said. "I'm just trying to figure out what's going on."

"I'd suggest you forget the whole thing. I don't want you snooping into our family's business."

"Well, I'm sorry I bothered you. I guess it must have been a prank."

"Apparently so," Thorn said. "Someone's got a strange sense of humor."

"*Very* strange," I replied. "Well, . . . thanks for the information, good-bye."

Mr. Thorn's revelation that his mother was dead stunned me. Either Robert Thorn was a liar, or I had been talking to a ghost. Not being a believer of the supernatural, I opted for the falsehood. I had no choice now but to find Melba Thorn, no matter how difficult that might be. As I was pondering my next move, the phone rang.

"I'm Martha Sweet from the office of the United States Postal Inspectors."

"Yes."

"We're conducting an investigation into the activities of Gena Lombardi and we understand you're her attorney."

"Well, I'm her bankruptcy attorney."

"We want to arrange a time to meet with you and her to discuss her case. We've gathered a lot of evidence, and we wanted to discuss the possibility of a plea bargain."

"Gee, I'd like to help you, but I'm not a criminal attorney. I'm just handling her bankruptcy."

"Well, we'd like to talk to someone so we can avoid having to go for an indictment."

"What did she do anyway?"

"We've got a lot of complaints from people out of state who sent her money for tickets and travel packages, but never got the merchandise. I guess you know it's a federal offense to use the United States mail in any kind of fraudulent scheme."

"Well, I'll call her and see if I can find out who's going to represent her in this matter. I think she has a criminal attorney. Maybe he'll be handling this."

"Let us know real soon, otherwise we'll just have no choice but to go for an indictment and arrest her."

"Okay, I'll call her right now."

"Thanks. Good-bye."

The last thing I wanted to do was call Gena, but I had no choice. I pulled out her file, found her number and called her. "I just got a call from Martha Sweet at the postal inspector's office," I said. "They say they're investigating you for mail fraud."

"What?" Gena replied. "I've already told that bitch that it wasn't my fault. You know, I told you about Tony taking all my money. Well, some of that money was from customers for tickets and hotel rooms and obviously since Tony took the money I couldn't buy them. There wasn't anything fraudulent about it."

"Well, it sounds like you may have a good defense, but you need to get your criminal attorney to call Martha Sweet."

"He won't take any more cases."

"Why?"

"I don't know. He's just a jerk. He says I'm not a good client, can you believe that?"

I laughed to myself. "No. Why aren't you a good client?"

"He says I don't listen to him and I don't pay my bills."

"Well, you can't blame him for wanting to get paid."

"I've already paid him over $5,000. You'd think he would cut me a little slack while I'm down."

"Well, you need to find someone to defend you."

"Why can't you do it?" Gena said.

"For starters, I don't practice criminal law, and secondly I'm kind of fond of getting paid myself."

"Well, that's okay, I've got another problem that you can handle."

"Oh really, what would that be."

"Did you look in your mail today? My mortgage company is trying to foreclose on my house."

"Have you paid them since we filed bankruptcy?"

"No."

"Well, I told you you've got to pay them each month from now on. The bankruptcy only takes care of the past arrearage."

"But I don't have the money."

"Then you'll have to let the house go."

"I can't do that. I've got to have the house."

"Then you better come up with money to pay the mortgage company, otherwise there's nothing I can do to help you."

"Great. You're a big help."

"I'm sorry, I just practice law, I don't perform miracles."

"Okay, I'll go try to scrape up some money somewhere."

"Good. See you later."

# THE RHINESTONE PROSPECT

It was Friday night and Rebekah had to work the night shift in the emergency room at North Central Receiving Hospital from three to eleven. This meant I had to get home early, feed the kids and amuse them the entire evening. While this was hard work, I loved the children so I really didn't mind it. They all were good kids and I had a lot of fun playing with them. I got home at 2:30 P.M. and Rebekah was dressed and ready to go.

"You all ready to go?" I asked.

"Just about," Rebekah replied. "I think Marcia needs her diaper changed. I was going to change it, but it's getting late."

"Go on, I'll take care of the little princess."

"How was work today?" Rebekah asked.

"Well, pretty interesting actually."

"How's that?"

"It seems that I have clients summoning me from the grave."

"What are you talking about?"

"Melba Thorn is dead," I said.

"Huh?"

"For two years."

"What'd they do, equip her casket with a telephone?"

"It's not funny," I said.

"Well, you'll have to explain this one to me later, honey.
I've got to go. I'll see you at 11:30. I love you."

"Bye-bye. Love ya too."

On Monday morning I got up early and drove to Love Field
to take the seven o'clock flight to Corpus Christi. Bird had
called me Friday and advised me that he needed some title
work done on a well not too far from Corpus Christi. He called
it Rhinestone Prospect. He said he would pick me up when
my flight landed at 9:10 A.M. because he wanted me to meet
his wife and see his home on Corpus Christi Bay before I got
to work. When I emerged from the ramp at gate eleven, Logan was there, with his very young and lovely wife, to greet me.

"Stan, . . . over here," Mr. Logan yelled.

"Hi Mr. Logan, thanks for coming to pick me up?"

"No problem. Hey, I want you to meet my wife, Sheila."

Sheila was medium height with a dark complexion. She
was wearing white jean shorts and a yellow halter tie sweater.
Her shoulder-length, dark brown hair was pulled back onto
her shoulders. We shook hands.

"Nice to meet you," I said.

"It's certainly a pleasure to meet you Mr. Turner," Sheila
replied.

Bird Logan must have been close to forty, I figured, and
Sheila couldn't have been a day over twenty-two. I wondered
why a beautiful young woman would marry a not-so-good-look-
ing, middle-aged man. More astonishing, however, was Bird's
behavior. Why would he ever do anything to jeopardize a mar-
riage to such a gorgeous woman?

"Come on, the car is parked out front," Bird said.

"Okay, lead the way."

We found Logan's car and loaded it up, and then he drove
us back to his beach house on the bay. It was a beautiful sunny
day with a cool southern breeze. The ocean was a deep alluring blue, and I was wishing I could have hired a deep-sea char-
ter rather than spend the day in the county clerk's office.

"Did you have a good flight Stan?" Sheila asked.

"Oh yes, it was smooth as silk and very relaxing," I replied.

"Have you ever been to Corpus Christi before?"

"I've passed through once or twice, but I've never stayed here. We've gone to South Padre a few times."

"So did you hear about Palmer #7?" Bird said.

"No, what about it?"

"It came in yesterday at eighty barrels a day."

"Wow! That's great," I said. "I bet the investors are happy."

"They ought to be, they're going to get back their investment in seven months and then it's pure profit."

"So how many Inca wells are in production now?"

"We've got nine now. Nine out of thirteen."

"That's a pretty good record," I said. "How do you think Parker #3 is going to do?"

"It looks like a sure thing. From the logs I've seen, it ought to produce a hundred barrels a day."

"Is there any chance that something could have happened to the oil since the well was capped twenty years ago?"

"All those wells on that pool were capped about the same time, so whatever oil was left should still be there. The only way it wouldn't be is if someone kept on pumping, and the records don't show that to be the case."

"So, Mr. Logan, how long have you been in the oil business?"

"You can call me Bird, Stan," Logan said. "About twenty-one years. I started out as a roughneck on one of the wells owned by the tribe."

"What tribe was that?"

"Comanche."

"Are you full blooded?"

"Almost, seven-eighths."

"Why did they call you Bird?"

"My real name is Blackbird, but my nickname is Bird," he said. "Indians name their children based on their feeling at the time of birth. Shortly after I was born a blackbird flew over my parent's teepee and screeched at them. They considered it a sign I should be called Blackbird."

"That's interesting," I said.

"I was lucky. I can live with the name Bird. It's kind of strange but not too bad. One of my friends wasn't so lucky."

"How's that?"

"His parents didn't want any more children. They already had six little braves. They were very angry and upset when their seventh child was born."

"Huh? So what did they name him?" I asked.

"Broken Rubber."

Bird and Sheila burst into laughter.

"Oh God, I think I've been set up."

"It's all right, Stan, Bird plays that joke on everyone he meets," Sheila said.

About that time Bird pulled us up into the driveway of his beach house. The house was on a man-made island that protruded out into Corpus Christi Bay. It faced the waterfront and had its own dock. A large yacht was tied up to it.

"That's a beautiful boat you have. Do you use it a lot?"

"I don't, Sheila's the mariner. I prefer horses or helicopters," Bird said.

"Yeah, Bird won't go sailing with me. He gets seasick," Sheila said.

"Really, I love to sail, I guess because I was born and raised near the sea in Ventura, California. I spent most of my spare time as a kid fishing off the pier," I said.

"Oh you can come sailing with me then," Sheila said.

"That would be great."

"Good, I'll go change my clothes and we can set sail."

"Now?" I said.

Sheila smiled. "Yes, Right now, I don't get too many opportunities to go out since Bird won't go."

"Well, I wish I could but I've got a lot of work to do in town at the county clerk's office," I replied.

"Take a few hours off, Stan," Bird said. "Those record books aren't going any place. I need to get rid of Sheila for a few hours so I can get some work done."

Bird's insistence that I go sailing shocked me. I had prepared myself for a boring day's labor pouring over deed records
in a dusty courthouse. The thought of cruising out in the bay
with a beautiful woman certainly was alluring.

"Are you sure?"

"I insist."

"But, if I don't get started at the courthouse soon, I may
not finish today."

"If you don't finish you can stay the night and finish in
the morning," Bird replied.

"Come on Stan. Let's get the ship loaded and get out of
here before Bird changes his mind," Sheila laughed.

"Okay, but I didn't really dress for sailing."

"There're some clothes in the guest room you can change
into if you want. I'll start loading up."

"Okay, I guess. I'll be right there."

Getting to go sailing on Corpus Christi Bay was a pleasant
surprise. I felt awkward and a little guilty taking Bird's incred-
ibly beautiful wife out to sea all alone, but I figured if Bird
didn't care then why should I worry about it. Sheila took the
helm and yelled at me to untie the boat and cast us off. I
untied both lines and pushed us away from the dock with my
foot. Sheila cranked the engine, and we began to slowly glide
toward the bay. After we cleared the dock, I joined Sheila at
the helm.

"Isn't this fun?" Sheila said.

"Boy is it ever," I replied. "I've never been on a private
yacht before."

"Is that right?"

"Well, I've gone deep-sea fishing, I've been on cruise ships
and lots of small ski boats, but nothing like this."

"I love it. I wish I could go out every day, but Bird won't
let me go alone. I'm so glad you wanted to go out. Hold onto
the wheel a minute, would you?"

"Okay."

Sheila pulled her sweater off over her head revealing a
bright yellow bikini top underneath. She was deeply tanned

all over and her stomach was flat and firm. She took back the wheel and smiled at me.

"Thank you, Stan. Isn't the air out here clean and fresh?"

"It sure is. I love the smell of the ocean," I said. "Where are we headed?"

"I thought we'd go to a little island I know about where we can swim and have a picnic."

"Great."

After about forty minutes, we approached an island about two acres in size with a white sandy beach.

"We can anchor here and then swim to shore," Sheila said. "We can come back later for the dinghy."

She put down the anchor, shut off the engine and then dove off the side of the boat toward shore. I stripped to my swimsuit and dove in after her. As I approached the beach, she splashed water on me and then swam away. I took that to be an invitation to pursue her so I did. When I caught her I grabbed her foot and pulled her toward me. She grabbed my head and tried to dunk me. We wrestled and played for a while until she got tired and went to lie on the beach. I watched her there on the sand for a while, wondering what was going through her head. Was this just an innocent adventure or did she have other things on her mind? She was so beautiful and so friendly I had the urge to go over and ravish her body. Unfortunately, her husband was back home waiting for her and, of course, I was a married man with four children. *Shit! How did I end up out here with such a temptation?*

Sheila looked over at me and smiled. "Would you put some suntan lotion on my back?" she said.

*Oh, Mother of God, why are you doing this to me?*

"Sure," I said.

I walked over to her and she handed me a tube of Coppertone. Then she unhooked the back of her top, exposing a portion of her breasts. I took a deep breath and began to rub the suntan lotion on her back. As I rubbed the lotion round and round on her soft supple skin, I got so aroused that if she had turned around I would have been quite embarrassed.

"Be sure you rub it in good all over. I don't want any streaks or patches," she said.

"Okay, I'll cover every inch of your body, don't worry."

She smiled as if she knew the torture I was feeling. Just then there was a garbled sound coming from the yacht.

"What's that?" I said.

"It's Bird calling us. I'll have to swim out and answer it."

Sheila jumped up, forgetting she had unhooked her swimsuit top. Her naked breasts were extraordinary. I gasped in delight at the sight. She smiled, grabbed her top, quickly put it back over her breasts and then turned and said, "Okay, Stan, put your eyes back in their sockets and hook this for me."

"Sure," I said.

After Sheila's top was secure, she ran toward the beach. I ran after her, and we raced each other to the boat. When I reached the yacht I quickly climbed aboard and helped her in. She gave me a bewitching little smile and climbed up to the helm to answer the radio.

"Blackbird One here," she said.

"Where have you been?" Bird said.

"On the beach having a picnic," Sheila replied.

"You need to get back here right away. The National Weather Service has issued a severe thunderstorm warning. You've only got about twenty minutes to get back before the storms start hitting."

"Okay, copy, we're on our way," she said.

"I can't believe we're going to have thunderstorms today, it looks so beautiful out here. There are hardly any clouds in the sky," I said.

"Well, these storms come up suddenly out here. Bird always keeps his ear on the radio when I go out sailing. He's very protective."

"Well, I can understand that. He has a beautiful wife to protect. I'd do the same. . . . Well, actually I wouldn't let you out of my sight."

"Listen, I'm not usually so careless with my clothing. Please don't say anything to Bird."

"Oh no, I didn't see anything. It was all just a wonderful dream."

Sheila smiled and started up the engines. We didn't say much on the way home. Our little outing had been very pleasant and quite memorable, although I could never tell anyone about it. As we approached the dock, Bird came outside and threw us a rope. We secured the boat and went inside.

"Did you two have fun?" Bird asked.

"Yes, it was beautiful out in the bay today," Sheila said.

"I was worried about you two when I heard the National Weather Service announce that severe thunderstorm warning."

As Bird was talking, it began to get dark outside and lightning could be seen in the distance.

"Looks like we got back just in the nick of time," I said. "I think I'll head on to the courthouse before the storm hits."

"You can take Sheila's jeep. Here are the keys," Bird said.

"Thanks, I'll be back around 5:30," I said.

"Good, we can go to Landry's for dinner," Sheila said. "They have the best seafood in Corpus."

"Sounds good to me. See you guys later."

Somehow I managed to beat the bad weather to the courthouse where I spent the rest of the day trying to work. Unfortunately I had difficulty concentrating as I kept daydreaming about Sheila and our morning cruise. The afternoon went fast and I barely finished before five o'clock when they shut down the clerk's office.

That night we all went out to Landry's before I had to take a late flight back to Dallas. Sheila was distracting in a short black slip dress with spaghetti straps. Bird was wearing a long black dress shirt with the top three buttons undone and a charcoal sport coat.

"So Bird, how did you and Tomlinson meet?" I asked.

"We're SMU fraternity brothers," he replied.

"Was Tex in your fraternity too?" I asked.

"Yes, he was, and we've all kept in touch with each other over the years," Bird replied. "When Tomlinson decided to start Inca, he called me and asked me to come aboard. At the time, I was working as a geologist for Mid-Continent Oil Company and the idea of doing a little wildcatting was quite attractive."

"I see," I said.

"What I want to know is when you're coming back down here, Stan, so we can take the yacht on a serious trip?" Sheila said. "I'm tired of just cruising the bay. I want to go to Mexico."

"That would take awhile. I doubt if Bird would turn you loose that long," I said.

"I don't know. Could I trust you two together for a week?" Bird said.

"I wouldn't if I were you, and I know my wife wouldn't trust me alone with Sheila for a minute," I replied.

Bird laughed. "Well Stan, at least you're honest."

I looked at Sheila and replied, "You have a very charming and beautiful wife. You're a lucky man."

"Thank you."

"When you come up to Dallas next time let me know and Rebekah and I will take you out to dinner," I said, as I looked at my watch. "Oh boy, it's getting late, I think I need to head back to the airport or I'll be sleeping on your sofa tonight."

"We've got an extra bedroom," Sheila said.

"Thanks, but if I don't get home and relieve Rebekah from the four monsters, she'll have my head."

"You have four kids?" Sheila said. "You don't look old enough to have children."

"That's what everybody says, but I assure you they're all mine."

Bird and Sheila took me back to the airport just in time to make my 8:45 P.M. flight back to Dallas. On the flight home I couldn't keep my thoughts off of Sheila. Wicked ideas crept into my mind. It occurred to me that if I came down again, I should bring Melissa, then I'd have Sheila all to myself. Before we touched down I managed to purge my mind of all depravity. I prayed silently for God to forgive me.

At 11:15 P.M. I walked into our house. Rebekah was in the family room watching TV.

"Stan! You're finally home," Rebekah said.

"Yeah, and you're lucky I'm here, I almost missed my flight."

"How come?"

"Bird and Sheila insisted on taking me to Landry's and we got to talking and lost track of time. I walked on the plane just as they were getting ready to secure the hatch."

"Oh. I would have been pissed if you missed your flight."

"I know, but I didn't. So how was your day?"

"Not too bad, Marcia threw up all over the sofa. It was a bitch to clean it, believe me."

"What happened, she eat something that didn't agree with her?"

"I don't know what it was," Rebekah said.

"Anybody call for me today?" I said.

"Yes, you got another call from your ghost client, Melba Thorn."

"You're kidding?"

"No, she called and asked for you. She was very disappointed when you weren't here."

"Did you talk to her at all?"

"I tried to, but it was like I was having a one-way conversation. I could hear her, but she couldn't hear me. I did find out where she was calling from though."

"How did you manage that?"

"She called collect, so I asked the operator where the call was coming from and she said Amarillo, Texas. I tried to get the number, but the operator said she couldn't give me that information."

"Amarillo . . . huh . . . I can't believe she called collect?

"She's obviously alive if she's in Amarillo," I said. "Unless Amarillo is Heaven."

"No, I always heard Amarillo was Hell," Rebekah replied.

"No, I think that's Odessa. Well at least now we know where to start looking."

"You're not going to go to Amarillo are you?"

"Well, not right away, but I may have to eventually."

"But you don't know if she's crazy or not, or whether she'll ever pay you."

"I know, but if her son is pretending she's dead, then something is seriously wrong, and I can't turn my back on it."

"Why didn't you just go to work for the legal aid society?" Rebekah said.

"And spend all my time doing divorces and child custody? No way. Besides, if it turns out she is rich and I rescue her, she'll be happy to pay me."

"Yeah, you're going to spend a hundred hours chasing her down just to find out she's some crazy old lady who's having delusions that she's Melba Thorn."

"Maybe so, but I guess that's a chance I'll just have to take."

That night, as I lay in my bed, my thoughts immediately ventured back to my encounter with Sheila Logan. Before long I fell asleep and found myself back in Corpus Christi.

*Sheila dropped the anchor, shut the engine and then dove off the side of the boat toward shore. I stripped to my swimsuit and dove in after her. As I approached the beach, she splashed water on me and then swam away. I swam after her and when I caught her I grabbed her foot and pulled her toward me. She grabbed my head and tried to dunk me. I escaped and wrapped my arms around her back and pressed her up against my body. She struggled to get away but I held her tightly. Finally I let her go and she strutted up on the beach and lay out on the sand. After a minute she turned over, looked at me and said, "Be a nice guy and go get me some Coppertone and bring the picnic basket."*

*I swam back to the ship, lowered the dinghy and dropped the picnic basket in it. Then I cast off and rowed to shore. After I had secured the dinghy, she called to me, "Rub some Coppertone on my back would you, Stan? . . . And bring me a beer."*

*"Okay," I said.*

*I grabbed two beers and the Coppertone and walked over to where Sheila was lying. I noticed she had unhooked her swim top to keep*

*from getting strap marks. Much to my delight, as she reached to take
her beer, she exposed a naked breast.*

*"Would you rub some of this on by back and legs, Stan," she said.*

*"Sure," I replied eagerly.*

*I began to gently rub the lotion on her back and shoulders. "Well,
Oh. . . . Umm. . . . Don't miss one inch of my body," she said. "I
don't want any streaks or blotches."*

*"I won't," I replied, as I began to caress her thighs with the lo-
tion. With every stroke my body became more aroused.*

*"Ohhh. . . . Ohhh. . . . Stan, that feels so good . . . don't stop."*

*I squeezed some more lotion on my hands and began to slowly rub
higher and higher on her leg until I reached her voluptuous bottom.
Since I had yet to meet any resistance, I slipped my hands under her
suit to see if there was any place that was off limits. She didn't resist
me, so I sat up and put my hand on her shoulder and gently turned
her over exposing her naked breasts. I leaned down and kissed them
tenderly. She put her arms around me and pulled me down on top of
her. We embraced and rolled wildly over and over in the warm white
sand. Her body felt so soft and succulent against me I could hardly
endure the pleasure. We interrupted our sexual frenzy just long enough
to remove our suits. Then we made love to the sound of the sea gulls
squawking above us and the pounding of the waves, until we reached
a plateau of ecstasy beyond imagination.*

*Suddenly the CB on the Yacht began to crackle. . . .*

*"It's time for the morning traffic report here at KPCS Country
Radio. There is a fender—"*

I hit the snooze button and rolled over, annoyed that my
dream had been interrupted. It seemed so real I could almost
smell Sheila's scent on my body. Once awakened, I wondered
if I was a fool not to make the dream a reality. I wanted Sheila
and I believed that she wanted me. I knew I could never have
her, but that only intensified my desire. So far I hadn't actually done anything wrong, but the carnal thoughts that engulfed
my mind made me feel guilty nonetheless. To ease my mind I
vowed to go to confession on Thursday.

# DEATH ON HIGHWAY 24

THE CLOCK RADIO BLARED its harsh refrain over and over every nine minutes starting at 7:30, but unconsciously I managed to hit the snooze button with equal regularity. Finally I opened my eyes and looked at the clock and saw the time.

"Shit! It's already 9:30."

Rebekah rolled over and looked at me. "I can't believe the kids are still asleep. They're usually up at 7:00."

"I've got to get out of here. I've got a 10:30 appointment with a new corporate client."

I flew out of bed, hit the shower and was out of the house in twenty minutes. When I walked in the office, General Burton was practicing his putting on a green carpet he usually kept rolled up in his closet.

"How's your game today?" I asked.

"Not worth a rat's ass, that's why I'm practicing."

"You going out today?"

"Rufus is picking me up at two," the general said. "So how was Corpus?"

"Beautiful. The guy I met down there has a beach house on the bay with his own yacht . . . and a wife that'd knock your socks off," I replied.

"Really?"

"Uh huh. . . . Oh, guess who called while I was gone?"

"Who?"

"The late Melba Thorn," I said. "And Rebekah found out where she's calling from."

"Where?"

"Amarillo."

"Amarillo? . . . Huh. What're you going to do now?"

"This afternoon I'm going to the library and check out all of the news stories on Melba's death. Then I'm going to see if I can find some of her old friends who can fill me in on some family history."

"I can probably help you there. I'll try to get you some names and phone numbers."

"Good, that'll be a big help."

As we were speaking, my 10:30 appointment walked in the door. After taking care of them, I checked my phone messages from the answering machine and saw I had a call from Cynthia Carson. I dialed the number and waited as the phone rang.

"Oh, hi Stan. Thanks for calling me back. Listen, Kurt's out of town and a couple of problems have come up. I need you to handle them for me."

"Sure, what are they?"

"Metro Leasing has been calling and threatening to re-possess the Rolls."

"What?" I said. "I didn't know the Rolls was leased."

"Yeah, Kurt leases everything. He doesn't believe in buying anything because he likes to preserve his capital."

"Do you know why he's behind on the payments?"

"No, I don't. . . . It must be some kind of oversight."

"Okay, I'll call them and calm them down until Kurt gets back."

"Thanks."

"What's the other problem?"

"You remember Pete Hall, one of the investors in the Pan-handle building?"

"Right."

"He wants to go over the deal with you again. His accountant has spooked him," Cynthia said.

"Sure, shall I call him?" I said.

"Please. Don't let him slip away. Kurt will be furious if he loses one of his investors."

"I'll talk to him. Don't worry."

"Thanks Stan, let me know if you need anything."

The calls from Metro Leasing disturbed me since I had always got the impression Kurt owned everything. I immediately called them to see what they were upset about.

"Mr. Weber, this is Stan Turner. Cynthia Carson asked me to call you regarding Kurt Harrison."

"Yes, is he going to pay up, or do we have to come out and pick up the Rolls?"

"Well, I wasn't aware he was behind. How much does he owe?"

"He's two months past due."

"So how much is that?"

"Eleven hundred and twenty-four dollars."

"Damn, those are pretty stiff payments."

"Well, it's a one hundred and twenty-five thousand dollar automobile."

My car had cost me $8,000 and change. I couldn't fathom paying over a hundred grand for a car.

"Kurt's out of town for a few days. When he gets back I'll be sure he drops off a check."

"We can't wait a few days. We need to get paid now or we're going to come repossess the car."

"Come on, you can wait a couple of days, can't you?"

"No, Mr. Harrison has never made a payment on time and were tired of it. We would rather just write off whatever our loss might be and never see Mr. Harrison again."

"Well, let me see if somehow I can scrape up the two payments due so we don't have to get entangled in litigation over this matter. I don't understand why you can't wait a few more days since you've waited this long."

"Well we can't, and if we don't get our money by Monday, we'll be over to pick up the Rolls," he said.

"It won't do you any good to go over there, the vehicle will be locked up and you can't breach the peace trying to repossess it. You'll have to file a writ of sequestration if you want the vehicle. By the time you get that put together Kurt will be back and will pay you. You might as well just wait."

It surprised me that Kurt was having problems with Metro Leasing since he was making so much money on his real estate ventures. Surely he could afford to pay his bills. I figured I would give him the benefit of the doubt anyway. Maybe he was just so busy he wasn't tending to his business the way he should.

That afternoon I went downtown to the Dallas Department of Vital Statistics to get Melba's death certificate, then to the public library where I started searching through old newspapers that were kept on microfilm. It didn't take long to find the story on Melba Thorn's death.

DALLAS PHILANTHROPIST KILLED IN FIERY CRASH

Melba Thorn, a wealthy Dallas resident, known for her generosity and love for the arts and education, died Monday in a fiery automobile crash on Highway 24 near Wilkerson Pass, Colorado. Mrs. Thorn, who had been vacationing in Colorado Springs at the renowned Winchester Hotel and Resort with her family, apparently was returning from a visit to the University of Colorado at Boulder when the 1977 Cadillac she was driving mysteriously spun out of control, plummeted off a cliff and then exploded into a fiery inferno. Sheriff Dick Barnett, from nearby Florissant, Colorado, indicated the victim's body was burnt beyond recognition.

Mrs. Thorn was the widow of the late real estate baron, Howard Thorn, who reportedly owned major downtown buildings in Dallas, Tyler, Ft. Worth and Amarillo. She was born in

London, England, in 1926 and immigrated to
the United States with her father, an unem-
ployed tailor, when she was only three. She attended the University of Texas from 1942-46
where she met and married Howard Thorn. She
is survived by her son, Robert Thorn, and daughter, Jane Thorn Brown. Funeral services will be
held Thursday in Dallas.

Mrs. Thorn was most known for her support
of SMU and the Dallas Fine Arts Institute. The
Dean of Southern Methodist University, when
asked about his reaction to Mrs. Thorn's un-
timely death, said, "She was a wonderful woman,
a great friend of the University and she will be
sorely missed."

It occurred to me that the incineration of Melba's body
was very unusual and convenient. If Melba was alive, I wondered who really died in that crash. I needed to find out all
about Melba Thorn, her friends, her enemies and who stood
to gain by the appearance of her death. Perhaps if I went to
SMU I would get some answers. I left the library and drove to
Highland Park where the university was situated. On the way I
devised a story to explain why I was interested in Mrs. Thorn.
The dean's office was the logical place to start since he had
been quoted in the newspaper. When I walked in, a well-dressed
middle-age receptionist greeted me. Luckily the dean was in
and I was able to see him.

"Can I help you?" Dean Pope asked.

"Yes sir, I'm Stan Turner and I wondered if I could ask you
some questions about Melba Thorn."

"Melba Thorn? Why would you be asking questions about
her?"

"I have a client that's thinking about setting up a scholarship fund to honor her. He wanted me to write a short story
about her life to put in the introductory materials that'd be
sent to applicants for the scholarship," I replied.

"How nice. Who is your client?"

"Well, he wants his participation to be anonymous so that the media will focus on Melba Thorn rather than him, since the purpose of the program is to honor her."

"I see. Well, what do you want to know?"

"When did Melba first start supporting the university?" I said.

"Shortly after her husband's death. You probably know the only thing Howard Thorn knew how to do was make money. He never gave any money away after he'd earned it," Dean Pope said.

"Really?"

"Did you know her personally?"

"Sure, she spent a lot of time here at the university. She was very much involved in the programs she supported financially. She loved the students and they loved her. Some of the students affectionately called her Grandma Thorn."

"It must have been a great tragedy when she died," I said.

"It was devastating," he said. "Not only did we lose a great friend and wonderful woman, but the financial loss to the university was overwhelming."

"Didn't the heirs pick up where Melba left off?"

"No, I'm afraid Robert Thorn took after his father."

"What about Jane?"

"I think if Jane controlled the fortune, she'd be a lot different. Regretfully, Robert and her husband, Taylor Brown, pretty much control what goes on."

"That's too bad. You'd think in deference to their mother they'd be a little more generous," I said.

"That would make sense," Dean Pope replied.

"Didn't you think the accident was a little strange?"

The Dean perked up in his chair. "What do you mean?"

"I don't know, it just seems a little strange to me that this rich old lady is up in Colorado with her family and runs off to Colorado Springs by herself. Why didn't someone go with her? What happened to her chauffeur."

"You know, you're right. It didn't make much sense. As a matter of fact, I called the sheriff to ask him about it."

"What did he say?"

"He said he did a thorough investigation and found nothing to make him think it was anything but an accident. Apparently all the members of the family were horseback riding fifty miles away when the accident occurred."

"Does anyone know why she went off that day alone?" I said.

"Apparently they thought her chauffeur was driving her to the university, but apparently he was getting the limo fixed. Mrs. Thorn decided to take her son's rented car and drive alone."

"What do you think of that?" I asked.

"That's really strange because I know Melba didn't like to drive. She was always driven by her chauffeur, and I can't imagine her driving on a treacherous mountain road all alone."

"Tell me about Jane's husband," I said.

"Taylor Brown? He runs a string of nursing homes around the state. That's about all I know about him"

"He doesn't happen to have one in Amarillo does he?"

"I don't know."

It was nearly five, so after talking to Dean Pope I went straight home. I was anxious to tell Rebekah what I had found out. She was in the laundry room washing clothes when I arrived.

"Hi, babe," I said.

"Wow! Did my watch stop?" she said.

"No, I came straight home to tell you what I found out about Melba Thorn."

"Oh, what?"

"Melba died in a single-vehicle car wreck on a mountain road in Colorado. Her body was incinerated while her family was horseback riding fifty miles away and her chauffeur was getting her limo fixed."

"That's pretty bizarre," Rebekah said.

"Yeah, particularly since she didn't like to drive and usually was driven every place she went."

"So why would she go out alone in the mountains?" Rebekah asked.

"Nobody seems to know or care," I said. "And get this. Melba's daughter is married to a man named Taylor Brown, who happens to own nursing homes all over the state."

"You don't think Melba is being held hostage in one of those nursing homes, do you?" Rebekah said.

"That idea occurred to me. I think tomorrow I'm going to call the Department of Health and find out if Mr. Brown owns a nursing home in Amarillo."

While Rebekah and I were talking, Peter came running around the corner.

"Mom, Reggie stole my fire truck!" he said before spotting me. "Daddy, you're home!"

"Yeah, come here big boy," I said. Peter ran over and raised his hands to be picked up. I pulled him up and held him in my arms. "Let's go see if I can rescue your truck."

"Okay, Reggie's mean."

We walked down the hall and entered Reggie's room. He had gathered a fleet of trucks that would have made any teamster proud.

"Wow, where did you get all those trucks?" I said.

"Hi Dad. How do you like my convoy?" Reggie replied.

"Pretty cool. . . . You didn't happen to see a stray fire truck did you?"

"Yeah, he joined the convoy in LA," Reggie said. "Well, how about if Peter takes her in for mechanical repairs in Frisco?"

"Dad I need all these trucks . . . especially a fire truck in case there's a crash on Highway 101."

"If there's a crash, you can get on your CB and call Peter, he'll be happy to respond," I said.

"Okay," Reggie said and then tossed the truck into the middle of the room.

I put Peter down and he picked up the fire truck, climbed up on the top bunk and began to play with it.

"Tell us a story, Daddy," Peter said.

"A story?" I replied.

"Yeah. Please, Daddy," Reggie joined in. "Tell us the story about you falling off the railroad bridge."

"Oh come on, you've heard it a dozen times," I said.

"Well tell us a new story then," Peter said.

"Hmm, . . . let me think, . . . okay," I said.

I climbed up onto the top bunk and lay down next to Peter. Reggie jumped on the bottom bunk and lay back to listen to the story. Mark wandered in and sat down in the middle of the room.

"Okay, once upon a time I was with my Boy Scout troop camping near Mt. Shasta in California. We had gotten up early to take a hike and were approaching a small creek. When we got to the creek, we all started looking for places to cross without getting wet. I spotted a big log that was lying across the entire creek so I started to cross it. Suddenly I looked down and saw that I was about to step on a water moccasin."

"Ahh!" Peter yelled.

I turned quickly to tickle him and suddenly the bunk collapsed. Peter and I looked at each other in shock. Suddenly I realized we were lying on top of Reggie. I bolted off the bed and tried to pull up the mattress, but Peter was still on it. "Peter, get off. Reggie's under there."

Peter began to laugh hysterically at his brother's plight. Reluctantly he crawled off the bed.

"Reggie! You okay?" Rebekah came running in the room. "What happened!" she screamed.

Reggie climbed out from underneath the mattress looking rather confused.

"You okay son?" I asked.

"Sure Dad. I'm fine. What happened?"

"Oh my God! Are you sure you're okay Reggie?" Rebekah moaned.

"I guess the bolts were loose on the supports," I said.

"Stan you had no business being up there!" Rebekah yelled. "You're just like a little kid sometimes!"

"Okay, I'm sorry, Reggie's fine. . . . Relax."

"Hey Dad," Reggie said. "Did the water moccasin bite you?"

"No, it turned out he had just swallowed a trout so he was harmless," I replied.

"Whew! That was lucky," Reggie said.

"Okay, dinner is ready, come on before your dad maims one of you," Rebekah said.

The next day I had an early appointment with Pete Hall. I didn't know exactly what we were going to talk about, but I was sure I could allay his fears a day or two until Kurt could get back. Pete was a short, red-faced man and very extroverted. When the door opened I jumped up to greet him. After getting coffee we sat down.

"Cynthia said you had some questions that you needed to get answered right away," I said.

"Yes, you know I've known Kurt for a long time," Pete said. "He used to date my daughter, Ruth."

"I didn't know that."

"Yeah, he set her up in the dry cleaning business, Hollywood Cleaners. You know, down on Turtle Creek."

"Oh yeah, I've gone by it."

"Kurt's a great guy and he's always been good to me and Ruth, but sometimes he gets in over his head in some of these deals."

"How do you mean?" I said.

"Well, Kurt's pretty shrewd, but every once in a while he deals with people smarter than he is . . . like Mohammed Bhangi."

"Who's he?"

"He's a guy from Beverly Hills that Kurt bought some apartments from last year. After the deal was made it turned out Mohammed had a partner he neglected to tell Kurt about. Mohammed disappeared and his partner sued Kurt."

"Gee. I didn't hear about any lawsuits."

"Anyway, I know that wasn't necessarily Kurt's fault, but I want to be sure this Panhandle Building deal is clean."

"You don't have to worry about that, you guys are going to get a title policy when the deal is closed."

"I know that Stan, but I just want you to make double sure everything's okay with this deal. I'm investing all of my retirement money and I can't afford to lose it."

"Well I've never seen the Panhandle Building, nor do I know anything about it as an investment. You guys have to make your own decision as to whether it's a good deal or not. I'll make sure you own it and all the legal work is done properly. After that, it's up to Kurt to rehab the building and then sell it for a big profit. You know better than I do that Kurt's awfully good at flipping property."

"Well, just keep your eyes open Stan. Protect me, okay. I really trust you."

"I'll have Kurt call you when he returns so he can discuss the specifics of the deal with you in more depth," I said.

"No, that's all right . . . I trust you. See you later."

I was upset by the meeting with Pete. It was like everything I said to him was meaningless. He obviously didn't come to ask me any questions or listen to anything I had to say. He simply wanted to tell me that he expected me to protect him. But that wasn't my job. I represented Kurt, and I told him and the other investors that, but they didn't listen. If anything went wrong, they were going to blame it on me.

I pondered what I could do to check out the investment to see if there were any holes in it. Perhaps I could convince Kurt to let my friend, Ron Johnson, close the deal at Big D Title Company. That way I would have much better control over the entire transaction. There really wasn't much else I could do.

On Thursday I went to work early so I could stop by St. Michael's Catholic Church to go to confession. I didn't tell Rebekah I was going, but I had been feeling guilty all week about my encounter with Sheila earlier in the week and needed to talk to someone about it. There were two priests receiving confessions. I choose Father Henry as he seemed the wiser of the two priests that served our parish. I waited for my turn and then entered the confessional.

"Forgive me father for I have sinned. It has been a year . . . well, maybe two years since my last confession."

"What brings you to seek the Lord's forgiveness after such a long time?" Father Henry asked.

"I've coveted another man's wife and nearly committed adultery?" I said.

"But you didn't?"

"No, but I have in my mind. I dream about making love to her almost every night."

"You must forget about her. The mind is strong, but the body is weak. Stay away from her. Cleanse your thoughts of her."

"But, she's the wife of one of my best clients, and I'm bound to see her again. What's worse, the way she looks at me, I think she wants to make love with me."

"Then tell your client you cannot work for him anymore; better to lose a client than a wife."

"But Father, you don't understand. I'm just starting out and I only have three clients."

"Better to lose all your clients than the love of God. You'll get other clients. Don't worry, my son. Now for your absolution, go do five Hail Marys, two Our Fathers and pray for God's forgiveness."

"Thank you, Father."

Confession made me feel a little better, but I couldn't bring myself to quit working for Inca Oil. They were too good a client, and I planned on making a big score on Parker #3 when it was drilled. I figured I would just have to stay clear of Sheila.

The next day I called over to see if Kurt had made it back in town. Cynthia answered the phone and told me that indeed Kurt had returned and that he wanted me to come over and report to him on my meeting with Pete Hall and conversations with Metro Leasing. When I arrived, Kurt was out in the front yard with two Doberman pinchers. After I parked my Pinto next to the Maserati I walked cautiously over to him. The dogs growled at me.

"Quiet down Ginger," Kurt said.

"Nice dogs," I said. "I didn't know you were a dog lover."

"These aren't pets. They are highly trained attack dogs. We've been having a problem with prowlers lately, and I'm teaching them to patrol the grounds."

"You don't have a solid fence around this place, so won't they just run off if you leave them?" I asked.

"No. They have a remote control device that gives them an electric shock if they go beyond a certain point," Kurt said. "After a few days they'll patrol the ground, but won't stray too close to the perimeter."

"What about people you invite over?"

Kurt smiled. "Well you better get to know them so they'll recognize you."

"Good idea. What are their names?" I said.

"Ginger and Pepper."

"Come here, Ginger," I said, as I knelt down and extended my hand. "Come here, Pepper."

The two dogs warily approached me, sniffing my feet and my legs. Slowly I moved my hand over their heads and began to pet them. They immediately warmed up to me and became very friendly.

"Well, they seem to like you. I don't think you'll have any trouble," Kurt said.

"No, dogs love me. I don't know why but they always do. I always had a dog when I was a kid. Rebekah doesn't like dogs so we don't have one now."

"Is that right? Well, come on in and tell me about Pete."

I followed Kurt through the house to the patio where Gwen was sitting and talking to Cynthia. Kurt sat down and told the maid to get me a drink.

"How was your trip?" I said.

"It went perfect. I got two new investors for sure and several excellent prospects. So what's Pete's problem?"

"He's just worried about the Panhandle Building deal," I said. "You know he's dropping all his retirement money into that project."

"Well you know who made him all that money?" Kurt asked. "I did. When I was dating his daughter he was penniless with no retirement at all. I put him in a couple of deals for peanuts and made him over one hundred thousand dollars."

"He mentioned something about that. I don't think he's going to be a problem, he's just a little scared and needed some reassurance."

"Well tell him if he sticks in this Panhandle deal, he'll triple his money in six months, plus get a tax write off that will make his profit almost tax free," Kurt said.

"You think it's going to be that good?" I said.

"I know it is. Once I rehab that building there'll be buyers lining up to buy it."

"Why is that?"

"Because none of these buyers want to go to all the trouble to locate a suitable building, hire a contractor and sink a lot of capital into a rehab project. They're too chicken to take that kind of gamble. But when I get the building done and have it all leased up, they'll be knocking at my door to buy it . . . and they'll pay me much more than the property is really worth."

"That makes sense, but what if you can't get the building leased up? Isn't downtown Amarillo dying?"

"That's a myth. Amarillo has one of the most dynamic downtown areas in Texas. They have an active civic association that's constantly doing things to promote the downtown area. We won't have any problems getting tenants because when we're done, we'll have one of the nicest buildings in Amarillo. And it won't be some modern skyscraper; it'll be a building with class and style."

"Well, you sold me," I said.

Kurt smiled and said, "You want in on this one, Stan?"

"No, I've got four kids that like to eat a lot so I pretty much spend everything I make."

"Well if you keep doing a good job, in six months you'll have lots of extra money. Maybe you can even afford a real car," Kurt said.

I didn't respond to Kurt's comment as I was a little hurt and embarrassed. Gwen sensed my embarrassment and changed the subject. "So I heard you went down to Corpus Christi," she said.

"Yeah, I did . . . had a little business down there," I replied.

"I love Corpus," Gwen said. "The bay is so beautiful."

"I love the deep blue water and salty smell in the air," I said.

"I hate the ocean," Kurt said. "I'll take the sweet scent of the city anytime."

"I guess I need to talk to you about Metro Leasing," I said.

"I took care of that little bastard already. If he sets one foot on this place, Ginger and Pepper will have him for lunch," Kurt said.

I didn't know how to respond to what Kurt said so I kept my mouth shut. I wondered if he meant he had paid Metro what he owed them, or he got Pepper and Ginger to guard the Rolls so it wouldn't be repossessed. I assumed it had to be the former.

"Listen Kurt, I wonder if you would do me a favor?" I said.

"What's that?" Kurt said as he gave me a curious look.

"I know you have a title company you usually use, but I've got this friend, Ron Johnson, who owns Big D Title Company, and who has been a big help to me getting my law practice off the ground. I was wondering if you would let Big D close the Panhandle Building deal?"

Kurt pondered my request for a moment and then said, "Why not? A title company is a title company . . . it doesn't matter what their name is, they're all underwritten by the same insurance companies. Anyway, Commercial Title has been kind of taking me for granted lately. It'll be good for them to realize I can go to any title company I want. Maybe they'll become a little more responsive to my needs in the future."

"Thank you. That's great," I said. "Well, I've got to get going. Nice seeing you again Gwen . . . Cynthia," I said.

"Don't forget the Panhandle deal has got to close in ten days. Be sure your guy at Big D is ready."

"No problem."

When I got back to the office I immediately called Ron Johnson and told him the good news. He was delighted he was going to get to close on a 2.5 million dollar office building, not just once but twice. I felt good because he had been so helpful to me when I needed him and now I was able to repay him. He assured me he would be ready for the closing in ten days.

That afternoon it began to rain and before long General Burton showed up. I wondered if he ever actually worked. I never saw him take a client to look at some real estate and he never talked about any properties he was trying to sell. The only thing I ever saw him do was go play golf or take some old friend out to lunch. My curiosity finally got the best of me so I asked him about it.

"General Burton, I know you're in the commercial real estate business, but I never hear you talking about any properties or projects you're working on."

"You know Stan, I've got a nice pension from the army so I don't need to make a lot of money, besides in my business you only need to make a sale once or twice a year to do well."

"I guess I'm in the wrong business."

"Well, most real estate agents work very hard, I'm just lucky because I'm a retired general, and I've got lots of friends who do most of my work for me."

"I guess you've earned it."

"I've paid my dues," General Burton said. "Hey. I've got some good news about Melba Thorn."

"What's that?"

"You wanted to talk to someone who knew her well."

"Yes," I said. "Well, we're having lunch today with Jane Thorn Brown."

"Her daughter?"

"Right, I used to see her quite a lot when I knew her parents so I just gave her a call," General Burton said. "She was really happy to hear from me so I invited her to lunch."

"Oh man, that's great. Now maybe we can find out what in the hell is going on."

# THE MERGER

At noon the door swung open and Jane Thorn Brown made her appearance. She was a slim brunette, about five foot four and appeared to be in her early thirties. General Burton took her into his office for a few minutes, for what purpose I wasn't sure, but shortly thereafter they appeared at my door.

"Jane, I want you to meet Stan Turner."

"Oh, I am delighted to meet you Mr. Turner. General Burton was just telling me about you."

"The pleasure is definitely mine."

"I hope you will go to lunch with us," Jane said.

"I'd love to."

"Well let's be off then," General Burton said. "We can take my car."

"Nonsense, my driver is out front with the limousine," Jane said.

"Okay, fine."

Jane introduced us to her driver, Ralph Hopkins. He was young, athletic and apparently very serious, as I never once saw him give even a hint of a smile.

"Ralph is a great driver. He's been with me now for over five years. I don't know what I would do without him," Jane said.

We rode in Jane's limousine to the Italian Alps, a five-star Italian restaurant well known for its exquisite Northern Italian cuisine. When the waiter spotted the general, he immediately took us to a corner table away from the usual bustle of the lunchtime crowd. After we were settled in and had given the waiter our orders, General Burton began to reminisce with Jane.

"I can remember you when you were in high school. Didn't you attend Immaculate Heart?" General Burton said.

"Yes, that was a long time ago," Jane said.

"Your mother was so proud of you. She wanted you to be a teacher as I recall."

"Actually she wanted me to be a college professor. She was really into education. She believed that education was the key to solving most of the world's ills."

"Well, I would tend to agree with her," General Burton said. "If there is any one force that can change the world for the better, it would certainly be our teachers."

"She was so disappointed when I refused to go to college. It was like I had betrayed her. She wouldn't talk to me for months."

"Why didn't you want to go to college?" I asked.

"I'm just not the intellectual type," Jane replied. "I was tired of school, I wanted to travel, to meet people and maybe work in my father's business or start a business of my own."

"I can identify with that, I never liked school much," I said. "I always felt like I would never use what they were teaching me. For instance I took six years of French and I haven't spoken a word of French to anyone in the past five years."

"Exactly, I was tired of learning. I wanted to experience, to taste life," Jane said.

"So, how did it work out?" I asked.

"Not so well. My dad wouldn't let me work in the business, he said a woman's place is at home. Of course, Mom was mad at me for not going to college so she made sure none of my travel plans got funded."

"She got over it though, didn't she?" General Burton said.

"Oh, of course, particularly after Dad died. We had to pull together to bear the tragedy."

"Yes, your father was a fine man and a great businessman. I don't know of anyone who could analyze the merits of a business deal so quickly and accurately as your father."

"You're very kind, General."

"I was doubly shocked to hear just the other day of your mother's sudden death," General Burton said. "And such a horrid way to die."

"I still can't believe it. Mom had been bugging Robert and me to bring our families to Colorado and vacation with her. She was so excited that we were finally all together and then all of sudden she's dead."

"Do you have any idea why she was driving alone in the mountains? That seemed uncharacteristic of your mother," General Burton asked.

"There had been a fight between Mom and Robert. She was upset and wanted to go for a drive. Her driver was out having the limo fixed, so she got in one of the rented Cadillacs and just took off. I figured she would calm down and return after a few hours, but when we all got back from horseback riding she was still gone. After four or five hours had passed I became very worried and called the police. It was then that they told me of the accident."

"I wonder what your mother and Robert could have been arguing about that would make her so upset that she would take off like that. Your mom was so mild mannered it just seems so strange," General Burton said.

"Robert was upset that Mom wouldn't let him run the business. He wanted more power; he didn't like the way Mom was giving away so much money to all her charities. He was frustrated because Mom would torpedo all his ideas for expansion and reorganization of the business. If I recall, at the time they were arguing something about a merger between Taylor's company and Thorn Realty. Taylor keeps me in the dark about his business so I'm not sure exactly what the argument was about, but it was very intense."

"General Burton mentioned your mother's death to me earlier, I'm very sorry," I said. "Did the police find out why your mom's car went out of control?"

"He thinks she hit a deer. They found one dead on the side of the road near where her car went off. Apparently as she came around a sharp turn, she was suddenly confronted by the deer. She veered to the right to avoid hitting it, however it was too late. When she hit it, she lost control of the car . . .," Jane said as she began to weep, "and . . . and it spun off the cliff."

"I am so sorry, Jane," General Burton said. "We shouldn't be talking about this. I'm sorry I brought it up."

"It's all right. I should be able to talk about it now. It's been over a year."

The waiter brought our food, and the conversation waned as we enjoyed the exquisite meal. Jane seemed like a nice woman who was deeply hurt by the loss of her mother and father. I could understand her grief, as I had lost my father recently as well, but I didn't quite understand all the inner-workings in the Thorn family so I pressed for more details.

"So is your brother running the business now?" I asked.

"Yes, . . . well, he and Taylor are actually. They merged their two businesses about a year ago," Jane said.

"So what are you doing now Jane?" General Burton said. "Do you have any children yet?"

"No, no children. I've been doing some of the traveling that I've always wanted to do."

"Does Taylor travel with you?" General Burton asked.

"Are you kidding? He's too wrapped up in the business for that. I usually take one of my friends and, of course, Ralph comes along to watch out for us. But, enough about me, what have you been doing, General?"

"Playing lots of golf," I noted.

General Burton gave me a wounded look. "Don't mind Stan, he's just jealous because he's just starting out in his career and has lots of hard work ahead of him. As you know, I'm coasting on the fruits of forty years of labor."

"Well no one deserves it more than you, General," Jane replied.

"I concur. I was just giving the general a bad time today about all the golf he played. He so eloquently pointed out to me, however, that the important thing in the business world was not how hard, but how smart you worked."

"Well, General Burton is a wise man so I recommend you listen carefully to everything he tells you," Jane said.

After lunch Ralph drove us back to the office. We had learned a lot, but the puzzle was far from complete. I didn't dare tell Jane that her mother, or someone claiming to be her mother, had been calling me. That would have to wait until I had confirmed that Melba was indeed alive. For now, I had to plan my next move. Where did I go from here to get closer to the truth?

It seemed I had three options: Go to Amarillo to scour all the nursing homes for evidence that Melba was being held in one of them, go to Colorado to find out more about the accident or confront Robert Thorn once again now that I had more information. Somehow I didn't feel ready for Robert Thorn so I opted to go to Colorado via Amarillo. My only problems were time and money, I didn't have either. Friday was a busy day; in the morning I had the big Panhandle Building closing, and in the afternoon Gena Lombardi's creditor's meeting. But even if I had the time, the money I had collected from Kurt Harrison for last month's billing was gone and there was no way I could afford a week's travel.

My only hope was if General Burton would fund the trip since he was as interested in solving the mystery of Melba Thorn as I was. When I told him of my dilemma he not only agreed to pay all my expenses, but also insisted his travel agent make all the arrangements. I told him it would have to wait until Monday, however, due to the Friday closing and Rebekah's weekend job at North Central Receiving Hospital.

During the afternoon I began final preparations for the Panhandle closing. While I was engrossed in my work, the phone rang. It was Bird.

"Hey listen, Sheila and I have to come up Friday to meet with Tomlinson. We thought we'd stay the weekend so I wanted to take you up on your dinner invitation."

"Oh, Saturday. Well, Rebekah works on the weekends so we'll have to work around her schedule."

"That's okay just check with her, and give me a call Friday over at Inca so we can coordinate our plans."

"Fine. What are you going to be doing with Tomlinson?"

"We're making final preparations on Parker #3. We want to start drilling in a couple of weeks."

"So you're telling me I've got to decide pretty quickly whether to cash in my chips or put them down on Parker #3."

"It looks that way, we've almost sold the well out, so Tomlinson is closing it to further investors on Friday. As a matter of fact, when you call me Friday let me know your decision. If you want to get paid, I'll have Tomlinson cut you a check, otherwise we'll need you to come by and sign an investor letter."

"I guess I've got some hard thinking to do," I said.

"It's only money, Stan. If you take the money, you're just going to spend it anyway. Take a little risk. If the well comes in and you're sitting on the outside looking in, you'll never forgive yourself."

"I don't know. I've got to talk to Rebekah about it. Money's kind of tight right now."

"Well, let us know. I'll talk to you on Friday," Bird said.

"Okay, say hello to Sheila."

Bird's call upset me. It was a bad weekend for him and Sheila to come to Dallas. Friday was already going to be a bitch of a day and now I had to make a decision on Parker #3 to boot. Then on Saturday Rebekah was going to meet Sheila. I had worried about that ever since I came back from Corpus. Rebekah was no dummy, she would sense the tension between Sheila and me immediately, and then when I got home I would get barraged with questions about my trip to Corpus Christi. What's going on between you and Sheila? she would want to

know. If she found out about the little excursion on Blackbird
One, I was a dead man.

As I was finishing up the Panhandle paperwork, I thought
I would call Kurt and Ron to see if everything was set for Friday. It was already Wednesday and if anything else had to be
done I needed to find out about it soon. I called Kurt first.
Gwen answered.

"Is Kurt around?"

"No, the president and loan officer from Worldwide Savings and Loan flew up in their corporate jet and picked up
Kurt on their way to Amarillo to check out the Panhandle Building before the closing on Friday."

"So everything looks good for Friday?"

"I guess. I overheard Kurt making luncheon reservations
for everybody at Pierre's Place at the Plaza of the Americas. I
think he intends it to be a closing party."

"A closing party. I never heard of that."

"Kurt likes to celebrate after important closings."

"Sounds good to me. Okay, well, tell Kurt if he needs me
to give me a call."

After I hung up I called Ron Johnson to see if everything
was ready for the closing. He advised me it was ready so I
packed up my briefcase to go home. I was about to leave when
I remembered I needed to call Gena Lombardi to remind her
of her creditor's meeting Friday. She was not at home so I left
her a message on her answering machine to meet me at the
federal courthouse fifteen minutes before the two o'clock hearing on Friday.

When I got home I had to go immediately to soccer practice with Reggie. When we returned dinner was ready, so the
family sat down together to eat. I thought it was a good time
to discuss coordination of our schedules for the next few days.

"Friday is going to be a busy day," I said.

"You've got your big closing don't you?" Rebekah said.

"Yes, but I also have a two o'clock creditor's meeting.
There's no way I can get home by two-thirty. Can your mother
come over until five?" I said.

"Probably, but I'll have to call her to be sure."

"I got a call from Bird Logan today. He wants us to have dinner with him and his wife Saturday."

"But I've got to work," Rebekah said.

"That's what I told him, but he wanted me to check with you anyway."

"Well, maybe I can get someone to trade shifts with me. I'll have to call the hospital and find out who's working Saturday."

"Don't knock yourself out. It's not critical that we have dinner with them. We can do it another time."

"I know it's important for you to socialize with your clients so you can get to know them better. Let me call around and see if someone will switch shifts with me."

"Okay, if you can, but it's no big deal."

Rebekah got up and went into the other room to make a phone call.

"Is Grandma going to baby-sit Friday?" Mark asked.

"That's right," I replied.

"Oh goody!"

Rebekah walked back into the room and sat down. She smiled and said, "I got my shift changed to seven to three."

"Good then, we're all set."

# THE PANHANDLE BUILDING

THE PARTIES BEGAN TO gather at Big D Title Company at 9:30 A.M. Ron Johnson had arranged two conference rooms, one for the sellers and one for the buyers. When I arrived, Cynthia Carson was talking to Pete Hall and George Sanders.

"Good morning," I said.

"Hi Stan," Cynthia replied.

Pete and George got up and we shook hands.

"You guys ready to put this deal to bed?" I said.

"I guess so," Pete replied.

"Did the people at Worldwide ever inspect the building?" George asked.

"Yes, they went out to Amarillo Wednesday and they were quite pleased with how it looked," Cynthia replied.

Just then Ron Johnson came in with a secretary. Ron was carrying a large stack of documents.

"Good morning gentlemen . . . Miss Carson," Ron said. "Here are all the closing documents for your review."

Ron placed a set of documents on the table, and then excused himself to go give a set to the sellers. Shortly after he left Tom Tower arrived.

"Good morning everybody," he said. "Is everybody ready to make some money?"

"I'm ready," Pete said.

"Have you read all these documents Stan?" George asked.

"Yes, but you all need to read them," I replied.

"If you've read them, I don't see why I should," George said. "What do we pay you for?"

"Well, actually you're not paying me, Kurt is, and it's just good business to read everything before you sign it," I said.

"Where is Kurt anyway?" Tom asked.

Cynthia went to the window, looked outside and said, "He should be here any minute."

I picked up the closing documents and started passing them around. "Go ahead and start looking these over, and if you have any questions, I'll be happy to answer them."

I looked at my watch and it was now 10:15. I wondered what had happened to Kurt. It was not unusual for him to be late, but this was an important closing and I was surprised he wasn't here. The parties began to get restless so Cynthia tried to call around to find Kurt. At 11:03 we were advised the sellers were going to leave in ten minutes if Kurt didn't show up. Several minutes later Ron Johnson came in and advised us that Kurt was on his way and would be there in five minutes. At 11:15 Kurt finally walked into the room.

"Good morning, gentlemen," Kurt said, as he walked over to the head of the table and opened his briefcase.

"It's damn near afternoon Kurt," George said.

"I'm sorry I'm late, but I had to do a little last minute negotiating with Worldwide Savings before we could close this deal," Kurt replied.

"I thought the financing was all worked out weeks ago?" Tom said.

"It was more or less, but they wanted me to pledge all of my profits against your note. I told them I couldn't do that because I needed that money to fund some of the rehabilitation costs on the building," Kurt said.

"So did you get it resolved?" I asked.

"Yes, they're going to let me take two-thirds of the money and put one-third in a CD and pledge it against the new note."

"How long will it take you to do the rehab?" George asked.

"Well, there are fifteen floors in the Panhandle Building, and seven floors have already been done and are ninety percent leased. So that means we have eight floors to totally rehab and then lease up. I would say that would take maybe six months. The nice thing is we're already cash flowing with the existing tenants."

Ron Johnson entered the room accompanied by two well-dressed men. "Excuse me, but I want to introduce Lawrence Wylie, the president of Worldwide Savings and his attorney, Mark Pointer," Ron said. "Okay, gentlemen. Are we ready to close?"

Everyone acknowledged they were ready, so Ron collected the three $100,000 checks from the buyers and began passing around documents for signature. When everything had been signed, Mr. Wylie went to the phone and called his office. When he got off the phone he said, "The loan proceeds are being wired as I speak."

Ron left the room and everyone began conversing with one another. During the break I took this opportunity to compliment Kurt on his dealings with Worldwide Savings.

"You're one hell of a salesman," I said. "I've never heard of a banker turning loose of collateral once he got his greasy palms on it."

"They wanted this deal, I could smell it," Kurt said. "That gave me a lot of leverage."

Ron Johnson came back into the room and asked for everyone's attention. "Gentlemen, the funds are in our account so the closing is complete. My secretary has a copy of all the documents for each of you. Thank you for closing with Big D Title and I hope we can serve you again soon."

Kurt then stood up and spoke to the gathering. "Before everyone leaves, I want to invite all of you to a luncheon celebration at Pierre's Place at the Plaza of the Americas at noon. This transaction is going to be lucrative for all of us, and I think we have good reason to celebrate. Pierre's has valet parking on the Pearl Street entrance, which I would recommend. So I hope to see all of you very soon."

The closing broke up and everyone headed downtown for the party. As I drove up in front of the Plaza of the Americas, I noticed Kurt right behind me in his Maserati. After they took my Pinto, I waited for him. The parking attendant's eyes lit up when he saw Kurt's car. Kurt got out, handed the attendant a $20 bill and said, "Take good care of this one. I don't want any scratches."

After everyone was seated in the restaurant, Kurt thanked them for their help putting the Panhandle Building deal together. He promised the buyers were going to make lots of money when the project was completed and resold. Then the waiters poured everyone a glass of champagne, and Kurt gave a toast to the new venture. After a lavish lunch Kurt handed me an envelope. I opened it to find twenty-five one-hundred-dollar bills along with a copy of my last statement for $2,122.50."

"Thank you Kurt. But that's more than you owed."

"The rest is a little bonus for the special attention you've given me. I know I'm not an easy client at times and I appreciate your patience. Oh, . . . and tell Ron Johnson that was an excellent closing, I may want to use Big D from time to time in the future."

"He's a great guy. He'll be glad to hear you were happy with the way things went," I said, as I looked down at my watch. "Oh, . . . I've got to get going. I've got a meeting a 2:00 P.M. at the Federal Building."

I got up, shook hands and left. The payment from Kurt was unexpected, but couldn't have come at a better time since Rebekah and I were virtually out of money. As I counted and recounted the money, I remembered I needed to call Bird to advise him about Saturday night and to tell him my decision on Parker #3. Now that I had a few dollars in my pocket, the decision of whether to gamble or not became more difficult. Had Kurt not paid me, I wouldn't have had any choice but to ask for a check. I figured if Inca paid me now it would be about twenty-five hundred dollars. That was a lot of money to me at the time; just three months earlier I had been making three hundred dollars a week.

By the time I got to the Federal Building I still didn't know what to do. I felt like Parker #3 was almost a sure thing based on the information I had seen, but I'd never had any luck gambling in the past so what made me think my luck would be any different now. In desperation I pulled out a coin and decided to flip for it, heads gamble, tails take the check. I threw the coin in the air and let it fall on the ground. I knelt down and saw that it was heads. A sick feeling came over me. Glancing at my watch, I saw it was nearly two o'clock so I went to a telephone booth to call Logan.

"Hey, Rebekah was able to switch around her shift so we'll be available Saturday night."

"Good, Sheila's really looking forward to meeting Rebekah."

"Rebekah's anxious to meet Sheila too. How about 7:30?"

"Fine."

"Listen, about Parker #3. I decided . . . to . . . ah, I decided to . . . I guess, go ahead and invest in the well," I said.

"You're going to invest?"

"Right."

"Great. I think that's a wise decision. You'll need to drop by and sign an investor letter. Or if you want, I'll just bring it by Saturday night to save you a trip over here."

"No, that's okay. I'll just drop by," I said.

"Good then, we'll see you and Rebekah tomorrow."

"Okay, see you then."

It was getting late so I took the elevator up to the ninth floor to the trustees' meeting room. Gena was leaning against the wall across from the doorway. She was wearing a short red baby doll dress and carried a matching purse. As I approached her, she stood up straight and smiled.

"Stan, you made it. I was worried you wouldn't come," Gena said.

"I told you I'd be here."

"I know, but I'm just nervous. Do you think any of my creditors will be here?"

"No, this should be real easy. All I am going to do is ask you if everything on your bankruptcy schedules is true and correct and why you had to file bankruptcy. There'll be five or ten other people having their creditor's meetings now too, so you won't be alone."

"Okay."

"Come on, we better get inside before they call your case."

We went inside and sat down amongst the crowd of debtors, creditors and attorneys. The trustee walked in with his secretary and sat down. He fumbled with his tape recorder, and after he got it going he commenced the meeting.

"Ladies and gentlemen, I'm Robert Olson. I have been appointed as interim trustee to administer your case. The cases will be called in the order in which they were filed. Everyone making an appearance will need to sign in. The first case is Gena Lombardi."

I stood up and motioned for Gena to come forward and sit at the table in front of the trustee. She reluctantly got up, walked to the table and sat down.

"This is case number 79-43217 in the United States District Court for the Northern District of Texas. The debtor is here with her counsel of record. Please state your name," the trustee said.

"Gena Lombardi."

"All right counsel, you may question the witness."

"Miss Lombardi, I'm going to show you the original petition that you filed in this case, along with the schedules attached to it. Is the information contained in these documents true and correct?"

"Yes."

I asked her the standard questions. There were no creditors present so the trustee took over questioning and went through his list of questions. I was relieved that the meeting had gone so smoothly. As we got up two well-dressed men approached Gena.

"Are you Gena Lombardi?" one of them asked.

"Yes," Gena replied.

"Miss Lombardi, you're under arrest. Please place your hands on the table."

"Under arrest! For what?" Gena said. "Stan, you can't let them do this."

"Who are you guys?" I asked.

"We're deputy U.S. marshals. . . . Now stand back and don't interfere."

One of the officers frisked Gena for weapons and then made her put her hands behind her back. Gena began to cry.

"Stan, come with me. Don't leave me alone, I'm scared."

"Okay, if they'll let me," I said. "Where are you taking her?"

"To the U.S. marshal's office on the sixteenth floor," the deputy said.

"I'll come up with you, Gena, don't worry."

I followed the marshals as they escorted Gena to the elevators. When the doors opened, they entered, but when I tried to follow them in, one of them said, "You'll have to take another elevator sir."

By the time I got to the sixteenth floor, Gena was nowhere to be found. I went to the main entrance to the U.S. marshal's office and entered. There was a deputy busy doing paperwork at a front desk.

"Did they just bring Gena Lombardi in here?" I said.

"I wouldn't know, they bring prisoners in the back door," he replied.

"Can you check and see if she's here?"

"Who are you?"

"I'm her attorney."

"Wait a minute, I'll go check."

After a few minutes the deputy returned and said, "She's here, but they're checking her in now, so you can't see her for thirty minutes or so."

"Can you tell me what the charges are?"

"Mail fraud," he said.

When he said mail fraud, I suddenly remembered the telephone call from the postal inspector's office. Obviously Gena had not contacted her criminal attorney after I had informed her of that call. I waited around about forty-five minutes, and finally the deputy said I could go see her. They led me into a small detention room where Gena was sitting behind a steel mesh screen. We had to talk through an intercom.

"You all right, Gena?"

"I guess," she replied.

"I'm sorry this happened to you. Didn't you call your criminal attorney about the postal inspectors that called me?"

"Yes, but he wouldn't do anything unless I brought him a $5,000 retainer."

"Oh no. Well, they have to give you a court appointed attorney," I said.

"Yeah, but court appointed attorneys are no good. Won't you defend me, Stan?"

"Me? . . . No way. I'm not a criminal attorney. The only criminal case I've been involved in was when I was tried for murder."

"You were charged with murder?"

"Yes, when I was in the Marine Corps."

"I can't believe my attorney was charged with murder! That is so cool."

"I was acquitted."

"Now, I definitely want you to defend me. I know you'll be better than anyone the court appoints. If it's the money, I promise you I'll pay you every cent of your fee no matter how much it is," Gena said.

"I'm sure you would try, but what if you were convicted and went to prison? You obviously couldn't pay me then."

"My mom would pay you."

"Just like she's sent me that five hundred dollar retainer on your bankruptcy."

Gena fell back in her chair and took a deep breath.

"I could kill Tony, that bastard. He better hope I never see his pretty face again."

"Maybe the trustee will find him and make him pay the twenty thousand dollars back."

"Oh Stan! I just remembered . . . my Corvette is down in the parking lot. You can't let them take it."

"I don't know if they'll let me have it," I said.

"Please, make them give it to you and keep it for me."

"Well, I guess I could take it and park it at your house."

"You can take it and drive it if you want, just don't let anyone take it away from me," Gena said.

"I'll go ask them about it. I've got to get going anyway I've got my mother-in-law at home baby-sitting."

"When can I get out of here?"

"I don't know for sure, but probably tomorrow morning after they set your bond if someone will post it. Your court appointed attorney will arrange to get you out."

"Would you call my mother for me?"

"Sure. You hang in there now. I'll take care of your car and call your mother."

"Thank you, Stan. You're the best attorney I've ever had."

"The cheapest too, I bet."

"Someday you'll make lots of money off me, don't you worry."

I was severely shaken by Gena's arrest. It was totally unexpected, and I felt guilty about not helping her with the postal inspectors. The marshal's office released Gena's car to me so I was now faced with the logistical problem of getting her car back to her house. I drove the Corvette home and then had my father-in-law drive me back downtown to pick up the Pinto. I thought about leaving it there, hoping it would get stolen, but figured with my luck it would just get towed off and I'd have to pay to get it released. It wasn't until nearly 6:30 that I finally got home and relieved my mother-in-law from baby-sitting.

With all the excitement of the afternoon I hadn't been able to stop at the bank and deposit the money Kurt had given me. After dinner I sat down on the sofa and began playing with the twenty-five one-hundred-dollar bills. Peter came over and sat down next to me to watch.

"Is that play money, Daddy?"

"No, actually this is real."

"Is that a million dollars?" Peter said.

"No, I'm afraid not," I replied.

"Are you sure? It looks like it, Dad."

"It's two thousand five hundred dollars. If you multiplied this by four hundred, it would be a million dollars," I said.

"Can I have it?" Peter said.

"No, we need it to pay bills and buy groceries."

Seeking to avoid further discussion about the money, I put it away and suggested we all play fish. I put Marcia in my lap and leaned against the sofa in front of the coffee table. The three boys sat around the table and the game began. We played about an hour until Reggie had beaten us all pretty badly. I didn't know why, but he was a whiz at any kind of game. It was late so I put Marcia and Peter to bed, and Mark, Reggie and I watched TV for another hour until it was their bedtime.

At 11:30 P.M. Rebekah came home. I was asleep on the sofa and didn't hear her come in. She sat down next to me and gave me a kiss. I opened my eyes, looked at her and smiled.

"Tough day, honey?" she said.

"Yeah, it was. How are you?"

"Upset."

I sat up and looked at Rebekah. "What's wrong?"

"There was a boating accident this afternoon at Lake Dallas. They brought in a man whose head had been sliced up pretty bad by a propeller."

"Oh no."

"He was damn near dead when he came in, but the doctors tried everything to keep him alive. His wife was hysterical, she kept asking me if he was okay. I told her we were doing everything we could, but I knew in my heart he would die."

"I'm sorry, honey."

"I kept thinking what if that were you or one of the kids. I don't want you or the kids to ever go skiing."

"Accidents can happen anytime, doing anything," I said.

"If you had seen what I did, you'd feel the same way."

"Maybe so."

"I'm kind of upset too," I said.

"Why?"

"Gena Lombardi got arrested today at her creditor's meeting."

"You're kidding?"

"No, it was horrible. . . . She was so upset. Of course, she was worried more about losing her yellow Corvette than being in jail. Oh, guess what else," I said.

"What?"

"Kurt paid me today, twenty-five one-hundred-dollar bills."

"Oh! That's nice."

"Peter thought it was a million dollars."

"That's a sweet thought."

"Oh. I guess I better tell you one other thing."

She looked at me intently. "I don't like the tone of your voice."

"I took the plunge on Parker #3."

"Oh shit! Stan, we could have really used that money. Now we might lose it all."

"I know, but since we never got it, we won't miss it. Maybe we'll get lucky and the well will come in."

"It better."

"Just think, over seven grand a month. Can you imagine getting that before you even get up in the morning? Wouldn't that be sweet?"

"You're a dreamer, Stan. It will never happen."

"Why not? It happens to other people."

# THE DINNER ENGAGEMENT

NATURALLY REBEKAH DIDN'T HAVE anything to wear for our dinner engagement with Bird and Sheila. This meant we had to rush out to the mall after Rebekah's Saturday shift, which ended at three. Shopping with Rebekah was a nightmare as she could never find anything she liked. She would try on dress after dress and reject each one for one enigmatic reason or another. She insisted that I hang around close by so I could give her my opinion on each garment, yet she rarely took my advice. After searching through racks and racks of women's clothing, Rebekah finally found something acceptable, not good, but something tolerable.

At six-thirty we drove to our rendezvous point with the Logans and found them waiting for us. We exchanged introductions and then Rebekah and I got in the back seat of the black Lincoln Town Car and we drove off.

Rebekah quickly surveyed Sheila's pretty face, smiled and said, "It's nice to meet you two. I love your car."

"Oh, it's not ours. We flew up and then rented it. It's a long drive from Corpus Christi to Dallas. We've done it a few times, but it's no fun," Sheila said.

"So where are we dining tonight, Bird?" Sheila asked.

"Anthony's, over near Northpark. It's got the best Italian food in Dallas."

"Oh, good," Sheila said. "So Rebekah, Stan said you're a nurse, I don't know how you can do that with four children."

"It's not easy, believe me," Rebekah replied. "I just work on the weekends when Stan can be home to watch the kids. If we had to get a baby-sitter, there wouldn't be any advantage to working. I'd just pay all the money I made to a baby-sitter."

Bird turned the Lincoln into the driveway at Anthony's and stopped the car in front of the valet parking sign. A young man hurried up to Bird's door and opened it. We all got out and entered the restaurant. A hostess immediately took us to a table near a large fountain encircled by marble pillars. We all sat down and began to look at the menu.

"I always hate having to decide between all these wonderful dishes. I wish I could order everything," Sheila said.

"I can never make up my mind either," Rebekah replied. "I usually wait until everyone has ordered then I order the first thing that comes into my mind."

After the girls finally settled on their selections from the menu, the waiter took our orders and vanished into the kitchen.

"We sure had a nice visit with Stan when he came down to do research at the Nueces County Courthouse," Sheila said.

"Yeah, Stan told me he had a good time. I understand you have quite a home on the bay," Rebekah replied.

"Oh yes, we love it. It was a wedding gift from my parents, along with the yacht," Sheila said rather nonchalantly.

Rebekah raised her eyebrows. "A yacht too? That's some wedding present."

Talk of the yacht sent shivers down my spine. I immediately sought to change the subject by asking Bird several questions in rapid succession. "So, Bird, when do you start drilling Parker #3?"

"If all goes well, we'll start drilling a week from Tuesday."

"How deep will you have to drill?"

"Probably six or seven thousand feet, I'd imagine. There are three prospective zones. The most promising one is about 5,400 feet."

Sheila gave me a bewildered look as a result of my sudden domination of the conversation. I smiled at her hoping she would get the hint and shut up about the yacht. Rebekah watched me curiously.

"How long do you think it will take to drill?" I continued.

Bird pondered the question for a moment and then replied, "Oh, it depends on what we find down there, but probably a week or ten days."

"That's pretty quick," I said.

"You know you ought to bring Rebekah and the kids out to the rig and watch the well come in. There's nothing more exciting than to see crude oil shooting twenty feet into the air, especially when you own part of it."

"That would be fun wouldn't it Rebekah?" I said. "We ought to do that."

"Well, it depends on when it is, I've got to work on the weekends," Rebekah said.

"We usually know about forty-eight hours in advance of when we expect to hit the productive formation so we'll call you as soon as we find out. Usually we have a good-size crowd so we have a barbecue and a big bonfire and you can camp if you want," Bird said.

"Oh, we've got to do that," I replied. "Rebekah will find someone to take her place if it comes in on the weekend, won't you, honey?"

"I guess I'll try," Rebekah replied.

"Good, then we'll plan on you being there. Oh, and don't bother to bring food or drink, you won't need it. Sheila always arranges enough food to feed Napoleon's army."

The conversation was briefly interrupted as the waiter appeared with a tray full of tantalizing Italian cuisine. I inhaled the sweet aroma of the fare and commented, "Umm, that smells good." Everyone agreed and began to eat.

"So, do you have a busy week coming up Stan?" Sheila asked.

"Well, I don't know how busy it'll be, but it should be interesting," I replied.

"Oh really?"

"Yes, I'm going ghost hunting," I said

Bird grimaced and said, "Ghost hunting?"

"Yeah, I've been getting phone calls from a lady who apparently is dead. Obviously if she's calling me, she must be very much alive, so we suspect someone has kidnapped her and is hiding her somewhere so that everyone will think she's dead."

"Oh! How exciting," Sheila said. "How are you going to find her?"

"Well, one of the calls came from Amarillo, so I'm going to check out the nursing homes there. One of our suspects owns a chain of nursing homes, and we think he might have her stashed away in one of them."

"If they are hiding her, they'll never acknowledge that she's there," Sheila said.

"True, so I've got to figure out some way to get access to the patient files. I don't know exactly how I'm going to do that, but I'll figure out something."

"One of my fantasies was to be a private investigator," Sheila said. "But there aren't too many female PIs I'm afraid."

"That's too bad, you probably would have made a great one," I replied.

"So, how long will you be in Amarillo?" Sheila said.

"A day or two then I'm going to Colorado to investigate the woman's accidental death," I said.

"How did she die?" Sheila asked.

"She ran off the road, over a cliff and then her car burst into blames. Her body was burnt beyond recognition. I figure the body in the car wasn't hers. Someone in her family wanted her to appear to be dead so they'd get control of all of her assets, including the company she owned."

"Who inherited the company when she supposedly died?" Bird asked.

"Her son and daughter," I replied.

"I think her son did it," Rebekah said. "He's a sleazy bastard from what Stan tells me."

"He's the most likely suspect since he didn't like the way his mother was running the company and wanted to run it himself. Of course, now he has what he wanted, complete control."

"Does he own the nursing homes?" Sheila asked.

"No, his brother-in-law does. It could be they're working together as they were involved in some kind of merger of their two companies when this all happened."

"That's really fascinating Stan. You've got to tell me how it all comes out," Sheila said.

"I'll certainly do that. Maybe I'll have it solved by the time we meet at Parker #3."

"You better have it solved because if you spend much more time chasing ghosts, we'll be filing bankruptcy and you'll have to go back to selling insurance," Rebekah said.

Bird and Sheila smiled and looked at each other.

"Never. I hate begging people to do business with me. I love practicing law because people immediately give you respect. I like that, and I like people coming to me and asking me to help them. We may be in for some rough times getting a law practice going, but at least I like what I'm doing," I said.

"Well, I think Tomlinson's going to be keeping you pretty busy, Stan, so I doubt if you'll be missing many meals," Bird said.

"That's good to hear," I replied.

The waiter came back to our table, took our plates and asked us if we wanted dessert. Everyone was too full to eat anything else so we got our check and left. The valet brought around the Lincoln and we departed. Bird took us back to our car where we talked for a few minutes before we parted company.

"So, we'll see you guys in a couple of weeks for a celebration at the well," Bird said.

"Absolutely, we wouldn't miss it. I've got a good feeling about Parker #3," I replied.

"It should be a big producer," Bird concurred.

"It was nice to meet you Rebekah," Sheila said.

"Make Stan bring you with him the next time he comes to Corpus," Bird added. "Sheila will take you out on the yacht and give you a tour of the bay like she did Stan."

Rebekah gave me a cool look then turned to Bird and said, "Oh, Sheila took Stan out on the yacht?"

"Yeah, didn't Stan tell you he and Sheila almost got caught out in a thunderstorm," Bird laughed.

Rebekah smiled, gave me an icy glare and replied, "No, he didn't tell me. It must have slipped his mind. That sounds like fun, I'll try to make it next time, if this tightwad will spring for the extra fare."

We watched the Lincoln pull away and then got into the Pinto. Rebekah was very quiet on the way home. This was her usual behavior when she was mad about something. I knew why she was mad, but I didn't want her to think I was feeling guilty so I said, "You're awfully quiet over there."

"What's there to talk about?" she replied.

"Didn't you enjoy dinner?"

"Dinner was fine."

"Isn't Bird a character?" I said.

"He's okay."

After five more minutes of silence I said, "Okay, I give up. What's wrong?"

"Nothing."

"Come on, we both know when you clam up like this something's wrong."

"I said, nothing."

Several minutes went by in silence as we cruised up North Central Expressway heading for Richardson. I hated to have Rebekah mad at me so I pressed for a confrontation.

"Is it something I said at dinner?"

"No, it's something you didn't say after you came back from Corpus."

"Something I didn't say?"

"Yeah, you never told me you went out on a yacht while you were in Corpus."

"Well, like you said, it slipped my mind. I just didn't think about it."

"Tell me I didn't hear what I thought I heard about your little cruise, Stan Turner."

"What do you mean?"

"Just who went on that little outing?"

"Just Sheila and I."

"That's what I thought I heard. What happened to Blackbeard or whatever the hell he calls himself?"

"Bird, doesn't like to sail much. He gets seasick."

"So you were alone with a beautiful young girl on a fancy yacht in middle of Corpus Christi Bay. Do I have it right?"

"Yeah, I guess so."

"And what was the captain wearing?"

"Gee, . . . I don't remember actually."

"Could it have been a string bikini like most of the girls wear down there?"

"Well, no . . . not actually . . . just a regular one."

"You dirty bastard! I'm at home cleaning dirty diapers and wiping snotty noses, and you're off sailing Corpus Christi Bay with a beautiful, naked woman."

"She's married. I would never do anything with a married woman."

"Oh, but if she'd been single, you would have fucked her brains out!"

"No! Of course not. I would never do that. I wasn't planning to go out in the yacht, it just came up and I couldn't get out of it."

As we drove in our driveway, Rebekah turned to me, looked me in the eye and said, "Stan Turner did you fuck her!" I stopped the car, shut off the engine and replied, "No! Nothing happened."

Rebekah stared at me for a moment and then started to get out of the car. She hesitated a moment and said, "I wish I could believe you." Then she slammed the door and stormed into the house. I fell back into my seat in despair. "Damn it! I knew this was going to happen."

Rebekah sent her mother home and went to bed without a word to me. I hated to have Rebekah mad at me so I snuggled up behind her and tried to get her to talk. She ignored me for quite a while, but when she sensed I was just about to give up and go to sleep she suddenly turned over and let me have it.

"I can't believe that little slut trying to get her hooks into you," Rebekah said.

"I don't think she's after me," I replied.

"Ha. You don't know women. I could see it in her eyes, she wants you."

"No. You're imagining things."

"You don't think for a minute she's interested in that old buzzard she's married to, do you?"

"I don't know, they must have loved each other if they got married."

"Oh come on, Stan, don't be stupid. She married him for some reason other than love."

"If he were rich and she were poor, then it would make sense, but she's the one from a wealthy family," I said. "What motive could she have other than love?" I said.

"I don't know, but I'm sure it was a good one."

"What I didn't understand is why Bird wanted her and me to go out. He doesn't know me that well, yet he insisted I go out with her alone on the yacht. He must really trust her."

"All I know, Stan Turner, is you better keep your distance from that bitch because if she messes with you, she'll have me to deal with."

I lay back and beckoned Rebekah to come to me. She scooted over and laid her head on my chest. I gently stroked her silky smooth hair and said, "Don't worry, no one's going to mess with me. You're the only woman I will ever love and no one is ever going to get between us."

She raised her head and gazed into my eyes and replied, "Do you promise?"

"I promise," I said, then I leaned down and gave her a tender kiss. She laid her head back on my chest and fell asleep.

As Rebekah slept I began to think of Parker #3 and how much easier our life would be if it came in. Slowly I drifted off into a semiconscious state and began to dream. My dream was interrupted by the sound of one of the children crying.

"Stan, get up, Peter's crying. He must have had a bad dream. Go take care of him," Rebekah said, and then rolled over and went back to sleep."

"Okay," I said.

I got up and went into Peter's room and lay down next to him. "What's wrong, tiger?" I said.

"My eyes hurt, Daddy," he said.

"Your eyes hurt?"

"They're burning me."

"Let me turn on the light and look at them."

I turned on the night lamp and looked at Peter's eyes, but they appeared normal.

"Let's go into the bathroom and rinse them with a little water, okay?"

"Okay."

We went into the bathroom and he threw some water on his face and then dried it with a towel.

"That feel better?" I asked.

"Yeah, sleep with me, Daddy."

"Okay, for a minute."

The next morning Rebekah came into Peter's room and woke us up. "Stan, what are you doing sleeping in Peter's bed?"

I opened my eyes and saw Rebekah standing over me with a puzzled look.

"I don't know. Oh, don't you remember you sent me in here when Peter started crying," I said.

"Well, I expected you to come back after you took care of his problem."

"I know, the weirdest thing happened last night."

"What?"

"I dreamt Parker #3 came in and you and I and the boys were at the well. Oil was pouring down from the sky drenching us all, then Peter began to cry because he was getting oil in his eyes."

"There's no hope for you, Stan. I'm going to make reservations for you at the home."

"No, that's not what was weird. Peter began to cry and you woke me up to go take care of him. When I got to him he was complaining about his eyes burning."

"What? You're trying to tell me that you and your son are having the same dreams?"

"We must, how else can you explain it?"

Rebekah shook her head and began to laugh. "You are crazy! I'm definitely making that phone call."

"Okay, but at least now I know that Parker #3 is going to come in."

"How do you know that?"

I walked over to Rebekah, put my hands on her shoulders and looked her in the eye. "What happened to me last night was not a dream, it was a vision, and my visions always come true."

Rebekah thought for a moment, smiled and then replied, "Well then, we better bring goggles for the kids when we go to Blackbeard's *comin'-in* party."

"Okay, you won't be laughing at me when we're pulling in five or ten thousand dollars a month in royalties," I said.

"Well, right now all I'm worried about is breakfast. Get your kids up so we can feed them."

"Yes ma'am," I said, and then proceeded to jump out of bed. Peter didn't stir.

"Before I do that, do you want to go back to bed for a little while?"

"I don't think so. I was there alone all night. I'm up now. Besides, Tom called and wants you to meet him at Frito Lay."

"Why?"

"I don't know. I just took the message."

Reluctantly I drove over to the Frito Lay offices. I couldn't imagine what Tom wanted.

"Well, how did you think the closing went Friday, Stan?" Tom asked.

"It seemed pretty smooth. That was some lunch Kurt gave us, wasn't it?"

"Yes, Kurt knows how to impress people," Tom replied.

"I guess you must be pretty excited about finally closing the deal," I said.

"Well, I am but I've got a lot riding on it so I'm a little worried. Did your friend Ron Johnson have anything to say about the closing?"

"No, he said everything looked great."

"Good."

"So what happens now?" I asked. "Is Kurt going to do the rest of the rehab or are you guys handling it?"

"No, Kurt's doing everything. All we were supposed to do was invest our money and guarantee the note."

"I suppose you went to Amarillo and checked out the building didn't you?" I asked.

"Well, actually no, I've never seen the building. Kurt's shown us some pictures."

"I haven't seen it either, but I'm going to be in Amarillo tomorrow so I thought I would go by and check it out," I said.

"Oh good, would you call me when you get back and tell me how it looks?" Tom asked.

"Sure, I'd be happy to. Don't look so worried, I'm sure everything will work out. Kurt seems to know what he's doing."

"My wife didn't want me to make this investment."

"Oh really?"

"She doesn't trust Kurt. If I lose this money, I'll probably end up divorced."

"Oh I doubt your wife would really divorce you over money," I said. "How long have you been married, twenty or thirty years?"

"Twenty-nine."

"Well if she's put up with you that many years, I think you're probably stuck with her until the day you die, no matter how the Panhandle Building deal turns out."

"I know, but I don't want this deal spoiling my retirement."

All the way home I wondered about the Panhandle Building project. All the investors seemed so paranoid about it, but if they didn't feel good about the deal, why did they each invest a hundred grand in it? It didn't make any sense. I discussed it with Rebekah when I got home.

"You're awfully quiet, Stan," Rebekah said.

"Tom and the other investors are so worried about this Panhandle deal. Now they've got me worried about it."

"What are they worried about?"

"I don't honestly know. It seems they just don't trust Kurt. They think he can make them lots of money, but I guess they realize he could just as easily screw them."

"Do you think he will?"

"No, but he did manage to talk Worldwide into releasing a million dollar CD," I said.

"You're kidding?"

"No, it was supposed to be pledged on the project, but somehow he talked them into releasing it."

"You won't get in trouble if the deal goes sour will you?"

"I don't think so, as far as I know the deal is legitimate."

"Now I'm worried," Rebekah said.

# AMARILLO

My FLIGHT ARRIVED IN Amarillo at 10:47 A.M. I rented a car and then went straight to a motel to get set up for my investigation. Before leaving I had contacted the Texas Facilities Commission to find out what nursing homes were owned by Taylor Brown. As it turned out, he owned four out of the seven nursing homes in the city. Timber Bluff Nursing Home was the biggest of the four. It seemed logical that I should check that one out first.

Before I ever came to Amarillo, I knew it would be difficult to find out if Melba Thorn were a patient. I struggled for some time for a ploy that would gain me access to each nursing home's census information. Of course I could pretend to be some government official doing an audit or investigation of some kind, but that would be illegal, and I didn't want to end up in jail or disbarred. I could go in as a computer repairman and gain access to their computer. I had taken computer courses in college and could probably pull off that ruse, but that was bordering on being illegal also and consequently I wasn't comfortable with that approach. Finally I decided the only way to legally and ethically gain the information I needed was from employees of the nursing homes. Obviously current employees would not be cooperative so I focused on former employees.

I called the personnel office of the Timber Bluffs Nursing Home first.

"Personnel," a female voice said.

"Yes, hi. Listen, I was visiting my aunt last week in Timber Bluffs and I met one of your employees. After we got to talking, it turned out we went to the same high school ten years ago. We were going to exchange telephone numbers and try to get together, but when I came in today to visit my aunt, she told me he had quit. I'm really embarrassed, but I've forgotten his name and I wonder if you might know who I was talking about."

"Let me see. Ronald Richardson quit last week and Harold Rogers was . . . well, . . . let go, shall we say. If you could give me a description I could probably tell you which one it was."

"Oh gee, you probably know them much better than I do, why don't you describe them, and then I should be able to figure out which one it was," I said.

"Well Harold Rogers is about twenty-five, tall with long blond hair. Ronald Richardson is about forty-five, overweight and has real short hair," she said.

"It must be Rogers, Richardson is too old. You wouldn't happen to have a phone number would you?"

"We're not allowed to give out phone numbers of our employees," she said.

"But he's no longer an employee."

"Huh. . . . I guess you're right . . . okay, I'll give it to you."

I wrote down the number on an envelope and then said, "Thanks for your help."

"No problem, hope you find him."

It seemed to me since Rogers had been let go he might be inclined to help me. I thought it best to just be straight with him and hope for the best so I placed the call.

"I don't work at Timber Bluffs anymore," he said.

"I know, that's why I'm calling you. If the person we're looking for is at Timber Bluffs, then she's there against her will and the management of the nursing home is not going to cooperate with us in finding her."

"Why would they be holding her against her will?"

"Well, it's a long story, but the bottom line is: She controls a big corporation and with her dead, or perceived to be dead, the kidnappers have control of the company."

"I see, that's pretty bizarre," Roger said.

"I know, but it may well be the case."

"What makes you think I'll help you?"

"You don't work there anymore so you have nothing to lose by helping us, right?"

"True."

"And, I imagine you're not too fond of Timber Bluffs since you were just fired, correct?"

"How'd you find that out?" he said.

"Oh, I've got my sources," I replied.

"Well, you're right. They've treated me like crap. Okay, so, how can I help you?"

"We're looking for a woman named Melba Thorn. She probably was not registered by that name. She should be about sixty-two years old, dark brown hair, five foot four, and about a hundred and forty pounds."

"That doesn't help a lot, that describes a number of our patients," Rogers said.

"She would have been brought in about a year ago by one of the owners of the nursing home, Taylor Brown."

"I know Taylor. He comes around once in a while, but I've never seen him check in a patient."

"Have you ever heard any patient claim they were Melba Thorn?"

"No, there's one who thinks he's General Patton and another one who's convinced he's Martin Luther King, but nobody has ever said they were Melba Thorn."

"Well okay. Do you think there's any chance Melba Thorn could be at Timber Bluffs?"

"I seriously doubt it. I knew most of the patients and their families, and no one fitting the description of Melba Thorn was ever there."

"Well, thanks for your help."

In the next two days I was able to check out two more of the nursing homes, but came up empty handed. This left me with just one nursing home to go. My approach at getting information had worked on three out of the four nursing homes in Amarillo, however, one of them hadn't had any employee turnover in several months, so I had to come up with another angle. It was a small nursing home, so I figured if I could get inside and look around, I could see if Melba was there. When I was at the library in Dallas I had made a copy of Melba's photograph from the newspaper article published after her accident, so I felt I would be able to recognize her if I saw her.

In order to get in and look around without arousing suspicion, I found an old man about seventy years old who was rummaging through a dumpster looking for aluminum cans. I paid him twenty dollars to pretend to be my grandfather. When we arrived at the home, I told them we were looking for a nursing home for my grandfather and wondered if we could look around their facility. They not only let us look around, but also insisted on giving us a grand tour and introduced us to most of the staff. During our visit I saw most of the patients, and was able to quiz some of the nurses about Melba Thorn. Unfortunately it didn't appear Mrs. Thorn had ever been a patient there.

Having come up empty handed, there wasn't much more to do in Amarillo, except to check out the Panhandle Building. Once I saw the building I could reassure the investors back in Dallas that everything was okay. I hadn't told Kurt I was coming to Amarillo because I didn't want him to think I didn't trust him. When I got back to Dallas I would just tell him I was in town and was just curious so I went to see it. It was Wednesday afternoon so I thought I would check out of the motel, stop by the Panhandle Building and then be on my way to Colorado Springs. I decided to drive since air service to Colorado Springs was not that great, and I had managed to get a good price on my rental car by taking it for the full week.

It was not hard to find the Panhandle Building since it was one of the largest in downtown Amarillo. I parked across the street and gazed at the building. It was a magnificent structure, built in 1922 when Amarillo was establishing itself as the hub of the cattle, oil and gas and grain industries for the region. I had never paid much attention to old buildings before, but working on this deal made me appreciate for the first time why the government had provided such nice tax incentives to rehabilitate them. If we were to learn from history and grow as a nation, we needed something to remind us of our heritage and these magnificent structures from bygone days sure did an excellent job of that.

I crossed the street and entered the Panhandle Building. The lobby had already been rehabilitated and was quite beautiful. It had a high ceiling, marble floors, brass elevator, exotic plants, a fountain and an extraordinary mural depicting the many different industries that made Amarillo such a great city. It was impressive and I was feeling relieved that the investor's concerns about the deal apparently were unfounded. I was so impressed, in fact, that I almost left the building right then. However, after giving it some thought, I decided I had better check out the entire edifice because I was sure to be thoroughly interrogated when I returned.

I wandered over to the elevators and pushed the up button. After a moment the door opened and an elevator operator smiled at me and said, "Going up?"

"Yes, thank you."

"What floor?" he asked.

"How about three," I replied.

"I'm sorry, sir, but that floor is closed to the public."

"Oh, okay then, take me to the next floor that's opened."

"There are only two floors that have tenants, sir."

"What? That's impossible, there're supposed to be seven fully completed floors," I said.

"Well, I'm sorry sir, but I can only take you to six or eleven. I don't have access to any of the other floors."

"Take me to six then," I replied.

The operator closed the door and the screen behind it and pulled a lever, which caused the elevator to move up slowly. A sick feeling came over me. When we got to the sixth floor I got out and started walking around. The decor on this floor was no less elegant than in the lobby and had exceeded my expectations. Now, however, I had to verify what the operator had told me, for if only two floors were finished out, then Kurt had grossly misrepresented the scope of the project and there wouldn't be enough money available to complete the project according to the plans and specifications.

I walked down the hall to the stairs and climbed up to the seventh floor. It appeared not only to be vacant, but someone had pretty much demolished the interior. I climbed up the stairs and inspected each floor and found them all to be pretty much identical. With the exception of the eleventh and sixth floors as well as the lobby, the building was totally empty and it would take considerably more money than had been budgeted to complete this project. To make matters worse the rent rolls submitted to the investors were obviously fake and there wouldn't be enough rent to cover the debt services to World-wide Savings and Loan.

What puzzled me was how Worldwide could have inspected the building and not discovered the deception. I started to panic as I realized that Worldwide and the investors might think I was a party to Kurt's fraud. Questions flooded my mind. Why would Kurt do this? He had everything going for him, why risk it all for a cheap scam? What was I going to do when I got to Dallas? Should I confront Kurt or keep my mouth shut and pretend I didn't know anything? These and count-less other questions kept running through my mind, but I had no answers.

# THE WARNING

THE RIDE TO COLORADO Springs was not pleasant, as I couldn't clear my mind of Kurt's deception. It did give me time, however, to recover from my initial panic and start to think of an appropriate course of action. As an attorney, under the canons of legal ethics, I couldn't disclose confidential confidences or communications of my client, but on the other hand I couldn't participate in a fraud. The only thing I could do would be to terminate the attorney-client relationship with Kurt immediately upon returning to Dallas, and then let the chips fall where they may.

My major concerns were the investors. If Worldwide Savings and Loan got defrauded, it was their own fault for not adequately inspecting the Panhandle Building and double-checking Kurt's numbers. The investors, however, were not sophisticated and basically put their trust in Kurt and, unfortunately, in me although I cautioned them that I did not represent them. I wished there were something I could do to protect them, but I didn't have a clue as to what it would be.

Once I got to Colorado Springs I tried to refocus my attention on Melba Thorn. She was out there somewhere being held as a prisoner and I had to find her. My first stop was the Winchester Hotel and Resort, a world-renowned getaway for the rich, known for its great food, elegant accommodations, spectacular golf course and fine equestrian facility. I couldn't afford to stay there, so I got a room a few miles away at a Holiday Inn and then drove over to see if anyone remembered Melba Thorn.

Not wanting to attract attention, I opted not to go to the manager, but decided instead to casually ask some of the housekeeping staff if they remembered Mrs. Thorn. After showing Melba's picture to eight or ten maids, I finally found one who remembered her. She wore a nametag indicating her name was Carmen.

"Ma'am, I'm Stan Turner and I'm looking for anyone who might remember one of the guests here, Mrs. Melba Thorn," I said, and then I flashed the photograph in front of her. "This is her photograph."

"Yes sir, I saw her. She was in the Palomino Suite."

"When was the first time you saw her?"

"When she got here I was across the courtyard working on south wing bungalows. We were told by Raul, our supervisor, that it was a big family reunion and we needed to take good care of them since they were rich and powerful people. She came with the first group in a limousine. She seemed so happy to be with her family. I was so envious because my family lives in Mexico."

"After they arrived did you have occasion to observe her anymore?"

"Yes, I saw her every day. I even talked to her a couple of times."

"Really? What about?"

"She asked me about my family and my job. She was a very nice lady. Not many guests go out of their way to be nice to the staff."

"Did you see her with any of her family?"

"Yes, her son and daughter and grandchildren."

"Did you see anything unusual happen at all between Mrs. Thorn and her family?"

"She argued with her son and son-in-law a lot."

"Could you tell what they were arguing about?"

"No, sir."

"I guess you know she was reportedly killed in an auto accident."

"Yes, I was sick about it. . . . Such a nice woman to die so violently."

"Did you ever see her drive an automobile while she was here?"

"No, sir."

"Did you see her on the day she died?"

"Yes, sir. I saw her come back to her room very upset on the morning of the accident. Raul said he saw her arguing with her son just before that."

"Did you see her leave her room?"

"No."

"Did you see her get in a car and leave?"

"No, sir."

"Was anyone with her or around her room when all this happened?"

"No, except one of the limousine drivers."

"Who was that?"

"The man who drove Mrs. Thorn's daughter, I don't remember his name."

"Is there anything else you can tell me about the day that Mrs. Thorn disappeared that was unusual or memorable?"

"No."

"Did you observe the reaction of her family after they found out she had been killed?"

"Yes I did. The grandchildren were very upset. You could tell they had really loved her. Mrs. Brown was so upset she didn't leave her room for several days. Mr. Thorn and Mr. Brown, well, . . . I don't know about them. I didn't see them that much since they stayed in a different part of the hotel. Raul said they met frequently and talked for hours. He said he overheard them laughing a couple of times."

"Carmen, you've been a great help to me," I said, as I pulled out a card and handed it to her. "If you think of anything else please give me a call. I'll be over at the Holiday Inn for a couple of days."

She took my card, studied it carefully and replied, "Yes sir, I will."

Before I left the Winchester I talked to Raul and one of the stable hands that had witnessed the confrontation between Melba and her son, Robert Thorn. They both agreed that Robert spent most of the day riding, and to their knowledge never left the hotel on the day of Melba's death. They didn't know, however, where Taylor Brown went after he quit riding about two in the afternoon.

Having exhausted all my leads at the Winchester, I decided to go inspect the site of the accident and talk to the sheriff, Dick Barnett, who had handled the investigation. I took Highway 24 to Florissant, Colorado, where the sheriff had his office. The sheriff wasn't in when I arrived so I sat down and waited. While I was waiting, a pretty young secretary engaged me in conversation.

"You're an attorney huh?" she said.

"Yeah, I am," I replied, as I stood up and extended my hand. "Stan Turner."

"Hi, I'm Claudia Robertson, it's nice to meet you."

"The pleasure is mine."

"I always wanted to be a lawyer," Claudia said.

"So why don't you do it?" I asked.

"Me, become a lawyer? . . . Why I'm not smart enough and I don't have the money to go to law school."

"I don't believe that."

"Huh. . . . What do mean you don't believe it? You think I'm lying to you?"

"No, that you're not smart enough. When I was a kid everyone told me I wasn't smart enough to be a lawyer but they were wrong. If you want to be a lawyer badly enough, you can be one. Trust me."

"Well, I don't know about that. So, what's a Dallas lawyer doing up here in the mountains anyway?"

"Do you remember a car wreck about a year ago where a prominent Dallas lady, Melba Thorn, was killed?"

"Uh huh, I remember that."

"Were you working for the sheriff back then?"

"Yes, I had just started as a matter of fact. I remember all the reporters that came by asking questions and interviewing the sheriff."

"Did any of the family stop in?"

"Yes, one of the children and a daughter-in-law, I don't remember their names. They stopped in and talked to the sheriff for a while. Then later on the daughter came by with her chauffeur."

"Do you know what they talked about?"

"No, I wasn't invited to the meeting. But the sheriff said later that they mainly wanted to know if it was an accident or not. Course the sheriff wanted to know why Mrs. Thorn was out driving alone."

"Was there any reason to suspect it wasn't an accident?"

"No, except there was more than one set of tire tracks near where the car left the road."

"Oh really? You mean skid marks?"

"Yes, there was fresh rubber from two different cars on the pavement."

"Did the sheriff investigate the possibility that someone might have murdered Melba Thorn?"

"No, he didn't have near enough evidence for that."

The door opened and Sheriff Burnett walked in. He looked at me and then his secretary.

"Who's your friend?"

"This is Stan Turner from Dallas. He's an attorney checking into Melba Thorn's death."

"You're a little late aren't you Mr. Turner? Mrs. Thorn died over a year ago, didn't she?"

"That's what I understand."

"Understand? Believe me Mr. Turner she was dead when we pulled that charred body out of her Caddy."

"I know the official report concluded her death was accidental, but what do you think?"

"I'll stick by the report."

"What about the extra skid marks?"

The sheriff glared at his secretary. "Those could have been left by someone earlier in the day, before this accident even happened."

"Was there anything else that would make you think maybe this wasn't an accident?"

"Before I answer that Mr. Turner, I'd like to know who your client is?"

"I'm not at liberty to disclose that information."

"Well then, this interview is over. When I give out information I want to know who's getting it."

The sheriff got up and gestured for me to leave.

"All right, I'll tell you if you promise to keep it confidential."

"Of course, I won't tell a soul. Who's your client?"

"Melba Thorn."

"Excuse me, is this some kind of joke? When I pulled Melba Thorn out of that Caddy she was dead, her body had been incinerated."

"But are you sure that was her?"

"Who else would it have been?" the sheriff replied.

"I don't know who it was, all I know is a woman keeps calling me up and saying that she's Melba Thorn and that I need to help her."

"You haven't met her though?"

"No."

"Then it may just be a prank, but it does make for interesting speculation."

"What do you mean?" I said.

"No one ever gave me a good explanation as to why Mrs. Thorn was out alone on a dangerous mountain road while the rest of her family was riding horseback fifty miles away," the sheriff said.

"Particularly since she didn't normally drive at all," I added.

"Let me go pull the file so I can refresh my memory. It's been a while since this all happened."

"That's a good idea."

The sheriff left the room and I looked over to his secretary and said, "I hope I didn't get you in trouble."

"No, this gives him a reason to dig a little deeper into this case. I don't think he ever believed it was an accident," she said.

The sheriff returned with a legal-size expansion file filled to the brim with papers. He set it down on his desk and began to look through it.

"Let's look at the autopsy report to see if they made a positive ID on Melba Thorn."

The sheriff pulled out a report and began to read it. "It says that a positive identification wasn't possible due to the condition of the body. Upon the request of the family no further effort was made since there was no reason to doubt that it was Mrs. Thorn."

"So it's possible someone else might have died in that crash?"

"It's possible, but who died down there then if it wasn't Mrs. Thorn," the sheriff said.

"I don't know, but the important thing is that Melba Thorn may well be alive."

"Anything's possible I guess," the sheriff said.

When I left the sheriff's office he agreed to reopen his investigation based on the telephone calls from Melba Thorn. He asked me to keep in touch and he promised to call me if anything turned up. I drove back to Colorado Springs that evening, ate dinner at Denny's and then went back to the Holiday Inn to get a good night's sleep for my trip back to Amarillo and then on to Dallas. Once I was in my room I decided to call Rebekah and see how she and the kids were doing. Just as I had picked up the phone I heard a knock on the door. I put down the phone and yelled, "Who is it?"

"Housekeeping, we've got an extra blanket for you," a female voice said.

"Okay, just a minute."

I walked over to the door and opened it. The door flung open and a tall man wearing a ski mask came barging in and grabbed me by the shoulder. He hit me hard in the stomach, knocking the wind out of me, then he struck my face with his knee, knocking me against the wall where I collapsed onto the ground. The pain was excruciating, blood came pouring out of my nose and I could hardly breathe. I looked up at him wondering what was behind this assault when he kicked me across the face with his big black boot. I fell onto the floor, everything was a blur and then as he was leaving I heard him say, "Forget Melba Thorn or the next time I'll kill you!" Then I heard screeching tires as they made their escape.

I must have passed out at that point because when I woke up I was in the hospital emergency room. I tried to sit up but the pain was too intense so I fell back onto the hospital bed. A nurse seeing me wake up came over to see how I was.

"Hey Cowboy, how you feeling?" she said.

"Not very good actually. Where am I?

"Colorado Springs County Hospital."

"How long have I been here?"

"Just about twelve hours. The doctor gave you a sedative since you were in so much pain."

"If you would like to sit up, I'll be happy to help you," she said.

"Thank you."

She leaned over, pushed a button and the head of the bed began to rise. She smiled and said, "You must've got someone real pissed off at you to knock you around the way they did."

"Apparently. How did I get here anyway?"

"Your neighbor at the motel heard the commotion in your room and called the police. They found you unconscious on the floor and called an ambulance. There's an officer outside who wants to interview you," the nurse said.

"Oh really, I don't feel like talking right now," I said.

"Well, he's been waiting about an hour so I expect you best talk to him."

"All right, tell him to come in."

The young officer entered the room, walked over to me and smiled. He took out a notepad and started asking me questions.

"Mr. Turner, I'm Officer Gray from the Colorado Springs Police Department. We're very sorry you were attacked, and want to assure you we will do everything possible to apprehend the persons responsible for this crime."

"Well, thank you. I appreciate your concern."

"I know you're probably not feeling too well right now, but I need to ask you some questions about what happened to you."

"Sure."

"Could you tell how many people assaulted you?" he asked.

"Two, a man and a woman."

"Can you describe them?"

"The man was tall, about six foot two and the woman was medium height, thin, maybe five foot four. They both were wearing blue jeans, the man had black boots and I didn't see what shoes the woman had on."

"Did you get a good look at their faces?"

"No, they both wore ski masks."

"Do you have any idea who they might have been?"

"Not really, they totally surprised me. It all happened so fast I'm afraid I didn't see much of anything."

"Did they steal anything?"

"I don't know, I haven't had a chance to look through my things, but I wasn't carrying anything valuable."

"What were you doing here in Colorado Springs anyway?"

"Just doing a little research for a client in Dallas."

"Maybe your client has some enemies he didn't tell you about?"

"Possibly, I really don't know."

"Okay, that's not much to go on, but we'll do our best to find your attackers."

"Thank you," I said.

In the morning I was released from the hospital so I picked up my baggage from the Holiday Inn and left for Amarillo. Before I left, however, I called Sheriff Barnett and reported the incident to him, hoping that would spur on his investigation. On the ride back to Amarillo I planned my activities for the following week. First I'd confront Kurt and then terminate any attorney-client relationship with him. I would then call each of the investors and explain the situation and strongly suggest they get independent counsel. Then I needed to go check on Gena Lombardi, who hopefully had managed to get out of jail by now. Finally, I had to get with General Burton and fill him in on the latest developments in the Melba Thorn case.

The plane ride back to DFW was short compared to the long drive from Colorado Springs to Amarillo. When the plane landed I wondered how Rebekah was going to react when she saw my physical condition. I hadn't told her about getting beat up because I didn't want her to worry. As I walked up the ramp from the plane, I saw her and the kids in the distance. When Reggie spotted me he broke away from Rebekah and ran toward me yelling, "Daddy! Daddy!"

He stopped when he was close enough to get a good look at me and said, "Daddy, what happened to you?"

"Oh, nothing, I'm okay. I'll tell you about it in a few minutes," I said, as Rebekah and the rest of the family reached us.

"Oh my God. What happened to you?" Rebekah exclaimed.

"I was attacked in my motel room last night," I said.

"Your eyes look terrible and you've got a horrible gash on your face."

"I'll be all right, don't worry," I said.

Rebekah began to cry. "Who did this to you? Oh, I'm so afraid that gash on your face will scar. I know a plastic surgeon you need to go see. Oh, . . . I can't believe they did this to your beautiful face. Does it hurt? Are you in pain?"

"No, the doctor gave me pain medication," I replied.

"You're never traveling again. It's too dangerous with all those maniacs out there. I can't believe this happened to you. What are we going to do?"

"Hey, relax. . . . I'm okay. I'll heal, don't worry."

"Daddy who beat you up?" Peter said.

"Somebody trying to rob me I guess," I replied.

I didn't dare tell Rebekah about the connection between my assailants and Melba Thorn, or she wouldn't let me keep working on the case. It seemed best for now just to leave that part out of my story. We got my luggage from the baggage claim area and then found Rebekah's car. On the ride back to Dallas I dumped the rest of the bad news about my trip on Rebekah.

"So now what are you going to do?" Rebekah said.

"I'm not sure, I've got to talk to General Burton and get his advice," I said.

"So did you find out anything of value on this trip, or did you get beat up for nothing?"

"Well, I'm afraid I haven't told you the worst yet."

"You're kidding? . . . There's more bad news?"

"I'm afraid so. Kurt's been lying to everybody about the Panhandle Building. It's not nearly as far along in the renovation as he told everybody. There's no way he's going to have enough money to complete the project."

"Oh shit! You mean Tom's going to lose his $100,000?"

"I don't know. He might."

"But he's such a nice man."

"I know. All of the investors are nice guys, but they got into a risky deal."

"They're going to blame it on you, Stan."

"I know, but what can I do?"

"You better call Kurt right now and get this straightened out," Rebekah said.

"I'm going to see him first thing Monday morning, but I don't expect I'm going to like what he has to say. I'm sure he figures he can get the money to cover the deficit on the building from some other source, but that's no excuse for outright fabrication of rent rolls and build-out reports."

"That bastard, how could he possibly think he could get away with something like this?" Rebekah said.

"It beats the shit out of me," I replied."

Rebekah shook her head. "Damn him."

I took Rebekah's hand and smiled trying to reassure her that everything would be okay. "So, did anything happen at home this week?"

"No, not really. Peter got two goals Tuesday night in his soccer game. You'd have been proud of him."

"Two goals! Wow. Way to go, Peter."

Peter leaned over the back to the front seat, smiled and giggled at me, basking in the recollection of his athletic accomplishment.

"Oh, your friend Blackbird called," Rebekah said.

"He called the house?"

"Yes, he said he couldn't get you at the office so he thought he'd try you at home."

"What did he want?"

"He says that Parker #3 is going to be completed next weekend, and he wanted to be sure we could be there."

"Oh good! What did you tell him?"

"I said I couldn't go, I've got to work and we don't have anyone to take care of the kids. I told him you couldn't go either because I didn't want you within a hundred yards of his wife."

"You didn't tell him that . . . give me a break," I said.

"Well, I almost did," Rebekah said. "You don't really want to go, do you?"

"Yes, I know the well is going to come in. I saw it in my dream and you and boys were there."

"Well, I'll have to see if Mom can baby-sit for Marcia."

"I'm sure she'll be happy to do it," I said.

"And I'll have to get someone to cover for me at the hospital for the weekend."

Rebekah shook her head and glared at me. "This is going to be a lot of damn trouble Stan Turner. That well better come in!"

"It will. I've already seen the oil raining from the sky. It's a sure thing."

"Right. Oh, you got another call too, from Gena Lombardi. She said she's still in jail and her court-appointed attorney sucks."

"Oh God, what does she want me to do?"

"Get her out of jail," Rebekah said.

"Well, if her criminal attorney couldn't get her out of jail, what makes her think I could," I replied.

"I don't know, but she thinks you're some kind of God or something. After all you saved her precious Corvette."

Finally we arrived home and parked the car in the garage. The kids opened their doors and rushed inside the house. I got my bags from the trunk and brought them in.

"Let's just go to bed and sleep right through next week, okay," I said.

"Sounds like a good plan to me."

# SECOND THOUGHTS

GETTING UP ON MONDAY morning was not an easy task. I wasn't anxious to confront Kurt nor to face the investors and tell them what I had discovered. To make matters worse, I was at a dead end with Melba Thorn and now Gena Lombardi was going to be pressuring me to represent her in her criminal case. I wondered why I ever wanted to be an attorney. The pressure had suddenly become overwhelming. Finally I rolled out of bed and hit the shower, hoping the hot water would relax the tightness that had developed in my neck and shoulders and produced an intense headache. Unfortunately, it didn't help so I opted for three aspirin. Before I got dressed I looked outside to see what the weather was like. It wasn't raining, but it was damp and foggy and the wind was from the north. A cold front must have come through during the night, I conjectured.

Rebekah tried to cheer me up, but nothing she could say could lessen the fear and guilt I felt over the Panhandle Building. Could I have done something to prevent what had happened? I suppose I could have confronted Kurt and got his assurances that everything was in order, but he still could have lied to me. If Kurt had any sinister plans, he certainly didn't relay them to me. Kurt's instructions were simply to do the paperwork for the deal. I took that to mean for me to be fair to all parties, which I tried to do.

I decided to go straight to Kurt's house rather than to the office. I wanted to get the confrontation over with immediately since it was weighing heavy on my mind. As I drove up to the front gate, I noticed it was locked. I pushed the bell but no one answered. I pushed the bell several more times, but still there was no response. I got out of the car to take a good look at the grounds to see if I could spot anyone. As I grabbed hold of the wrought-iron gate, one of Kurt's dogs suddenly appeared and attacked me. Luckily I jerked my leg away from the fence fast enough to narrowly miss having my leg ripped apart by the Doberman's sharp teeth.

"Pepper! It's me," I yelled. "Come on boy calm down. I'm just looking for your master."

Pepper quit barking and began to wag her tail once she recognized me. I stuck my hand through the fence to pet her. Ginger came charging across the yard and joined us. I got up and took one last look at the grounds, but did not see anyone.

Slightly shaken and extremely frustrated, I got back into my car and went to the office. When I arrived, General Burton was at his desk filling out a contract. When he saw me enter, he smiled, squinted and then jumped out of his seat and approached me.

"Stan, what happened to you? You look terrible."

"As you can see, someone doesn't want me to find Melba Thorn."

"What do you mean?" the general asked.

I told him the story.

"I guess that proves Melba is alive," General Burton said.

"I don't know about that, but it does prove that someone doesn't want us to find out the truth."

"What are you going to do now?"

"I was going to ask you for some suggestions."

"Boy, I don't know. Maybe you should contact the authorities."

"And tell them what, that a ghost has been calling me? I don't have a shred of evidence to back up my suspicions. Anyway, I did manage to get the sheriff up in Florissant, Colorado, to reopen the investigation of Melba Thorn's death. He apparently had been suspicious all along, but didn't have anything to go on. Now he's convinced, especially since I got beat up, that something's not right."

"Well, that's one positive accomplishment anyway," the general said.

"In the meantime, I've got some other problems to deal with, ones that developed while I was gone, so I better get to work."

"Well, don't let me stop you. I'm so sorry you got beat up, Stan. I hope it's not too painful."

"No, it looks worse than it feels," I said.

After talking to General Burton I decided to try to call Kurt. I dialed the number, but it rang and rang with no answer. I decided to try to get a hold of Cynthia Carson, hoping she would know where Kurt went. I didn't have her home number so I called information. She wasn't listed in her full name, but there were a few C. Carsons, so I tried them. After three tries I got lucky.

"Oh hi Stan, where have you been? Kurt was looking for you."

"He was?"

"Yes, he had to go to Brazil to meet some investors and he wanted you to take care of something while he was gone."

"How long's he going to be away?"

"I don't know, maybe a couple of weeks."

"Oh shit, I can't believe this."

"What's wrong?"

"I was in Amarillo and I visited the Panhandle Building."

"Oh, you did. How did you like it?"

"Well, the lobby and the floors that are completed look great. Unfortunately, I discovered . . . well, . . . the information Kurt's been giving us about the finish-out is not accurate."

"How is that?" Cynthia said.

"There are only two floors complete instead of seven, and the rent rolls he gave us are pure fabrication."

"What? I can't believe that. The manager mailed me those rent rolls himself. Why would he fake them?"

"I have no idea, but we need to get ahold of Kurt and get this straightened out immediately," I said. "Do you have a telephone number where we can reach him?"

"No, he's staying with some investors. He didn't give me a number."

"Shit. What I can't believe is how the people from Worldwide Savings could have inspected the building and still closed the deal."

"This doesn't make sense, there must be some mistake, Kurt wouldn't do something like this," Cynthia said.

"I hope there's some explanation, but I took a look at every floor in that building and there're only two floors that are finished," I replied.

"I don't know what to say, Stan. It just doesn't seem possible."

"I know, but it's happening and you and I are in hot water if we can't get it straightened out."

"Why would we be in hot water?"

"Because the bank's going to think you and I were in on it."

"But it's not true."

"You and I know that, but to Worldwide and the FBI it's not so clear."

"What can we do?"

"I don't know yet. Just sit tight, and if you hear from Kurt, don't say anything to him. Just tell him I need to talk to him immediately."

"Okay, I will," Cynthia said.

That's all I needed, Kurt disappearing on me all of a sudden, just when I had to get some answers. The question now was could I afford to wait a couple of weeks for Kurt to resurface? After considerable soul-searching I decided the situation wouldn't get any worse in two weeks. The damage had already been done. I guess I owed it to my client to let him explain what was going on.

# MAKING BAIL

AFTER TALKING TO CYNTHIA I decided I better go visit Gena, who by now had been in jail over a week. I couldn't understand why her criminal attorney had been unable to get her out on bail. When I got to the Criminal Justice Building I obtained a visitor's pass and walked down the long corridor to the main cellblock. When I got to the entrance I pushed a button and stuck my visitor's pass up against the glass. After a minute a bell rang and the big steel gate opened and I entered. Once inside I followed a yellow stripe, which led to a visitor's room. I went inside, sat down at one of the stations and waited. After a minute Gena was escorted into the visiting room and sat down in front of me. She was a knockout even in her orange jumpsuit.

"Stan, where have you been?" Gena said.

"I've been out of town," I replied.

"Well, I've been rotting in my cell while you've been out gallivanting around."

"Wait a minute, I'm not even your criminal attorney, so what difference does it make what I've been doing?"

Gena took a deep breath. "I know. I'm sorry for jumping on you, I'm just frustrated that I haven't got out on bail yet. Stan, you've got to defend me. That feeble-ass attorney they've appointed for me doesn't understand English. He insists I plead guilty, but I've told him over and over again that I am innocent. All he does is patronize me. If he defends me, I'm going to get screwed, I know it."

"Gena, I am not a criminal attorney, I don't know the procedures for criminal court and I barely passed my criminal law course in law school. You'd be in worse shape if I represented you."

Gena leaned over, next to the glass that separated us, and gazed at me with her beautiful brown eyes.

"No I wouldn't, at least you believe in me and if you believe me, then so will the jury."

"Who said I believe you?"

"Come on Stan, I know you believe me, otherwise you wouldn't be here. I can tell by the way you talk to me and listen to what I have to say that you respect me. Most men look at me like I'm another piece of ass they'd like to fuck. But you look at me like you care and you've always treated me with dignity and respect. I'd trust you with my life, Stan, without giving it a second thought."

"Gena, I believe you're innocent of this crime. I do have a lot of respect for you, despite your reputation and your wild lifestyle. Deep down inside of you is a wonderful person, I can feel it and I believe it. And I know, for some reason that I will never understand, that you've had to put up this tough facade, perhaps just to survive, I don't know, nor does it matter. But this isn't a question of my belief in you, it's a question of competence. I'm not a criminal attorney, I never wanted to be a criminal attorney and I don't intend to become a criminal attorney."

Gena sat back with a frustrated look on her face, stared at me silently for a moment and then she smiled. She leaned back toward the glass that separated us and said, "Okay, we'll let the feeble asshole defend me, but you've got to help him."

I shook my head in dismay at Gena's relentless pursuit of her objective. I knew I had lost the battle, there was no telling this lady no.

"Please Stan, come on, at least you can do that."

"Okay, okay. I give up. I'll help him, what in hell is his name?"

"Thank you Stan, I knew you wouldn't let me down. You're wonderful. I love you."

"You may not love me so much if I botch your case."

"You won't. I feel so much better now Stan. Finally now I'm going to be able to sleep."

"That's good, but what's asshole's name so I can call and tell him he's going to have a co-counsel?"

"Syd Brim, his number is 555-4411."

"Did Syd say why he hasn't been able to get you out of jail yet?"

"He says he can't get anyone to put up my bond."

"How much is it?"

"Twenty-five thousand."

"What about your mother?"

"He says she's refused to do it, but I don't believe that. Mom has always come through when I needed her to."

"Have you talked to her?"

"No, they don't let you use the phone too much, and every time I've called she's been out. She works two jobs you know, so she's not home much. Asshole says he's talked to her but she won't help."

"What about your father?"

"Shit, I haven't seen him in fifteen years."

"Well, I'll talk to your mother again and see if she'll help. I've got to go now. Hopefully the next time we meet it'll be to get you out of this place."

"Thanks, Stan."

Leaving the jail I felt good that I had given Gena hope, but on the other hand, I felt kind of sick now that I was going to have to help defend her in an arena I knew nothing about. As I thought about it further on the drive home, I began to get excited. I realized with Syd as lead counsel I didn't have to worry about procedure or my lack of experience in handling

criminal cases. All I had to do was convince him she was innocent and search for evidence to prove it. It was really an ideal
situation, and who knows, maybe the experience might change
my mind about practicing criminal law.

When I got to the office I called Syd Brim to break the
news to him.

"Yeah," Brim said.

"We have a mutual client, Gena Lombardi."

"Okay."

"I represent her in a bankruptcy proceeding," I said. "And,
well anyway, I went to visit her today and she asked me if I'd
help you in her criminal defense."

"I'm her court-appointed attorney. The government's not
going to pay for two attorneys. Anyway, we're just going to
plead her out, so I really don't need your help."

"She believes she's innocent."

"You know her story will never hold up. I told her she
needs to just take the best deal I can get her."

"Why don't you think her story will hold up?"

"Because it's a bunch of bullshit!"

"Are you sure, have you checked it out?"

"Of course I've checked it out. It won't hold water."

"Well, if she wants to plead innocent, she has a right to do
that, and I guarantee you she won't agree to a plea. You might
as well let me help you. Don't worry about splitting your fee,
she'll pay me herself some day when she gets back on her feet."

"Yeah, right. Okay, I don't give a shit if you want to do
some pro bono work."

"Do you mind if I try to get someone to put up her bond?"

"I've already tried, but go right ahead. Good luck."

"Thanks. I'll get to work on that right away. I'll be in
touch and don't hesitate to call me if you think of some way I
can help out."

After talking to Syd I understood now why she felt the way
she did about him. His attitude wouldn't be very comforting
to someone in trouble. Now, however, the ball was in my court.

I had to figure out a way to get Gena out of jail. The first thing that came to my mind was my experience with getting Ron Johnson out of jail on his DWI charge. Alliance Bonding, that's who I needed to call. I got out the phone book, got the number and dialed it. A girl answered and put me through to Roger Rand.

"I've got a young woman in on a federal mail fraud charge. Her bond is twenty-five thousand dollars and I wondered what it would take to get you to put it up," I said.

"Well, it would be twenty-five hundred cash plus we'd need some collateral or a good co-signer."

"Well I might be able to get her mother to do it. She lives in Michigan."

"We need a local co-signer. There's no way we're going to chase someone up in Michigan for the bond money if your client skips out on us."

"Okay, thanks, I'll try to see if I can scrape up the money and find someone local to co-sign."

"Let me know Stan. We'd like to help if we can."

"I appreciate that . . . thanks. Bye."

"Okay, bye."

My conversation with Roger didn't make me feel so great. Maybe Syd had done all he could to get Gena out of jail after all. What had I gotten myself into? Shit, I was always a sucker for a pretty face and beautiful brown eyes. Damn it, why didn't I just tell her no?

After sitting awhile in a dejected state I picked up the phone to call Gena's mother. I wasn't feeling very confident, but I knew I had to be positive when I talked to her. I got Gena's file, found her mother's number and dialed the telephone.

"Hello."

"Hi, this is Stan Turner. Is this Mrs. Lombardi?"

"No, this is her daughter, Cindy."

"Cindy, oh, . . . Gena's sister?"

"Yeah, how did you know?"

"Well, actually I didn't know she had a sister until this moment. . . . So, is your mom in?"

"No, she's at work."

"Listen, this is an emergency. I'm trying to get your sister out of jail and I need your mother's help."

"She won't help. Gena's always in trouble and Mom's fed up with it."

"I know she's had some hot check charges and stuff, but this is serious. She could go to the federal penitentiary, plus I think she's innocent."

"Don't bet on it," Cindy said.

"Really, do I sense a little bitterness between you and Gena?"

"She's no good, she's always in trouble and causing Mama grief."

"I know it must be tough on both of you, but I'm sure she doesn't intend to hurt you or your mom. Can you just give me her work number so I can talk to her?"

"She can't take calls at work."

"Well, give it to me anyway please, they might make an exception under the circumstances."

"Oh, all right, it won't do you any good though, Mom won't give Gena another dime. Her number is 555-4903."

"Thanks a lot Cindy. You've been a big help."

Feeling even less confident I dialed Mrs. Lombardi's work number. After some difficulty I got through to her.

"Oh, I already sent the $500, didn't you get it?" she said.

"Well, no actually, when did you send it?"

"Last week," Mrs. Lombardi said.

"I'll probably get it any day now then, but that's not why I called. I guess you know your daughter is in jail."

"Yes, some asshole attorney named Syd called me and told me. He said he needed five thousand dollars for Gena's defense. I told him there is no way in hell I could scrape up five thousand dollars even if I wanted to."

"That's strange since he's being paid by the state and the bond isn't five thousand dollars. Well, anyway I don't need quite that much. I just need twenty-five hundred dollars for Gena's bond."

"Five thousand dollars or twenty-five hundred dollars, what difference does it make? Where am I going to come up with that kind of money? I'm working two jobs just to scrape by. You know I've got a daughter I'm still raising, don't you?"

"I understand, I know it's hard on you and Cindy struggling on your own. Are there any other family members that might help?"

"No, there's no one."

"Is there some property you have that maybe you don't need and you could sell it?"

"No, everything of value has been taken to the pawn shop long ago."

"How about life insurance?" I said.

"Life insurance?"

"Yeah, some life insurance has cash value that you can borrow."

"Well, I have an old policy on my husband. He deserted me fifteen years ago. I figured someday when he died I'd collect a hundred thousand dollars and that would compensate me a little for all the hell the bastard has put me through."

"When you get home, find the policy and call me. I bet it has more than $2,500 cash value. You could borrow that money pretty quick if it does."

"Okay, I'll do that . . . and Mr. Turner, I'm sorry I was kind of short with you, I love Gena and I want to help her. She's told me how good you've been to her and have tried to help her. I just want you to know I appreciate what you're doing. Maybe after this is all over Gena can get her life straightened out."

"I hope so Mrs. Lombardi, I really do. Good-bye."

"Good-bye."

# THE GUARANTY

It didn't take us thirty minutes to spend the thirty-one hundred dollars that Kurt had paid us several weeks earlier. We had paid the most critical of our bills at that time, but they were coming due again and we had fallen a month behind on our mortgage payment. I had received a hundred dollars the day before for a will I had done for one of Rebekah's friends at the hospital. With that money I had gone by Lone Star Gas and paid that bill just in time to avoid a disconnection. Later that afternoon I got a frantic call from Rebekah.

"Stan, some man came by from the mortgage company. He said we're two months late on our mortgage payment and if we fall three months behind, they'll foreclose."

"Why did he come by the house? They haven't even sent us a nasty letter yet."

"Yes, they did. Didn't you see it? I put it on your desk at home."

"Oh really, I guess it got lost in the bill drawer. Even so, why come by the house?"

"He said the mortgage company wanted to know the condition of the house in case they decided to foreclose."

"Great. So, what did he say when he left?"

"He gave me a number to call so we could advise them of our intentions."

"Well, I'll call them tomorrow."

"What are we going to tell them?"

"You get paid next week and I should get something pretty soon from Mrs. Lombardi. She said she put five hundred dollars in the mail to me several days ago. That'll be enough for one mortgage payment and food for next week."

"Stan, I hate living like this! You're a lawyer for godsake. We shouldn't have to be worrying about money."

"I know, but things are starting to roll. The money will start coming in on a more regular basis soon. It won't be too long before Kurt pays me again."

"Yeah, if he happens to come back from Brazil. Then you'll have to go beg him for the money."

"I don't think so. He'll probably just send me a check this time."

"Uh huh, sure."

Rebekah was right. Money wasn't supposed to be a problem. After all, one of the reasons I became a lawyer was because they were supposed to make so much money. For a brief moment I wished I had gone to work for a big firm. At least I'd have a steady paycheck. Then I felt a rush of optimism and quickly dismissed the big firm idea. I knew independence was one of the greatest treasures a man could acquire. I had obtained it already and I wasn't about to give it up.

As I continued to contemplate my economic plight, the phone rang and Mrs. Lombardi was on the line.

"Hey, you were right. I managed to get a twenty-five hundred dollar cash advance on the insurance policy."

"Fabulous! Can you wire it to me?

"I sent it by overnight mail. Oh, and I don't know what happened, but I found your five hundred dollar check on my desk. It must have got mixed in with some old bills. I thought I had sent it to you."

"Oh, really?"

"Yeah, anyway it's in the package too."

"Good, I'll look for it tomorrow then."

"Yes. Thanks again Stan. I really appreciate what you're doing."

With that hurdle overcome, my only problem now was to get a co-signer on the bond. My only hope was if Gena's boyfriend, Tony, or her ex-best friend, Bridgett, would help. If Tony had taken all of Gena's money, maybe he would feel guilty enough to help get her out of jail. Likewise, maybe Bridgett would have enough remorse about what had happened to help out. After a long and tedious search to find them, I finally got Tony on the phone just before noon the following day.

"What does that bitch want now?" Tony said.

"Well, you may have heard she's in jail for mail fraud. She claims she took some ticket order money and deposited it in a joint account that she had with you. She said that you took the money out, which prevented her from paying for the tickets and delivering them to the buyers."

"Is that what she told you? That lying bitch! She owed me that money. When we started the business I put up all the money, and when we decided to split I just took what was mine."

"I understand there are two sides to every story, and Gena's not looking to recover the money from you. She just wants some help getting out of jail so she can better defend herself."

"She can rot in jail as far as I'm concerned."

"Why do you hate her so much?"

"She's been trying to turn Bridgett against me. She keeps calling Bridgett and telling her that I'm no good. She follows us sometimes, spies on us and just won't leave Bridgett or me alone."

"Well, I guess you can understand why she was upset over what happened."

"Maybe so, but it happened, and there's nothing she can do about it. I hope she gets convicted so Bridgett and I can have some peace."

"Can I talk to Bridgett?"

"No way, good-bye," he said and hung up.

After the fiasco with Tony my only hope was to convince Roger Rand to waive a co-signer on the bond. In desperation I called him.

"I got the twenty-five hundred on that bond I talked to you about."

"Great, come on by and we'll write her up."

"I've just got one problem."

"What's that?"

"Well, I can't get anyone local to co-sign the bond."

"Oh, well that is a problem."

"Is there anything else we can do? Couldn't you let her mother in Michigan co-sign?"

"No, her guarantee would be a waste of time."

"There must be something we can do?"

"Why don't you guarantee it?" Roger said.

"What, me guarantee it?"

"Yeah, we trust you."

"But if she skips, I'm out twenty-five thousand dollars."

"Well, just keep a close eye on her."

"I'll have to think on that one. I'll get back with you."

My stomach began to turn as I realized it was possible now to get Gena out of jail. All I had to do was risk twenty-five thousand dollars. Shit, Rebekah would divorce me in two seconds if I guaranteed Gena's bond. I just couldn't do that. I'd just have to tell Gena that I couldn't get her out of jail. I started to get up and go to the courthouse to tell Gena the bad news, but I suddenly realized I was wasting my time. She'd just convince me to co-sign the bond if I went to see her. I couldn't resist her charm. Anyway, Gena wouldn't skip town. At least I don't think she would. If she did, well, . . . I could take her Corvette as collateral. That would be an ironclad guarantee that she'd never leave town. I picked up the phone and called Roger.

"Will you take a second lien on a Corvette as collateral."

"How much equity does she have in it?" Roger said.

"I don't know, five or six thousand," I replied.

"No, I'm afraid not, the first lien holder would grab the car if she skipped out on the bond and we'd end up with nothing."

"Oh really, shit!"

"I'm sorry Stan, but we've got to be really careful how we collateralize these bonds. Bonding is a very risky business."

"I know, damn it! . . . Okay, I'll guarantee the bond."

"Really, what made you change your mind."

"Well, I know this girl and if I've got her car, there's no way she'd ever skip out."

"Okay, come on by and we'll do the paperwork."

"I'll be right over."

After I had Gena's bond in hand, I went to the sheriff's office, got it approved and then went to the jail to see Gena. As she walked through the door to the visiting room, her eyes lit up and she smiled joyfully. She sat down and immediately said, "I knew you would come through for me."

"What makes you so sure I came to get you out of here?" I said.

"I can tell by the look on your face and besides you wouldn't be here so soon unless you had good news."

"Well you're very perceptive," I said, as I pulled the bond out of my briefcase. "Here's your bond which I need you to sign."

"Oh Stan, I'm so excited. I knew I could count on you. "

"Well, you can thank your mother, she came up with the twenty-five hundred premium for the bond."

"See, I told you Mom wouldn't let me down."

"Oh, there's one little thing. I had to co-sign this little sucker to get you out of here so I'd like your Corvette as collateral."

"You co-signed my bond for me?"

"Yeah, I had to or they wouldn't issue it."

"That is so sweet. No one has ever believed in me the way you have, Stan. I'll never forget this."

"It's all right. But I do want you to pledge your car on the bond."

"That's okay, I already told you to keep it for me."

"I don't need to keep it, just sign this paper giving me a second lien on it."

"Fine."

I slid the bond and the assignment through a small slot in the window. "Just sign these papers and I'll have you out of here in no time."

Gena signed the documents and slid them back to me through the window. "Okay, when do I get out?"

"Right now. Just go back to your cell and someone will come get you in a few minutes."

"Oh, I'm so excited! This is the happiest day of my life."

I left the visiting room and took the bond to the desk sergeant. He said to have a seat and they would get the prisoner. As I sat in the waiting room, I felt a great sense of accomplishment. It was the best I had felt in weeks. Suddenly the door to the jail opened and there stood Gena retrieving her valuables from one of the jailers. She looked over at me and smiled. Then the jailer nodded that she could leave, and she quickly made her exit, ran over to me and embraced me.

"Thank you Stan. I am so happy I could kiss you."

With that she pressed her lips to mine and kissed me passionately. For a few seconds I enjoyed her passion and then I gently pushed her away and said, "That's okay Gena, I know you're grateful."

"Oh Stan, it was horrible in there, you just don't know how terrible it was," Gena said.

"It's the loneliness that's really tough," I said.

"Oh, that's right, you've had some experience serving jail time."

"Yes, unfortunately," I said. "If you've got everything, let's get out of this place."

"I'm ready. Let's go."

We left the criminal justice building and entered the parking garage. I stopped in front of my Pinto and Gena gave me a puzzled look.

"You drive this piece of shit?" she said.

"As a matter of fact I do," I replied.

"But you're a lawyer, you should have a Mercedes or a Porsche."

"Well, as you might recall, I just started law practice and haven't struck it rich yet."

"I'm sorry. I just wished you had a better car. You deserve it."

"Well, some day I will."

"I sure hope so. This is pathetic."

We drove back to Gena's house and I let her off. Her Corvette was still in the driveway, thank God. She smiled and thanked me again and then got out and ran over to it and jumped in.

"You want to come for a ride, Stan?" she yelled.

"No thanks, I've got to get back to the office. You go ahead, have fun."

"Okay," she said, then the Corvette tore off down the street.

I sat in my car and watched her as she disappeared. I could still taste her sweet lips and smell the pleasant odor of her body. I almost wished I could have gone with her, as there was no doubt she would have given me anything I wanted that night. After a while I regained my senses and drove back to the office.

## PARKER #3

On Saturday morning we packed up all the kids, left Marcia with Rebekah's mother and commenced our journey west on Interstate 20 to Cisco. We arrived there about noon and had lunch at the Dairy Queen. From Cisco, getting to the well was not an easy task as the well was located far from any major highway. Bird had given me detailed instructions on how to get to it, but somehow we missed a number of his landmarks. By 3:00 P.M. we were traveling aimlessly down a dirt road in the middle of West Texas.

"I knew this wasn't a good idea," Rebekah said. "Now we're lost out in the middle of nowhere on a dirt road with no one around for miles."

"Don't panic, we'll find someone to give us directions. Someone's bound to come along soon," I said.

"Daddy, where's the oil well?" Reggie said.

"I don't know son, it's out here somewhere. We'll find it."

"I've got to go to the bathroom Daddy," Peter said.

"Okay, you'll have to go behind a bush," I said.

"Why don't you take me to a bathroom Daddy?" Peter said.

"They don't have bathrooms out here, Peter."

I got out of the car and opened Peter's door. "Okay, come on," I said.

We walked off the road and behind some bushes. "Okay, Peter you can pee here."

"Right on the ground?" Peter said.

"Yeah, right here."

"Oh cool!" Peter said, and then unzipped his pants eagerly.

As we were walking back to the car, I saw some dust on the horizon behind us. I put Peter back in the car and waited for the approaching vehicle.

"Honey, there's someone coming. Maybe they can help us."

"Thank God," Rebekah said.

After a few minutes a large tanker truck appeared spraying water on the thick layer of dust that had settled on the roadway. As it approached, it slowed down and stopped. The driver got out and said, "You all having car trouble?"

"No, no, we're just lost. You don't know where Parker #3 is do you?" I asked."

"Sure, I'm heading right by there, just follow me," he said.

We followed the water truck several miles down the road, then as we reached a fork in the road, the truck stopped and the driver got out.

"Okay, just take that road about two miles and you'll be able to see the rig," the driver said.

"Thank you very much," I replied.

We followed the road as instructed and before long could hear the hum of an oil rig in the distance. After two miles, just as promised, we saw Parker #3 in the distance. As we drove toward the camp, we saw a makeshift parking lot ahead so we drove in and parked our Montego. We all got out and walked toward the rig. There were lots of people mingling around drinking beer and conversing with one another. I didn't see anyone we knew until I heard a familiar voice from behind me."

"Stan and Rebekah, there you are," Sheila said.

I turned around in response to the voice, and there stood Sheila Logan, just as gorgeous as ever, with a bottle of beer in her hand.

"We were wondering if you got lost or maybe you couldn't get off work," Sheila said.

"Huh. We did actually," Rebekah said. "You'd think an Eagle Scout could read a map."

"Well, Bird's maps aren't that great. I've gotten lost a few times trying to follow them," Sheila replied.

"I was on the right road, I just didn't go far enough," I said.

"Well anyway, you're here now. I hope they gave you the whole weekend off because after the party tonight you're not going to feel like getting up early tomorrow," Sheila said.

"Unfortunately, I've got to work seven to eleven tomorrow."

"P.M. I hope."

"Yes, if it were A.M., we wouldn't be here."

"Are these your boys?"

"Yes, this is Reggie, Peter and Mark. We left Marcia with Grandma," Rebekah said.

"Great, well, we're roasting a pig and it's almost done. I hope you're hungry."

"Oh yes, the kids are starved, we had an early lunch," Rebekah said.

"Good, we've got plenty. Go grab a beer and enjoy yourself . . . I think they have about twenty or thirty feet to go until the well is supposed to come in."

"Okay, thanks Sheila," I said.

We walked over to the barbecue pit and watched the pig turn round and round over the hot charcoal. The kids were quiet as they watched.

"Daddy, are we going to eat that pig?" Reggie said.

"Of course," I replied.

"I'm not eating a pig," Reggie said.

"Why not, pork chops come from pigs."

"They do?"

"Sure, so does ham and bacon. You kids want a Coke?"

"Uh huh," said Peter.

After we had been at Parker #3 for a couple of hours, it began to get dark. Thirty minutes after sunset a large bank of lights was turned on over the rig so the drilling could continue twenty-four hours a day. Some roughnecks made a big pile of wood and ignited it with gasoline. As the barbecue progressed, a small band situated near the rig began to play country music. We loaded up everybody's plates and sat down at one of many picnic tables that had been set up for the party. As we were eating, I spotted Bird and Mr. Tomlinson approaching.

"Hey Stan. I'm glad you could make it," Mr. Tomlinson said. "Is this your family?"

"Yes, most of it. This is my wife, Rebekah, and my children, Reggie, Mark and Peter. We left the baby at home with Grandma."

"Well, I hope you're enjoying the food," Mr. Tomlinson said.

"We are, it's great," I replied.

"Mrs. Turner, I think you're going to be happy your husband invested in this well. It's looking mighty good," Mr. Tomlinson said.

"I hope so," Rebekah replied.

"Listen Stan, Bird and I will be going back to Dallas tomorrow afternoon, and we'd like to meet with you first thing Monday morning to finalize a couple of things," Mr. Tomlinson said.

"Sure, ten o'clock?"

"Fine, we'll see you then."

After Bird and Tomlinson left, we decided to go sit around the campfire. The air was a little nippy so the warmth of the fire felt good. By now most of the other guests were mingling around, talking, drinking beer and wine and waiting. The intense sound of the rig was becoming annoying so I left Rebekah a moment to go see how much farther they had to drill. Several roughnecks were working diligently, locking pipe after pipe in place over the well and watching them disappear into the earth.

Someone yelled from the platform that surrounded the rig that they only had ten feet to go. Everyone jumped out of their seats and rushed over to the rig. I went over to Rebekah, grabbed her by the hand and took her and the boys over to where the crowd had assembled. The excitement and anticipation of the gathering was intense. The boys stuck their fingers in their ears to lessen the discomfort from the whining of the generators and the pounding of the rig in operation. The man on the rig came out of his little control room and yelled, "Five feet!"

Everyone watched the grease-laden roughnecks lift the last pipe, set it over the well and lock it into place. The crowd came alive as the pipe sank slowly beneath the earth. Suddenly the ground began to rumble and a gushing sound could be heard. I squeezed Rebekah and pulled the kids around us. Then from out of the earth came a stream of oil so strong it was sent fifty feet into the air. The crowd erupted into pandemonium and everyone began to dance and scream with delight until the oil began drenching us. We ran from the well in hysterical delight as oil saturated our hair and ran down our faces. Then Peter began to cry, "Mom, I've got oil in my eyes! It's burning."

I stopped momentarily and wiped the oil from Peter's face and then I picked him up and held him. "Can you believe this Rebekah, we're going to be rich!"

"No, I can't believe it. Are you sure this is really happening?"

"Well, you've got oil all over you to prove it," I replied.

Everyone watched the roughnecks as they worked to cap the well. Within thirty minutes the oil had stopped and then the celebrating really began. Bird had several coolers of champagne brought out. Now that the rig had shut down, you could actually hear the sound of the band playing. People began to dance and have a good time. Rebekah seemed stunned by the events of the evening and was unusually quiet.

"Come on honey, let's go get some champagne," I said.

"Okay," Rebekah replied.

We walked over to where they were pouring the champagne, grabbed a couple of glasses and had them filled up.

"Can I have some Daddy?" Reggie said.

"No, this isn't for kids," I replied. "I'll get you another Coke."

The roughnecks began circulating amongst the crowd, refilling their glasses just as soon as they became empty. Rebekah sipped her champagne very slowly, as she didn't really like its taste that much. I loved champagne so consequently my glass was refilled many times. After a while I began to get rather light headed and the bonfire began to become a blur. Having drunk so much, I felt the urge to go to the bathroom so I excused myself and started to search for the Port O' Let. Upon successfully locating it and relieving myself, I was returning to the crowd when I ran into Bird.

"Stan, you having a good time?" Bird asked.

"Yeah, this is great. I'll never forget this night," I replied.

"I guarantee you won't," Bird said. "Hey, Sheila was looking for you. She's over by the guard shack."

"Oh, okay. Thanks."

I walked over behind the rig to the guard shack and sure enough Sheila was there.

"Hi Stan. Isn't this wonderful. I'm so excited," Sheila said.

"Oh, I know it. I still can't believe it," I replied. "I've always been poor. It's going to be so different with a few bucks in the bank."

"I must say you surprised me a little tonight, Stan, but I'm glad it turned out this way."

"Huh?"

"Come here, I want to give you something," Sheila said.

Sheila grabbed my hand and escorted me to the door of the guard shack. Then she opened it up and stepped inside.

"What are you going to give me?" I said.

"Be patient, it's a surprise. Come on in."

"Why, what's in there?"

"Just come on in," Sheila said, as she pulled me in and then pushed the door closed.

Once inside I looked around the small room that was modestly furnished with a bed, a small table and chairs and a kerosene lamp. Sheila put her arms around me and said, "I know you've wanted this. I could tell by looking in your eyes."

Then she pressed her lips against mine and began to caress my tongue with hers. As my mental capacity had been greatly impaired by the effects of the champagne, my animal instincts took over and I began to reciprocate with great fervor. Sheila pulled off her blouse exposing her exquisite breasts. I ripped off my shirt in eager anticipation of feeling her naked body next to mine. Our passion became so intense we knocked over the kerosene lamp and the floor suddenly became ablaze. I quickly grabbed a blanket and put out the fire before there was any serious damage.

Sheila was greatly amused by the fire and by this time had reclined on the bunk, beckoning me to ravish her. The sudden flash of fire, however, had awakened my mental capacities and I realized it was time to retreat. I put on my shirt and opened the door to leave. Much to my shock Bird and Rebekah were standing in front of the doorway. Rebekah peered in the shack and saw Sheila naked from the waste up. She looked at me, then turned and stomped off.

"Oh shit," I said as I looked at Bird. "Nothing happened we've just had too much to drink."

I ran after Rebekah who, by this time, had gathered up the kids and was heading for the car.

"Rebekah, stop. I don't know what happened. I'm wasted. I'm sorry."

"I'm going to kill her! She'll curse the day she ever met you," Rebekah said.

As we walked back to the car, I tried to explain to her what happened, but she didn't respond. We got in the car and drove off. Rebekah wouldn't talk to me at all during the five-hour trip home. It was after 2:00 A.M. when we walked in the door so we carried the kids, who were asleep in the car, into the house and put them to bed. Rebekah then put on her nightgown and went to bed without a saying a word.

Feeling very guilty and rather sick over what had happened, I tried again to get Rebekah to talk to me. Finally she responded.

"That little bitch won't be satisfied until she steals you away from me. I could see it in her eyes the first time I met her. I don't want you to ever lay your eyes on her again. And if I ever see her again, I'll kill her," Rebekah exclaimed.

"Don't worry, I'm going to stay clear of that woman. You're right, she's nothing but trouble. I'm really sorry, honey, I just drank too much and lost control of my senses for a minute."

"I just wonder what would have happened had you not set the place on fire," Rebekah said. "How did you manage that anyway?"

"I accidentally knocked over the kerosene lamp, I guess."

"I haven't seen that kind of passion around our bedroom lately."

"I'm sorry, honey."

On Sunday Rebekah didn't mention the incident with Sheila. I was relieved I had dodged that bullet. Rebekah did bring up Parker #3. "Are we really going to get $90,000 per year from that well?"

"Well, it could be more or less, depending on what the production from the well finally turns out to be."

"That'll be so wonderful if we finally get some steady money we can count on. You need a new car and the kids need lots of clothes."

"Yeah, I could rent a real law office and hire a secretary. We could even take a Hawaiian cruise."

"That would be nice? I just won't believe it though until I see it," Rebekah said.

"You saw the oil shooting up into the sky."

"I know but it just seems like a dream."

"You've got an oil-stained dress to prove it was real."

"True, but still . . . until I see a big check I won't believe it."

"Whatever. I think it will take two or three months however, before we see any actual money."

# MURDER

THAT NIGHT REBEKAH LEFT for work at 6:30 P.M., and I settled back to enjoy the evening with the kids. For the first time in a long while, I felt really confident about the future. Finally we were going to have some money so we wouldn't have to worry so much about bills, we'd always have enough money for the mortgage payment and food. Maybe we could set up an IRA or Keogh plan and even start building a stock portfolio. My excitement grew as I contemplated what to do with our newfound fortune. I got out a legal pad and mapped out a strategy. When it was done I wished Rebekah were home to share it with her. I put it aside and anxiously awaited her return.

I heard the garage door go up at 11:05 P.M. I knew it must be Rebekah, but she was way too early so I sensed something must be wrong. I rushed to the door to open it for her and as I swung the door open Rebekah was getting out of the car. She looked at me but didn't smile. I could instantly see she was upset. Her face was pale, her eyes were swollen and she looked exhausted.

"Honey, what's wrong with you?"

"Oh Stan, the most horrible thing happened tonight."

I put my arms around Rebekah and began to walk her inside.

"What happened? Come on in and sit down and tell me all about it. Can I get you a cup of coffee?"

I sat Rebekah down at the kitchen table and stood there waiting for her response.

"No, just some water."

"Okay, just a minute."

I got the water and set it down next to Rebekah. She took a drink and then looked up at me. Tears were running down her eyes.

"Honey, tell me what happened?"

"Okay," she said, and then took another drink of water. "About nine o'clock I was helping a doctor sew up a man who'd cut his finger slicing lemons with a sharp knife. We were almost finished when we got word of a lady coming in who had been in an accident on Central Expressway. She reportedly had a bad concussion and was unconscious. Dr. Meade told me to get a table ready, which I did. When the medics brought the lady in, much to my shock, it was Sheila Logan."

"What?"

"That's right, Sheila Logan."

Obviously I was shaken, considering what had happened Saturday night. Rebekah continued, "Dr. Meade noticed my distress and asked me what was wrong. I told him I knew this woman and I couldn't assist him. He shrugged his shoulders and told me to go relieve someone else and send them over to assist him. I found another nurse on duty, Glenda Barnes, and asked her to switch with me. She didn't understand the problem, but there wasn't time to explain, so she went ahead and switched with me anyway.

"After they treated Sheila, they took her up and admitted her. Dr. Meade told me she would probably be all right. She was still unconscious, but he expected she would come out of it okay. As Dr. Meade walked away, I saw Bird staring at me through the doorway to the waiting room. I didn't want to, but I felt I had to go talk to him. As I approached him, he smiled anxiously and said he was hoping I'd be on duty tonight. Then he asked me how Sheila was doing.

"I told him the doctor said she should be all right although she was still unconscious, and Bird was relieved to hear that.

"Then I asked him what had happened and he told me they had just returned from the well. They'd eaten dinner and were going to the Sheraton Hotel on Mockingbird. Bird said he was a little tired so he rubbed his eyes just for a second, and when he looked up a large German shepherd was running across the freeway in front of them. Bird slammed on the brakes to avoid hitting the dog and actually missed him, but the man behind them had been tailgating and rammed into them pretty hard. Bird said he was holding on to the steering wheel so he didn't get hurt. Sheila, unfortunately, was caught completely by surprise and was thrown up against the windshield. Bird said she was then jolted again in the opposite direction when the pickup hit them.

"Bird said it was horrible. When he looked over at Sheila, her body was limp. He said he was panicky, he thought he had lost her. He checked for a pulse and, thank God, she had one. The paramedics got there pretty fast and Bird rode with them to the hospital. Then he said again how glad he was that I was on duty.

"I couldn't help it, I asked him about last night. And he told me not to worry about it, he said you and Sheila just had too much to drink. He said Sheila's a lot younger than he is and he probably doesn't take care of all her needs. He said he knows she loves him, but he can understand if she has an attraction for a younger man, like you.

"Well, I told him I don't feel the same way. Commitment is commitment. I said that I wouldn't have forgiven you if you had made love to Sheila. And I said that I wouldn't have forgiven Sheila either.

"Bird said that it was a good thing it didn't happened.

"Then I apologized because this was no time to be talking about this. I told Bird to go up to the medical-surgical waiting room and I'd come by every once in a while and keep him abreast of Sheila's progress.

"Bird wanted to know why she wasn't in intensive care so I explained that her vital signs were stable, she wasn't in any danger, she just hadn't regained consciousness yet. I explained that there was really no reason for her to be in ICU.

"Bird didn't say anything, but I could see he wasn't convinced by my assurances. I told him I'd check on her every thirty minutes, and when my shift ended I'd get one of the other nurses to do the same thing. He thanked me and said he'd really appreciate that.

"After talking to Bird, I went up to Sheila's room to check or her. She was lying peacefully in her bed with an IV bottle hanging beside her. I checked her chart to be sure that everything was normal and then inspected her IV to be sure it was flowing properly. After my inspection I found the nurse on duty and asked her to take special care of Sheila because she was a friend. I told her to call me if anything unusual happened.

"When I got downstairs, Dr. Meade called for me so I went to assist him with some new patients that had been admitted. I didn't see Bird again. After forty-five minutes I got a call from the charge nurse on the medical-surgical floor. She said to come up immediately as Sheila was arresting. As I ran up the stairs, I heard them call a code blue. When I got to the medical-surgical floor, doctors and nurses were rushing in and out of Sheila's room. I stepped inside and saw a staff doctor holding two paddles trying to resuscitate her. He placed the paddles on her chest and yelled for everyone to clear. Sheila's body was jolted by the charge, but she didn't respond.

"I heard the doctor say that she was gone, it was no use. Then I heard him ask who was the nurse in charge on that floor, he said he wanted to see her immediately!

"I followed the doctor down the corridor. The charge nurse came running up to the doctor and said she heard he wanted to see her. The doctor took her into a storage room where they could talk in private. I inched up close to the door so I could overhear their conversation.

"I head him say, 'Somebody fucked up in there and I want to know who it was and how it happened! There's no reason why that lady should have died.'

"Then I heard the nurse say they were watching her very closely, every thirty minutes someone was in there, and everything seemed normal. She said when she went in to check Sheila a few minutes before she arrested, she observed her having shortness of breath, a rapid pulse and swelling of her arm where the IV had been positioned. The nurse said it looked to her like someone had tampered with the IV.

"The doctor said he wanted the names of everyone who went in the room. He said he would question them all personally, first thing the next morning. Then I heard him say he needed to go report the death to the chief of staff because the chief might want to call the police.

"At that point I quickly left so the doctor wouldn't see I had been eavesdropping. I immediately went back to the emergency room. Dr. Meade asked me what was going on upstairs so I filled him in on what I had seen.

"He asked me how I knew Sheila, and I told him she was the wife of one of your clients.

"Then he asked if I knew her well, and I said we'd gone out together a few times. Stan, then I broke down and began to cry and asked if he minded if I went home.

"Dr Meade was really nice, he said my shift was almost over anyway, I could go ahead and go.

"I thanked him and left the hospital and drove straight home," Rebekah concluded.

"I'm so sorry baby. You must be feeling terrible. Why don't you come into the bedroom and lie down," I said.

I helped Rebekah up, guided her into the bedroom, helped her out of her uniform and then put her into bed.

"I just can't believe this," I said. "Just yesterday Sheila was so alive. I just can't believe she's dead."

"Why did this have to happen to me? Why couldn't she die in some other hospital!" Rebekah exclaimed, as tears rolled down her cheek.

I got up and brought Rebekah some tissues. She wiped her eyes and laid her head on the pillow. After a while she fell asleep. I lay down next to her but couldn't sleep. The events of the past weekend were just too overwhelming. My thoughts turned to Bird and how he must be feeling. What if it were Rebekah who had died, how would I feel? Around two o'clock exhaustion finally overcame me and I dozed off.

The next morning when Rebekah was arrested for Sheila's murder, I was frantic. I didn't know what to do. After the squad car disappeared around the corner, I called Rebekah's mother and told her to come over immediately and take care of the children. When she arrived, I briefly explained the situation and then got in my car and drove to the police station where they were holding Rebekah. As I sat in the waiting room, I tried to think rationally about what I should do. It was obvious I needed a good criminal attorney immediately. I wondered who in the hell I could get.

My mind raced, trying to remember a criminal attorney I might be able to hire. My criminal law professor in law school was also in active practice. He was good, but how could I come up with his twenty-five thousand minimum retainer. Then I remembered Ron Johnson, he told me about the attorney he used from McKinney. Maybe he would take it easy on me under the circumstances.

Immediately I got up and went to the phone. I looked up Big D Title Company and called Ron Johnson.

"Ron Johnson."

"Ron, this is Stan Turner, something terrible has happened."

"What is it?" he said.

"Rebekah has been arrested," I said.

"You're kidding! For what?"

"Murder!"

"Oh my God! What happened?"

"It's a long story, but right now I need a good criminal attorney. What about the guy you're using for your DWI?"

"Ken Sherlock?"

"Yeah, he's good isn't he?"

"Sure, I think he's great, but I don't know if he handles murder cases."

"Would you call him and see if he'll take the case? I don't have much money, but an oil well I invested in just came in so I'll be getting some good money in a few months."

"I'm sure if he handles murder cases, he'd do it for you as a matter of professional courtesy. I'll call him right now. Give me the number you're at so I can call you back."

After a few minutes one of the police officers motioned for me to pick up the phone.

"Hello."

"Stan."

"Yes."

"This is Ron."

"Yeah."

"I talked to Ken. He says he'll do it. He's on his way down there right now."

"Thank you Ron. I owe you one."

# SETTING BAIL

SINCE REBEKAH HAD BEEN arrested during the day, getting her out of jail was a bit easier than it had been for Ron Johnson and Gena Lombardi. Ken Sherlock had already contacted the district attorney's office by the time he met me at city jail. When he entered the room, I recognized him immediately from Ron's description.

"Hi, Mr. Sherlock. Thank you for coming down here so quickly."

"It's okay, have you seen your wife yet?"

"No, she's still being processed."

"Did you have any idea she was a suspect in Sheila Logan's murder?"

"No, it never even occurred to me."

"Has your wife ever been in trouble before?"

"No, absolutely not. She would never break the law. This murder charge is totally ridiculous."

"Well, the assistant DA assigned to the case seems to think he's got some solid evidence. I couldn't get too much out of him, but he seemed pretty confident."

"What do we have to do to get her out of here?"

"There's a bond hearing set at eleven. Do you have a bondsman?"

"Yes, Alliance Bonding."

"Good, I'm pretty sure we can get a bond since your wife has a clean record and you're established in the community. I just hope the bond isn't so high you can't afford to post it."

"Oh God, I've got to keep her out of here. She couldn't handle jail; she'd go bananas."

"Well, keep your fingers crossed that the judge is in a good mood."

"Oh man, I'm serious. Rebekah can't go to jail! We've got four kids at home."

"I realize that, Stan, but you've got to understand this is a murder charge, and the judge doesn't have to set a bond. I think he will, but it could be pretty high."

"How high?"

"A hundred or maybe a hundred and fifty thousand dollars."

"Oh shit, I'm not sure I could post a bond like that."

"Well, don't fret over it now. Let's just wait and see what happens."

Around ten o'clock I was able to see Rebekah. She was shaking pretty badly when the jailer escorted her into the small visitor's booth. Her eyes were swollen and she was very pale. Seeing her so distraught upset me. I couldn't hold back the tears that had been swelling in my eyes since I had first laid eyes on her. Of course, seeing me cry set her off again.

"Rebekah, are you okay?"

"No, do I look okay?"

"I'm sorry, honey. We're going to get you out of here real soon. Ken Sherlock has agreed to defend you. He's a friend of Ron Johnson and he's very good."

"Really? How soon until I get out, I don't want to go back in there. The people in there are scary."

"I know, honey. There's a bond hearing at eleven and once the bond is set then we can get you out of jail."

"I didn't kill Sheila, you've got to believe me."

"Honey, I know you didn't kill her. You would never kill anyone, I know that."

"She was okay the last time I saw her," Rebekah said. "I looked at her chart and everything was normal. Her IV was running just fine, I checked it."

"Somebody must have got to her after you left."

"How could they, the floor was packed with people? How could anyone just walk in there and tamper with the IV?"

"I don't know."

"That's why they think I did it. No one would suspect a nurse going in and out of the room. I'm so scared Stan, what if they convict me?"

"They won't, that's ridiculous. Don't even think like that."

"How are my babies? Oh my God, can you imagine what they thought seeing their mother arrested. They're going to be emotionally scarred for life."

"No, I explained to them it was all some kind of a mistake. I promised them you'd be back home tonight."

Rebekah began to cry hysterically, "I want my babies. Get me out of here, Stan, get me out of here!"

"I will, honey. I will. I promise."

Hearing the commotion from our visitor's station, the jailer came over and escorted Rebekah back to the holding cell. I found Ken in the lobby making phone calls. He hung up as he saw me approaching.

"How is she?"

"Not too good. She's pretty upset."

"I can imagine. Let's head on over to the courthouse and maybe we'll get lucky and get her out of this dump."

"God, I hope so."

At precisely eleven o'clock Judge Robert Wendall Stone took the bench. He was a distinguished-looking jurist in his early sixties with white hair, a mustache and sky blue eyes. Ken advised us that Judge Stone was a tough but fair judge. Ken was pleased he had been assigned to the case. The bailiff called Rebekah's case and she was escorted by a jailer in front of the bench. Ken and Paul Snyder, the assistant DA assigned to the case, joined her in front of the bench.

"All right, what do we have here?" the judge said.

"Your honor, Mrs. Turner is charged with first degree murder," Mr. Snyder advised. "The victim was a patient at North Central Receiving Hospital. The defendant was a nurse at the hospital and was seen going in and out of the victim's room. We intend to prove that the defendant injected a lethal poison into the patient's IV, causing her to arrest."

"What was the motive?" the judge asked.

"We will show that the victim was having an affair with her husband, your honor."

"Oh, I see," the judge said. "So do you oppose bond?" the judge asked.

"Yes, your honor, the people feel that it would be an unacceptable risk to the public to have Mrs. Turner back in the hospital tending to patients when it's very likely she took advantage of her position in the hospital to kill Sheila Logan."

"Would you object if she agreed not to go back to work?"

"No, your honor, the people feel that due to the heinous nature of this killing, the defendant should be denied bond."

"Okay, Mr. Sherlock, what do you have to say about all of this?"

"Your honor, Mrs. Turner has no criminal history, she owns a home, she's got four children, a husband who is a practicing attorney in this community and her parents live close by in DeSoto. There is absolutely no risk of flight and she certainly poses no threat to patients at Central Receiving Hospital."

"Do you think it's fair to allow her to go back to work at the hospital when these charges are outstanding?"

"Fair to whom, your honor. Mrs. Turner has a right to make a living. She's not a wealthy woman."

"All right, you both can go ahead and put on your testimony and then I'll make my ruling," the judge said.

Snyder called several witnesses from the hospital that testified as to how the murder was perpetrated. Ken put on Rebekah's parents and her parish priest. I volunteered to testify, but Ken didn't think it would be a good idea since it was my alleged affair that was supposedly the motive behind the crime. When all the testimony had been presented, the judge made his ruling.

"Okay, I don't see any great risk that the defendant will flee given her strong ties to the community. I don't want her working at Central Receiving Hospital, however, during the pendency of this case. The testimony has shown that the Turners are not well off financially, so if I set a very large bond it would be tantamount to not allowing bond at all. On the other hand Mrs. Turner is charged with first degree murder, which is obviously a very serious charge and could result in a sentence of life in prison. Taking all of this in consideration I'm setting bond at $50,000. The defendant is remanded into the custody of the county sheriff until the bond has been posted."

The judge banged his gavel and then got up and left the courtroom. I was relieved that bond had been set, but I had no clue how I could get a bond for such a large amount. I called Roger Rand and told him the situation. He indicated that he could cover the bond if I could come up with $5,000 and talk Rebekah's parents into signing a personal guaranty. Luckily Rebekah's parents came through, and before Rebekah was transported to the county jail, we had her out on bail.

It was a great relief having Rebekah back home again. Although she had spent less than one day in jail, the experience had shaken her up so badly I thought it best if her mother stayed with her and the kids during the day while I was at work. During the first week Rebekah was home, she became obsessed with looking after the children. She spent every minute seeing to their every need or whim. Getting her away from them for even a minute was impossible. When I confronted her with this obsession, she said no matter what happened, no one would ever take her babies away from her, she wouldn't let them. Not wanting to deal with that possibility yet, I dropped the subject.

# DEALING WITH DECEPTION

AFTER STAYING HOME SEVERAL days with Rebekah, I had to get back to work because the cost of a murder trial would be staggering, and I needed to earn every cent I could to fund it. General Burton felt really bad about what happened to Rebekah and offered to help me out any way he could. He told me not to worry about the rent until the trial was over and I had gotten back on my feet. All our neighbors and friends were very supportive and I felt fortunate to have them.

One afternoon General Burton and I were discussing what to do next on the Melba Thorn case when we were interrupted by the telephone. It was Worldwide's attorney, Mark Pointer.

"We've been trying to get hold of Kurt Harrison, you wouldn't know where he is, would you?" he said.

"Well, as a matter of fact I've been looking for him myself. His secretary says he went out of town for a couple of weeks."

"Mr. Wylie at Worldwide is getting very nervous because the investors haven't made their first payment on the Panhandle Building loan yet. It's already fifteen days past due. We contacted the investors directly, and they told us Kurt was supposed to be making that payment."

General Burton, apparently not wanting to eavesdrop anymore on the conversation, got up and left the room.

"That's what I understood too."

"Do you represent the investors?"

"No, no, . . . I just represent Kurt. I'm sure he'll be back any day now and take care of everything. I'll try again to get in contact with him and call you back."

"Good, it looks really bad for a loan to be in default on the first payment. Please contact me just as soon as you talk to Kurt."

"I will, thanks for calling."

The call from Mark Pointer stimulated me to make a greater effort to find Kurt. I contacted Cynthia Carson again to see if she had heard from Kurt, but she had not. Then I called Tom Tower to see if he knew anything.

"Tom, this is Stan Turner."

"Oh Stan, I read about your wife in the newspaper. Is she okay?"

"Yes, she's holding up pretty well. Her mother's staying with her."

"Well good, if there's anything I can do to help, please let me know."

"You're very kind, thank you. Listen, I wondered if you've heard from Kurt lately?"

"Well no, and the fellow over at Worldwide Savings and Loan called me the other day wanting the first payment on the note. I told him Kurt was handling all that."

"So you haven't heard from him at all?"

"No. Is there a problem?"

"I hope not, but Kurt has disappeared and the first note payment is overdue. Cynthia said he went to Brazil to see some investors and is due back any day now, but I'm not so sure."

"Why? What aren't you telling me?"

"Nothing, I just have some bad vibrations about the Panhandle deal."

"Stan, you were supposed to watch out for us."

"This isn't something I could have anticipated. . . . Anyway there's no need to panic yet. Kurt might show up tomorrow. Let's just wait a day or two. Worldwide won't do anything until the note is thirty days past due."

"Is there anything I can do to help?"

"No, other than ask the other investors if they've heard from Kurt lately."

"I'll do that and I'll call you immediately if I find anything out."

I hadn't hung up the phone for thirty seconds when it rang again.

"This is Arnold Weber, Metro Leasing."

"Oh. Right."

"I guess you know why I'm calling."

"No, you'll have to enlighten me."

"Your client, Kurt, is behind again on his lease payments on the Rolls."

"How far?"

"Three months."

"Gee, Kurt's due back in town any day now, I'm sure he'll take care of it then."

"No, no, this has to be handled immediately! If you don't tell me right now how I'm going to get paid, I'm turning this over to my attorney."

"I guess you'll have to do that then because I don't have a clue where Kurt Harrison is and I don't give a rat's ass about your Rolls-Royce!"

"Well, huh. Then I'll see you in court."

"Fine."

I closed my eyes and rubbed by eyelids with the palms of my hand. General Burton came back in the room and sat down.

"You all right Stan?" he said.

"No, actually I'm not. Your friend, Rufus Green, has gotten me in a big mess," I said.

"How's that?" the general said.

"He referred me to a guy named Kurt Harrison who's turning out to be crooked and I don't know how to deal with it."

"Oh, I'm sorry Stan, I had no idea that Kurt wasn't legit."

"Oh it's not your fault. I should have seen it coming. There were numerous warning signs, I just needed the business so bad I ignored them."

"What are you going to do?"

"Find Kurt Harrison.  That's what I'm going to have to do if it means going to Brazil.  I'm going to find that weasel and make him find a way for everybody to get out of this mess."

"Good, I'll call Rufus Green and see if he has any idea where Kurt is."

"Thanks."

"Now I believe we were talking about Melba Thorn when we were interrupted."

"Yes, we're at a dead end.  I really don't know what to do next," I said.

"Why don't you call Sheriff Burton and see if he's come up with anything."

"Good idea, I'll call him right now.  Go get on the other extension."

General Burton left to go to his office and listen in on the conversation.  I looked through my notes and found Sheriff Barnett's telephone number.  I dialed the number and waited. "Sheriff's office," a female voice said.

"Hi, is this Claudia?"

"Yes, who is this?"

"Stan Turner."

"Oh, hi Stan, how are you?  Oh, I am so sorry to hear about your wife."

"You heard about her all the way up there in Colorado?"

"Well, it was just a small story buried in the *Denver Gazette*, but the headline got my attention."

"What did it say."

"I believe it read: ATTORNEY'S WIFE CHARGED IN DEATH OF LOVER."

"Oh my God.  Shit.  Well, anyway she's home and doing okay for now.  Thanks for asking.  Is the sheriff in?"

"Sure, I'll get him."

"Hello, Barnett speaking."

"Sheriff Barnett, this is Stan Turner."

"Oh hi Stan, I'm glad you called, I was going to have to track you down."

"Oh really, what's up?"

"After you called and told me about being accosted at the Holiday Inn in Colorado Springs, I sent over a forensic team to the motel to check for fingerprints, tire tracks and any other evidence that might have been left by your assailants. They didn't find any prints, but they did find some tracks where your assailants peeled a little rubber in their haste to make their escape."

"So, did they come up with anything?"

"Yes, as a matter of fact the tire tracks left at the Holiday Inn match the second set of tracts up on Highway 24. Now that's not conclusive, but it's damn good evidence that your assailants were involved in the murder of Melba Thorn."

"That's great news, so now you're convinced she was murdered?"

"Yes, after that we had no choice but to formally reopen the investigation."

"Good, so what happens now?"

"Well, one of the first things we did was to request the Dallas medical examiner to exhume Mrs. Thorn's body so we could get a positive ID."

"Have they done that yet?"

"Yes, they did, and they've determined from dental records that the body in the car was definitely Melba Thorn."

"What? But how could that be? What about the phone calls?"

"Somebody else must've made those calls."

"So what are you going to do now?"

"We've already got a warrant out for the arrest of Taylor Brown."

"Already?"

"That's right, the tire tracks from the Holiday Inn and the scene of the accident were matched to a limousine belonging to Mr. Brown. While we were digging around into Mr. Brown's affairs, we found out that Mrs. Thorn's driver disappeared about six months ago. We contacted the Fort Worth police and suggested they get a warrant and search Mrs. Thorn's limousine. Sure enough they found traces of blood in the trunk. The blood is the same blood type as their limousine driver."

"Have they found a body?"

"Not yet, but one is sure to turn up pretty soon."

"So do you think Taylor Brown acted alone?"

"We're pretty sure Robert Thorn was involved, but we don't have enough to arrest him yet unless Taylor Brown implicates him."

"Wow, I'm really impressed, Sheriff."

"Well, if you hadn't come up here and jerked my chain, the murderer would have gotten away with it."

"Yeah, but I still don't understand the phone calls. If they weren't from Melba Thorn, who made the calls?"

"That's bothered me a lot too. I figure it must've been a witness to the accident who was afraid to get involved or perhaps someone who overhead Taylor Brown and Robert Thorn plotting to kill Melba Thorn. You've got to admit it was pretty creative to call you and put you on the hunt."

"I guess, but somehow it still doesn't fit."

"It fits Stan, Taylor Brown and Robert Thorn took over control of a multi-million-dollar corporation the minute Melba Thorn died. It's a classic case of greed turning to murder."

"Well, I hope you're right. Does the DA think he'll have any trouble getting a conviction?"

"Without a body it's going to be tough."

"That's what I was thinking."

"Hey, I'm sorry you didn't find Mrs. Thorn alive. I know if you had, you might've got paid for all your trouble."

"Oh well, I guess every attorney has to do a little pro bono work from time to time, right?"

"Yeah, I expect so. Okay, I'll let you go, I wish your Mrs. good luck."

"Thanks, good-bye."

"Bye now."

I was glad the sheriff had apparently solved the mystery of Melba Thorn's death, but for some reason I had an empty feeling inside. Maybe it was just all the other problems I was facing at the time that made it difficult for me to celebrate, or maybe I still didn't understand how all the pieces of the puzzle fit together. At any rate, for now I was done with the Melba Thorn matter and could turn my attention elsewhere.

# ESCAPE TO BRAZIL

It had been several days and I hadn't heard from Kurt Harrison. With each passing day the situation got more critical. I wasn't sure what the bank would do about the quick default on the Panhandle Building loan, but I knew it wouldn't be pleasant. I knew that once the bank gave up on getting the first payment on the loan, it could accelerate the note and demand its payment in full. This would pave the way for a foreclosure, which would mean the investors would lose everything, plus face a big deficiency claim if the bank lost money. To make matters worse, the bank could send the investors an IRS Form 1099 for any debt that was forgiven. The net effect would be the investors could lose their entire hundred thousand dollar investment, be sued for several hundred thousand dollars and then get hit with a massive income tax liability. If these thoughts hadn't totally stressed me out, the next call did.

"Hello, this is Stan Turner."

"Yes, Mr. Turner, this is Special Agent Howard Henderson of the FBI," he said.

I hesitated as I struggled to breathe. "FBI? Oh, yes, what can I do for you?"

"We're looking for Kurt Harrison. You wouldn't have any idea where he might be, would you?"

"No sir, as a matter of fact I've been looking for him myself. Why are you trying to find him?"

"We're not at liberty to discuss an ongoing investigation, but suffice it say, it's imperative that he contact us immediately."

"Like I said, I don't know where he is or how to contact him, but if you'll give me your telephone number, I'll be sure to give it to him should he contact me."

The agent gave me his phone number and I wrote it on a legal pad and then hung up. Somehow I had to find Kurt, but how could I do it? On the way home that night I drove by Kurt's house to see if anyone was at home. Much to my shock the house was lit up like a Las Vegas casino. The gate was unlocked so I drove my car up into the circular driveway. The only car parked in front was a red Cadillac convertible. I walked to the front door and pushed the doorbell. The chimes resounded throughout the house, but no one answered. I waited a few moments and tried again. This time I observed a young lady dressed in gray fleece shorts and a white sweatshirt walking down the circular staircases. As she got closer, I recognized her to be Gwen Dove. She opened the door and said, "Stan, what are you doing here?"

"I'm looking for Kurt. May I come in?"

"Sure, but I don't know where Kurt is right now."

I came inside, Gwen closed the door behind me and then she walked over to a white satin sofa and sat down. "Have a seat," she said.

"Thank you. Did Kurt return from Brazil?" I said

"Brazil?"

"Yeah, Brazil."

"How do you know he's in Brazil?"

"That's where Cynthia said he was."

"Why that low-down, two-timing, son of a bitch!"

"What are you talking about?"

"Kurt told me he was going to California to work on some deals with Dan Kelley."

"Oh, really?"

"Yes, I was supposed to go to St. Louis and spend a week with my sister while her husband was out of town, but his trip got canceled so I didn't go. Kurt didn't think I would be at home this week, I bet."

"Why would he lie to you?" I said.

"He's had his eye on this Portuguese girl from Rio, Heloisa something, I don't remember her last name. She's the daughter of one of his foreign investors. I don't know exactly what he does, but he's filthy rich."

"Huh."

"When they were in town last week, Kurt couldn't keep his eyes off her."

I shook my head and said, "I can't believe that, you are so beautiful and such a nice person. I don't know why he would even look at another woman."

"Thank you Stan, that was nice of you, but what was that I was reading about in the newspaper about your wife being arrested for killing your girlfriend?" Gwen said.

"That's a lie, she wasn't my girlfriend or my lover, and Rebekah didn't kill her. It's all a big mistake. I don't know who killed Sheila, but it wasn't Rebekah."

"The story sounded pretty bizarre. How's your wife taking it?"

"She's doing better, we're going to see her lawyer tomorrow to start working on her defense."

"Tell her I wish her well."

"Thank you, I will."

"I'm surprised Cynthia told you that Kurt was in Brazil. She and Dan Kelley usually cover for him."

"I think I scared her pretty bad."

"Why?"

"I found out the Panhandle Building is far less complete than it was represented, and now Kurt has missed his first note payment."

"Oh, shit."

"Yeah, the attorney for Worldwide Savings & Loan has contacted me, and just today the FBI called looking for Kurt."

"Oh, my God. I knew Kurt was eventually going to get into serious trouble. What are you going to do?"

"I've got to find him. If he cooperates and we work quickly, we may be able to get things back on track and avoid a total disaster," I said, and then stood up, walked to the window and stared into the courtyard. "You don't think he's gone to Brazil for good, do you?"

Gwen shook her head casually and said, "No, he'll come back when he gets tired of fucking Heloisa."

"It doesn't sound like this is the first time this has happened."

"I wish I could say it was."

"Why do you stay with him?"

"I love him."

"Oh. I guess that's a good reason," I said, and then turned and went back and sat on the sofa next to Gwen. "You and I might still be able to save him if we can just find him and talk to him."

"I know how we can tell if he's planning to come back," Gwen said.

"How's that?"

"Come with me."

Gwen got up and I followed her to the den. She sat down at Kurt's desk, flipped up the corner of the carpet and began opening the safe. After she got the safe opened she looked up and said, "We're in trouble. He took all his money."

"The briefcase is gone?"

"Yes, he usually keeps two hundred and fifty thousand dollars in there as emergency money. He never takes it with him when he travels. I'm afraid he's not coming back."

"Shit! Now what are we going to do?" I said.

"I know where Kurt kept Heloisa's address and telephone number," Gwen said.

"You do, that's great. Where is it?"

Gwen got up and walked over to a file cabinet, opened it and pulled out a black book. "He keeps this address book of all his investors. Her father's name is in here somewhere. . . . Let me see. . . . Here it is."

Gwen handed me the book and pointed to a phone number. I took it away from her, walked to the phone and said, "Good, let's give Heloisa a call right now." I dialed the operator and asked her to place the call for me. In about five minutes she came back on the line and said she had made the connection.

"Alo," a male voice said.

"Hello, does anyone there speak English?"

"Ah. One momento."

"Hello, this is Carla. Who is this?"

"Yes, Carla, this is Stan Turner, I'm an attorney in Dallas. I'm looking for Kurt Harrison, I'm his attorney."

"Oh yes, Kurt, he is not here right now. Heloisa and he went to the beach."

"Would you have him call me just as soon as he gets back. It's an emergency. If he comes back in the next thirty minutes, tell him to call his house, otherwise he can call me at home or at my office."

"Okay, I will tell him," Carla said.

I put the phone down and looked at Gwen. "They're at the beach."

"I can imagine what they're doing on the beach," Gwen said.

"Is it a public beach?"

"No, it's quite private from what I understand. Heloisa's father gave us a detailed description of his estate and all its amenities, including the private beach."

Gwen and I commiserated about our problems for a while until we were interrupted by the telephone ringing. Gwen answered the phone and stiffened up when she found out it was Kurt. She argued with him for a few minutes about Heloisa and then finally Gwen handed me the phone and stomped off.

"You want a drink Stan?" she said before she left the room.

"Sure," I replied, and then put the phone to my ear. "Hello, Kurt."

"Stan, what's going on?"

"That's what I wanted to ask you. The attorney for Worldwide called and said they haven't got the first note payment yet on the Panhandle Building."

"That can't be right," Kurt replied. "The manager was supposed to send it."

"You mean the same manager that sent us the phony rent rolls?"

"What are you talking about?"

"I saw the Panhandle Building Kurt, it's not fifty percent leased like the rent rolls say. At best it's twenty percent leased."

"The manager told me it was fifty percent leased. I can't believe he would lie to me," Kurt said.

"Kurt, give me a break, I've been to the Panhandle Building, there are only three completed floors instead of seven."

"I swear, he told me it was fifty percent complete."

"Kurt, I'm not one of your naive investors. You obviously knew exactly how much of the Panhandle Building was finished out. Now, quit lying to me and let's level with one another. I've already got a call from Worldwide and they are totally pissed off. Apparently they've called the FBI because they called me looking for you."

"The FBI?"

"Yes, the fucking FBI has been called in on the case. They've already contacted Cynthia and all the investors. I don't think they know about the false rent rolls or other misrepresentations yet, but they will, just as soon as they go to Amarillo and talk to your manager."

There was a moment of silence and then Kurt said, "What do you suggest I do?"

"For starters you could wire me $24,642, which would pay the first payment that's past due and also next month's payment. That would certainly take the heat off."

"I don't have the money right now."

"Give me a break, you put a million bucks in your pocket when you closed the Panhandle deal, plus you've got the two hundred and fifty thousand that you kept in your safe."

"I had commitments. The million dollars is gone. All I have is the quarter million and I need it to live on down here."

"You mean you're not coming back?"

"I don't know. If I came up with two payments, do you think the FBI will back off?"

"I can't promise anything, but I'll do my best to convince everyone it was just a misunderstanding with you and the manager. But I will only do that if you swear you'll finish up the project like you promised. You'll need to raise the necessary funds and put them in escrow."

"Where am I going to find the money?"

"I don't know, you're the expert at raising money."

"It's not going to be easy coming up with the kind of money it will take to finish the Panhandle Building."

"You mean you never intended to do it? This whole thing was a big scam?"

"No! Things just didn't work out like I expected."

"Well, they haven't worked out like Tom Tower expected either. I thought he was your friend?"

"You don't know what you're asking. It'll take half a million easy to do the finish out, and then there's no guarantee we can lease the space."

"Well, you're the one who dreamed up this project for godsake. I can't believe this? Forget it. I'll just go to the FBI and tell them the whole thing was a scam."

"No! No. Don't do that. I'll wire you the twenty-four grand, but I need time to raise the other money."

"Well, don't take too long. Once the FBI discovers what you did, you might as well stay down there and have kids with Heloisa."

"Okay, I'll arrange to wire you the money in a couple of days. I'll call you next week about the rest."

"Good, if you move fast I think we can salvage the situation. Good luck."

"All right, thanks."

I put down the phone and looked up. Gwen had returned, kicked off her shoes and was relaxing in an overstuffed chair and sipping a margarita. I couldn't help but admire her long silky legs; they were exquisite.

"Your drink's on the table Stan," Gwen said.

I reached over and picked it up and smiled at her. "Well, I think he got the message. He's wiring me the twenty-four thousand we need immediately and supposedly working on getting the rest."

"How much money will it take to finish the Panhandle Building anyway?"

"I don't really know, he says half a million, but I'm not sure we can rely on his estimate at this point. I'll have to get a couple of contractors out there to give us some bids."

"He didn't say when he was coming back did he?" Gwen said.

"No, he didn't . . . I'm sorry. Didn't he tell you when you talked to him?"

"No, he said he'd come back when he got good and ready and that we weren't married so he could screw other women if he wanted to."

"Do you think he loves you?"

"I don't know, I'm beginning to wonder about it. I kept thinking he would settle down as he got older and eventually we'd get married. Now I don't know, I may have wasted five years of my life."

"Hopefully he'll come to his senses and return home to you."

"I don't know. . . . He may be afraid to come home now."

"I'm sorry Gwen, I really am," I said. "Listen, I better be running."

I got up and started to leave. Gwen got up and grabbed onto my arm. "Don't leave me now, Stan. I don't want to be alone."

I walked over to Gwen, sat down and put my arms around her. She embraced me and put her head on my shoulder and began to sob. After a moment she looked up and gazed at me sadly. I wanted to kiss her, to pick her up and carry her up the spiral staircase to her magnificent bed and then to make her forget that Kurt ever existed. Our lips were drawn closer and closer, so close I could smell her sweet breath . . . but then somehow I stopped myself.

"No! . . . We can't do this . . . I better go. . . . This isn't right."

"Please stay with me Stan. We'll just talk."

"No, it's too dangerous. I don't trust myself around such a beautiful woman, particularly with you being pissed off at Kurt. I'll call you tomorrow."

Gwen took a deep breath, sighed and replied, "Okay then, I'll talk to you tomorrow."

I left Gwen and went home feeling a little better about the Panhandle Building situation. For the sake of the investors and myself, I sincerely hoped Kurt would come through. I hated to think of what might happen if he didn't.

Rebekah seemed in pretty good spirits when I got home. I thanked her mother again for staying with her and she left.

"How are you feeling, babe?" I said.

"Okay, I guess," Rebekah replied.

"I know tomorrow we're going to make a lot of progress on your defense. I can just feel it."

"I hope so. I've been so worried about it."

"Your attorney's really good. He'll get you off."

"So, how was your day?" Rebekah asked.

"I finally found Kurt Harrison, and he's sending us a couple payments on the Panhandle Building."

"Oh that's wonderful," Rebekah said. "I'm so relieved."

"Well, until I actually see the cash I won't feel a whole lot better."

"Do you think he might not send it?"

"No, I think he will. It's the rest of the money I'm worried about. The twenty-four thousand he's sending will just buy us a little time, thirty days at the most."

"I'm so worried," Rebekah said. "What would we do if we both ended up in prison? Who would take care of the children?"

"That's not going to happen. Neither of us is going to jail."

"I hope not."

"Oh, guess what?" I said.

"What?"

"The sheriff up in Colorado has finally figured out that Melba Thorn was murdered.  He's got a warrant out for Taylor Brown's arrest."

"Is that right?"

"Yeah."  I told Rebekah about my conversation with the Sheriff.

"Why did they call you, I wonder?"

"I don't know, they must have gotten my name from one of my clients or one of our friends.  Who knows?"

That night when we went to bed Rebekah seemed in much better spirits so I cuddled up to her and began to stroke her stomach gently.  She didn't respond at all so I slid my hand down into her panties and began playing.  After a minute she slapped my hand and said, "Cut it out, I'm not in the mood."

I withdrew my hand and began stroking her breasts.  She grabbed my hand, tossed it aside and said, "I told you, I didn't feel like it."

"Yeah, but I know how to get you in the mood."

"Oh, . . . how's that?"

"Your neck . . . one bite and you're mine," I said, as I dug my teeth gently into Rebekah's sweet succulent neck.

"Ahhhh! . . . Oh!" she moaned.

"See, what did I tell you?"

# DEFENSE COUNSEL

The next morning Rebekah's sister watched the kids while I took Rebekah to see her attorney, Ken Sherlock. Ken had an office in an old mansion in McKinney, Texas, which had been renovated and made into offices. It was situated on a heavily wooded street, not three blocks from downtown McKinney and the Collin County Courthouse. We opened the front door and were greeted by the receptionist.

"Good morning. You must be the Turners."

"Yes, we're here to see Mr. Sherlock," Rebekah replied.

The receptionist stood up. "I'll tell him you're here," she said, as she began walking toward the back of the house through a hallway that, in days past, must've led to the kitchen. In a few moments she returned and invited us back to Mr. Sherlock's office. We followed her back through the hall to a large office furnished with antique furniture, photographs of several Texas courthouses, the head of a fifteen-point buck and a lunker black bass. Ken stood up when we entered the room and gave us a warm smile.

"Well, let me fill you in on what I know so far. I've talked to the DA and I think the evidence they have is a little shaky."

"What evidence do they have anyway?" I asked.

"Of course, Rebekah's fingerprints are all over the room, but I told the DA that's to be expected since Blackbird Logan

asked you to keep an eye on Sheila. Then there is the IV bottle
. . . her prints are on it too."

"I checked the IV to make sure it was flowing properly,"
Rebekah said.

"Was it?" Ken asked.

"Yes, it was doing just fine."

"Apparently the murderer removed the IV from Mrs.
Logan's arm, contaminated the needle and reinserted it im-
properly so that she would go into shock," Ken said. "The
person may have also injected something into the IV solution
or directly into Mrs. Logan's veins. So far the medical examiner is not sure exactly what happened."

"Since we know Rebekah didn't do it, who else would've
had an opportunity to kill Sheila?" I said.

"It could've been anyone on the medical staff or anyone
who was at the hospital that night. I suppose the logical person would be Bird Logan himself," Ken replied.

"Do the police consider him a suspect?" I asked.

"No, a lot of witnesses in the waiting room saw him during
the evening, and he was pretty distressed when he found out his
wife had died. He's either innocent or a good actor," Ken said.

"Maybe I should check into Bird's accident that night.
Something seems fishy about it," I said.

"If you want to help, that'll be fine. Start with the police
report, see if there were any witnesses, check out other people
in the waiting room that night and look into Mr. Logan's past
if you can," Ken said.

"Okay, I'll be happy to," I replied.

The receptionist returned with two cups of coffee and set
them on the desk in front of us.

"Other than Mr. Logan, do you know of anyone else that
might have wanted Sheila dead?" Ken asked.

"Well, Bird and his secretary had something going. I think
she'll sleep better now that Sheila's dead."

"Oh really, what's her name?"

"Ah, . . . Melissa something. I don't remember her last
name."

"Huh. All right I'll get someone to check her out."

"Anybody else?"

"Not that I know of, but I didn't know Bird and Sheila that well. There could be others who wanted her out of the way."

"Okay, that's a start. Now, what I need is a minute-by-minute account of what happened that night. You've got to think back and tell me every detail and, if you don't mind, I'm going to tape it so I can replay it later to make sure I haven't missed anything."

Rebekah repeated her story to Ken, as he listened intently and took copious notes. When she was finished Ken stood up, grabbed a pipe and walked toward a window that overlooked the backyard. He lit the pipe and then turned to us and smiled.

"Well, looks like we've got lots of work to do to prove your innocence Mrs. Turner, but I feel good about this case. I think we can beat this thing," Ken said. "Oh, there is just one thing I guess we need to cover though before you leave. I always hate to bring this up, but I will need a retainer and a cost advance."

"How much?" I asked.

"Well you know investigating a murder case can take a lot of time, and private investigators don't come cheap. I think a five thousand dollar cost advance and maybe a ten thousand dollar retainer to start would be appropriate," Ken replied.

"Well, I can give you a couple thousand right now, but it may be a few weeks before I can come up with the other $13,000. I can get it, it will just take a little time."

"Pardon me for asking, but where do you plan to get it?"

"Well, thank God all of our luck has not been bad lately. We had an oil well come in a couple weeks ago and we're expecting a pretty good-sized royalty check coming in each month starting in thirty to sixty days."

"That's good, I'll just take an assignment on your royalty interest to secure the payment of my fees."

"You want collateral?"

"Yes, don't take it personal. This is business. You're asking me to extend you a substantial amount of credit. If I were a banker, you'd expect to give me collateral, right?"

"I suppose."

"Well, until you've got the cash to pay me, I'm just like the bank. For every dollar I bill that you can't immediately pay, I'm making a loan to you."

"Okay, that'll be fine. I'll get with Inca Oil Company and draw up the paperwork."

"Good then. I'll call you when I hear something about your case. In the meantime don't worry about it. That's my job," Ken said, as he stood up and shook hands good-bye.

After I got Rebekah home, I went to the police department and got a copy of the police report. Then I went to the office to study it. The police report didn't list any witnesses so I decided to put an ad in the *Dallas Morning News*, asking if anyone observed the accident that night. I figured, on a busy freeway someone had to have seen it. I wrote out a short little article for the weekend paper.

H*E*L*P, IF ANYONE SAW THE ACCIDENT AT CENTRAL EXPRESSWAY AND ROYAL LANE ON MONDAY NIGHT, MAY 18, 1979, PLEASE CONTACT STAN TURNER AT 555-2222. REWARD.

After I had placed the ad, I went to my bank to see if the money had arrived from Kurt. It wasn't there yet, so I went to my office to try to get some work done. On the way there I pondered whether I should put a call into the bank's attorney, Mark Pointer, just to let him know the money was coming. After weighing the pros and cons, I finally decided to make the call.

"Oh Stan, have you heard from Kurt?"

"Yes, and as a matter of fact, I've got good news for you."

"I could use some good news," Mark said.

"Kurt is wiring May and June's payment to me in the next day or two."

"Well, that is good news. When can I pick it up?"

"I'll call you just as soon as it comes in, hopefully tomorrow."

"Okay, I'll send a runner over just as soon as you have the money in hand."

"Listen, before you go . . . what's this FBI call I got?"

"We're required by law to inform the FBI of any suspicious transactions. When we loan a couple million dollars and don't even get the first payment, we get a little concerned."

"Will you notify them to back off when you've got your payments?" I asked.

"Once I get the money you've promised, I'll try, but once the FBI takes a referral it's not easy to call them off."

"Please try, I've had a long talk with Kurt, and he's going to fire his manager up in Amarillo and get someone else to oversee construction on the project for him."

"I'll do my best."

"Thanks a lot, I really appreciate it."

As I was praying for the funds to arrive, General Burton walked in the front door. He smiled, said hello and then hurried into his office. I heard him dial the phone and talk excitedly to whomever he had called. When he was done he came into my office and sat down in a side chair facing my desk.

"Hi Stan, how are you doing?" the general said.

"Better, things are beginning to turn around," I said.

"Good, I've been worried about you and Rebekah."

"Rebekah's attorney seems to really know what he's doing. I think he's going to be good. All I've got to do now is find $13,000 to pay him."

"Well, if you don't have the money, I can introduce you to a good banker."

"I appreciate that, but I'm supposed to start getting some money from Parker #3 pretty soon.

"You don't happen to know any good contractors in Amarillo, do you?"

"Not right off hand, but I can check around for you."

"I'm looking for a good finish-out contractor to do a building rehab."

"I know some brokers in Amarillo I can call and maybe get a referral"

"That would be great."

"No problem."

As we were speaking, we heard the newspaper boy drop the *Ft. Worth Star Telegram* off in front of our office. General Burton got up, walked outside and picked it up. When he returned he was engrossed in a story on the front page.

"What's so interesting?" I asked.

"They've indicted Taylor Brown for the murder of his partner's chauffeur," General Burton said, as he laid the paper down in front of me. "The headlines reads: 'FT. WORTH BUSINESSMAN INDICTED FOR MURDER.'"

"Damn, it didn't take them long did it?" I said.

General Burton picked up the story and began to read it aloud.

> A Fort Worth grand jury today indicted Taylor Brown, a wealthy real estate developer and major shareholder of Thorn Enterprises, Inc., for the murder of his chauffeur, Ronald Sage. The alleged murder took place approximately six months ago near Brown's ranch in Johnson County, Texas. The indictment came about as the result of an investigation triggered by a tip from a Colorado sheriff. The informant said that Brown was involved in a conspiracy to murder Brown's mother-in-law, Melba Thorn, who at the time was the controlling shareholder in Thorn Enterprises, Inc.
>
> Mrs. Thorn met a fiery death when her car spun out of control on Highway 24 near Florissant, Colorado. Authorities now believe that the crash was not an accident, but a conspiracy between Brown and the decedent's son, Robert Thorn, to gain control of Thorn Enterprises. Authorities report that they are looking for Robert Thorn to question him about the two murders, but they haven't been able to find him as yet. In a bizarre twist the *Ft. Worth Star Telegram* has learned that the conspiracy was actually uncovered by a local attorney, Stan Turner,

who claims to have received telephone calls from someone who said she was the deceased, Melba Thorn. The *Telegraph* has been unable to make contact with Mr. Turner for his comments.

"Jesus, how did they find out about that, I wonder?"

"Your sheriff friend up in Colorado must have told someone."

As we were speaking, the door opened and two men came in, one was carrying a camera. Before anyone spoke, the man with the camera said, "Smile," and then took my picture. Then the other one pulled a small tablet from his pocket and began talking and writing at the same time.

"You're Stan Turner, I presume," he said.

"Yes."

"Hi, I'm Walter Benjamin from the *Ft. Worth Star Telegram* and this is my photographer, Paul Myers. I guess you read the story in today's paper," Mr. Benjamin said.

"Well yes, just now in fact," I replied.

"Is it true you were contacted by the ghost of Melba Thorn?"

"Someone called me claiming to be Melba Thorn. She said she was being held hostage and wanted me to help her."

"Did you ever meet this woman who called you?"

"No, she didn't tell me where she was being held," I said. "I searched for her but never found her."

"How did you crack the conspiracy between Brown and Thorn?"

While I was briefly explaining to them what had happened, the door flew open and a television crew came bursting into the office. Following right behind them were other reporters and cameramen. Bedlam broke out and General Burton finally fought his way to a telephone and called security. In a few minutes several uniformed security men arrived and cleared the office. As the last reporter was escorted out of my office, I looked at General Burton and began to laugh.

"Holy shit! Can you believe that?" I said.

"No, those bastards damn nearly destroyed my office."

"I'm sorry, I'll pay for any damage."

"Don't worry about it, it's not your fault. I'll send a bill to each and every one of them."

General Burton turned around and limped back to his office. "You weren't hurt were you?" I asked.

"No, I just pulled a muscle in my back wrestling with one of those gorillas," he replied. "I'll be all right."

"Tell me which one it was and I'll sue him for you."

"That's all right, forget it."

The telephone began to ring incessantly. I knew the calls were about the story so I disconnected the phone line. I wondered how long this was going to last. I might have to get an unlisted number if I ever wanted to be able to use the phone again. What if Kurt tried to call me and he couldn't get through, or what if prospective clients called? Then I remembered I needed to call Inca Oil to arrange for my collateral. I plugged the phone back in the jack and quickly dialed before it started ringing.

"Mr. Tomlinson, this is Stan Turner." For several seconds there was no response, then finally Brice responded.

"Hi Stan. How's your wife?"

"She's okay. Listen Rebekah didn't kill Sheila, I promise you."

"Well, I guess that's the district attorney's problem now, not mine."

"How's Bird doing?"

"He's pretty upset. He went down to Corpus to be alone for a while."

"I am really sorry, Sheila was a wonderful person."

"What was going on between you two anyway?"

"Nothing, we were just a little infatuated with each other, what can I say? Nothing really happened. I tried to steer clear of her since we were both married and I love Rebekah, but we just got out of control there for a brief moment, you know, with the well coming in and the party and everything."

"I guess it's water under the bridge now. Why did you call?"

"How's Parker #3 coming along? I need money for Rebekah's defense."

"Didn't you get the letter?"

"What letter?"

"Parker #3 has been shut down."

"What! Why?"

"For about twenty-four hours we were getting some good production. There was quite a bit of salt water in the oil, but that's not a big deal as long as there's plenty of oil too. We can separate the water from the oil and haul it off or drill an injection well. Unfortunately, the percentage of oil began to drop drastically, until ninety-nine percent of what we were pumping out was salt water."

"Oh shit! How could that be when the production reports said they were pumping out two hundred barrels of oil a day when the well was shut in."

"Maybe there was an offset well drilled somewhere that we didn't know about."

"Oh my God, what am I going to do now?"

"I'm sorry, Stan. It really looked like a good prospect."

"Damn. . . . Well, okay, I'll talk to you later."

"Oh Stan, under the circumstances, I think it would be better if we used another attorney for a while until this thing with your wife is resolved. Send me a final bill and I'll see to it that it's paid immediately."

"Sure, bye," I said, and then slammed down the phone. "I can't believe this."

Just as I hung up the phone it rang. Forgetting momentarily that I needed to disconnect it, I answered it.

"Stan, this is Jane Brown."

"Oh, Jane. Hi. I'm sorry about your husband being arrested."

"I guess we both have something in common now," Jane said.

"That's true."

"I just now read in the newspaper about how you've been investigating my mother's death," Jane said. "I take it then, our luncheon a few weeks ago wasn't really a social occasion."

"Well, I'm sorry about that, but I was at a dead end and needed some information in order to continue the investigation."

"I just can't believe Robert and Taylor would kill Mom. I pray to God the sheriff is wrong and someone else did this horrible thing. I've been so sick since Taylor was arrested."

"I hope you're not mad at me for digging into this mess, but I didn't know what to do when I kept getting those calls."

"No, you did what you had to do. If Mom was murdered, the persons responsible should be brought to justice, no matter who it is. And, I want you to know that if it turns out Mom was murdered, Thorn Industries will pay you for all your time and trouble in bringing it out in the open."

"Thank you. I really appreciate that."

"Let's have lunch in a few weeks, I want you to tell me all about your investigation."

"Sure, give me a call when you'd like to do it."

"I will, good-bye."

"Bye."

The bad news about Parker #3 had drained every ounce of energy I had in me. It was only four o'clock, but I was so wiped out I decided to go home. Rebekah and her mother were happy to see me home early, as they were beginning to run out of things to say to each other and the kids were driving them nuts. After Mom left, I took over entertaining the boys, and Rebekah put Marcia in her high chair and began making supper. Rebekah was in such good spirits I couldn't tell her about Parker #3 so I kept my mouth shut. I figured I would tell her when the time was right.

That night I couldn't sleep, worrying about how I was going to pay Ken Sherlock the rest of his thirteen thousand dollar retainer. I remembered General Burton's offer to introduce me to his banker, but upon careful analysis, I realized that would never work in my current situation. Of course, an obvious source of funds would be from relatives, but in scanning my brain for all known relatives with available cash, none came to mind. I finally decided if I couldn't come up with the money, I'd have to defend her myself.

# THE CONFERENCE

THE FOLLOWING DAY I went by the bank, but Kurt's money still hadn't arrived. When I got to the office there was a message from Mark Pointer. I tried to ignore it for a while, but finally I picked up the phone and began dialing his number.

"You got the money yet," he asked.

"Well, no. Not quite yet. I went by the bank but it wasn't there. I'm sure it'll be there tomorrow."

"Well, we need to have a meeting with you and the investors so we can get this thing straightened out."

"That shouldn't be necessary, I'm sure the money will be there tomorrow."

"Maybe so, but let's go ahead and set up a meeting for tomorrow anyway. We can cancel it if the money shows up."

"Well, I don't know if I can line up the investors or not. They're not really my clients."

"I'm sure you can arrange it. Ten o'clock at my office, okay?"

"All right. I'll try to set it up."

The conversation with Mark Pointer shook me up pretty badly. Suddenly I was faced with the prospect of having to contact all of the investors and explain to them why they were being summoned for a meeting with the bank. Obviously they would have lots of questions. If I wasn't careful, Kurt's scam would be uncovered and it would be all over. To make things worse, if I made any statements that were untrue or said anything misleading at the meeting, I would pay for it later if the truth came out. For a brief moment, I thought maybe I should join Kurt in Brazil.

There was no way I could tell Rebekah what was going on. She had enough to worry about with her own trial. After several hours of pondering my predicament, I decided I could pull off the meeting if I just listened and didn't say much. I contacted the investors and gave them the bad news. They were all very upset, but agreed to the meeting. At precisely ten o'clock the next morning, I walked into the offices of Pointer, Blasingame and Merrill for the meeting. Tom, Pete and George were already seated in the reception area and they looked pretty pale. They greeted me with a barrage of questions for which I had very few answers. Before long we were summoned into the conference room for the meeting.

Mark Pointer was sitting at the end of the long conference table. He whispered something to Henderson and then began the meeting.

"Gentlemen, thank you for coming today. As you may remember, I'm Mark Pointer, counsel to Worldwide Savings and Loan. I think you've met Mr. Wylie. Here to my left is Howard Henderson from the FBI. We also invited Brian Walls, chief of bank security, and one of the associates in our firm, Paul Wize, to sit in on the meeting."

Mr. Pointer paused for a moment and then continued. "As you know, the bank has not received its first payment on the promissory note that was executed less than sixty days ago. When we contacted each of you about this, it was explained that Kurt Harrison was supposed to be taking care of these payments. Unfortunately, Kurt hasn't made the first payment and soon a second payment will be due."

"Now, Mr. Turner has advised us that he had managed to reach Mr. Harrison and a couple payments are supposedly due in momentarily. Unfortunately we don't have those funds yet and frankly, I'm not convinced we'll ever see them."

"I feel like the funds will be here," I said. "Kurt was pretty definite about sending the money."

"I hope you're right, Stan, but I wanted to have this meeting to make sure the partners understood the gravity of this situation. Worldwide Savings and Loan is a federally chartered institution, and any misrepresentations or fraud committed against the bank would be a federal offense."

"I beg your pardon," Tom said. "Are you insinuating that we've done something wrong?"

"No, not at all, but I want you to understand that if Kurt doesn't live up to his agreement with each of you, then you would be well advised to make these payments yourself. The consequences of a default on this loan at this stage could be quite severe."

"What do you mean?" Tom said.

"Well, the bank would be forced to assume there was never any intent to pay back the loan since not a single payment was made," Mr. Pointer replied. "That could only mean that the loan was fraudulent and merely a pretext to steal money from the bank. I honestly don't think any of you did that, but if no payments are ever made on the note, that would be the only conclusion we could draw. The net effect would be that we'd have to turn the matter over to the FBI. If that happens, things will get ugly, believe me."

"I don't know about the others, but I don't have sufficient income to make my third of the note payments each month. It's just not feasible. Kurt promised us he'd make all the payments," Pete said.

"I think his plan was to use the income from the building to service the debt, and just subsidize the project until it became self-sufficient," I said. "You guys wouldn't have to come up with the whole payment, only the deficiency."

"That may be true, I don't know," Mr. Pointer said. "Anyway, will you all make these payments if Kurt doesn't come through in the next three days? That's what we need to know. If we can't get that commitment, I'm just going to turn this matter over to Mr. Henderson right now."

"That won't be necessary. Will it, gentlemen?" I replied.

There was a brief pause and then Tom said, "I guess we don't have any choice. Somehow we'll have to make the payments."

"Pete, George. Do you concur?" I said.

"Yes, but I'm going to kick some Harrison ass if I have to sink any more money into this deal!" George said. "This is ridiculous."

"That's right," Pete added. "Stan, you can tell Kurt that he'll be looking at a major lawsuit if he doesn't adhere to our agreement. I can't afford to be pumping a lot of money into this deal. It's not right."

"Good then," I said. "If Kurt comes through, everything's okay; if not, the partners will work something out to get the loan payments made each month."

"Fine," Mr. Pointer said. "Then we'll expert to hear from you, Stan, real soon."

"Yes, one way or another I'll be calling you."

"Well, thank you, gentlemen, for coming. I hope we don't have to meet again."

"Tell me about it," Pete said.

I left the meeting feeling like I had dodged a bullet. Now all I had to do was get Kurt to wire me the money like he promised and everything would be okay for a few weeks.

The next morning I went by the bank fully expecting the money to be there. I got in line at the teller's window and when it was my turn asked her, "Can you check and see if a wire transfer came in for me today from Brazil?"

"Sure."

I handed her a slip of paper with my account number on it and she went into the back room. After a moment she returned. "Nothing today, Mr. Turner."

"Damn, I can't believe it. It was supposed to be here."

"I'm sorry, if you'll leave me your phone number, I'll call you when it comes in."

"Oh, would you? That would be great."

"Sure, no problem."

# BEYOND A REASONABLE DOUBT

WHEN I GOT TO work it suddenly occurred to me I hadn't seen or heard from Gena Lombardi lately, and nothing had been done to prepare for her trial. I decided to call Syd Brim to see if he'd got a trial setting yet. I dialed the number and waited.

"Law office," a female voice said.

"Syd Brim, please," I said.

"Let me see if he's in a meeting. Who is this?"

"Stan Turner."

"Okay, hang on."

The annoying elevator music came on as she put me on hold. After a several minutes she came back on the line.

"Sorry, he's in a meeting."

"Maybe you can help me."

"What do you want?"

"I just need to find out if you've got a trial setting yet on Gena Lombardi's federal criminal case."

"We can't give out information about clients," she said.

"I'm co-counsel with Syd, I just need to know if there's a trial setting yet."

"Okay, let me look . . . yes, June 3, 1979," she said.

"Huh, . . . that's less than thirty days. . . . Okay, thanks."

"Good-bye."

It was clear Syd wasn't going out of his way to prove Gena innocent so I knew I had better figure out a way to do it. It seemed after talking to Tony and Bridgett that Gena was telling the truth. She had acted in good faith in selling tickets and collecting the money for them. It was Tony who discovered money in the account and withdrew it, preventing Gena from filling her orders. It suddenly occurred to me if Tony hadn't spent the money, I could file a preference action in Gena's bankruptcy and recover the money he took. Then, if I provided for the reimbursement of the ticket buyers, and proved to the DA that there was no intent to defraud the ticket buyers, the DA might drop the charges. After all, he had to prove his case beyond a reasonable doubt, which would be difficult given the evidence I would have gathered by the time of trial.

After careful thought I determined that I needed Gena's bank records to show the deposit of the money and the withdrawal by Tony. Gena wouldn't have any records so I would have to get them from the bank. This often took time so I decided to get a subpoena out immediately. Then I prepared an adversary proceeding to be filed against Tony for withdrawing money owed to him within ninety days of Gena's bankruptcy filing. The preference statutes were designed to make sure all creditors were treated equally. Obviously Tony got paid much more than the other creditors so the preference action was an appropriate threat. Wouldn't he be surprised when he got the suit in the mail?

While I was thinking about Gena's defense, my thoughts were strangely drawn to Gena's mother. She had been deserted by her husband, but nevertheless kept a hundred thousand dollar insurance policy in force. How would she know if he died so she could collect the money? I remembered seeing an advertisement in the *Texas Bar Journal* for a firm called International Tracers. What was interesting was that they didn't charge you anything if they couldn't find the person for whom you were looking. Since I didn't have anything to lose, I called them and got them started looking for Michael Roman Lombardi, age fifty-two, greasy black hair, standing five foot eleven with a slight limp from an old war wound. His last known address was his wife's current residence, which I provided them. They advised me that since this was such an old address it may take them a little longer to track him down, but they were confident they could do it.

I was feeling pretty good about Gena's case after working on it for a couple of hours so I decided to call her and tell her what I was planning to do. I called her business but no one answered. I thought that a little strange since it was the middle of the day. Then I tried her at home but the phone had been disconnected. My heart began to pound as I was cognizant of the fact that I had co-signed on her bond. After trying her at her business again, I decided to swing by her house on the way home to see if there was any sign of her.

On the way there I remembered I hadn't told Rebekah about Gena's bond. She was going to have a stroke. The thought occurred to me that I might want to go home and pack my bags, for Rebekah was surely going to kick me out of the house when she found out not only was I about to lose $25,000 on Gena's bond, but that Parker #3 had washed out as well. As I approached Gena's house, I held my breath that I would spot the yellow Corvette for which she was so fond. If it was in the driveway then Gena had to be close by. Unfortunately the driveway was deserted. I got out of my car and went up to the front door. I rang the doorbell although I didn't really expect an answer. After a minute I peered through the windows and was relieved to see that the furniture was still there.

By the time I got home, I had decided not to tell Rebekah anything yet, as I wasn't sure about Gena nor had I given up on finding the $13,000 needed for her defense. One nice thing about practicing law, you never knew when someone might drop in and dump a nice retainer on you. When I arrived home Rebekah met me at the door obviously excited about something.

"What's going on babe?" I said.

"You won't believe it, but we got a call on your advertisement about Bird's accident. A guy called and said he drove by the accident almost immediately after it happened. Mom is on her way over to watch the kids. We're meeting this guy at the Denny's in Richardson at 7:30."

"Oh that's great, babe. I hope he saw something that'll help."

Several minutes later Mom arrived and we left for Denny's. When we arrived, the man wasn't there yet so we got a booth and waited. "So how was your day, babe," I asked.

"Pretty good, Mark came home with a smiley face today. He was the best citizen in his class."

"I bet he was proud of himself."

"He certainly was. Marcia was fussy all day. She wouldn't eat anything and she refused to sleep. I think she must be teething."

"Hmm."

As we were talking, a short, stout, bald-headed man walked into the restaurant. He talked to the waitress and she pointed toward us. The man walked over. "Hello, are you the Turners?"

"Yes," Rebekah said.

"Hi, I'm Paul Singleton . . . I called about your ad."

"Please have a seat," I said.

Mr. Singleton sat down in the booth across from Rebekah and me and smiled.

"Rebekah tells me you saw the accident on Central Expressway the other night," I said.

"Yes, I got there just after it had happened."

"So what exactly did you see?"

"Well, as I approached the two cars, the man driving the rear car got out. He was a little shaken but seemed all right," Singleton said. "It was a few minutes before the other man got out of his car."

"That would have been Bird," I said.

"Is that his name?" Singleton asked.

"Right."

"I parked on the side of the road and observed what was going on just in case I would be needed as a witness. I remember that the man driving the rear car was very upset and wanted to know why Bird suddenly stopped. I overheard Bird claim a dog ran in front of him."

"Did you see any dog?"

"No, but he could've run off by the time I got there."

"How did Bird react to the accident?" I said.

"He attended to his wife, as you would expect, until the paramedics showed up, but he didn't cry or anything. He was really nervous though, and had trouble talking coherently to the paramedics and police when they arrived."

"I suppose he could have been in shock over the accident," I said.

"Was Sheila Logan unconscious after the accident?" Rebekah asked.

"I think so, I never saw her move or say anything."

"Well, did you see anything else that might be significant?"

"No, . . . well, just something kind of curious," Mr. Singleton said.

"What?"

"Bird was real concerned about his wife's purse. He made the driver of the ambulance wait while he went back to get it. They told him to forget it, but he insisted his wife had to have it."

"Maybe she was carrying a lot of money or something," I said.

"I don't know but it was kind of weird," Mr. Singleton said.

"Well, thanks for your help. Rebekah's got your address and telephone number so we'll call you if we need you at the time of trial," I said, and then pulled an envelope out of my pocket. "Here's the reward we mentioned in the ad. It's a hundred dollars."

"Thank you, I appreciate this very much."

Rebekah's spirits had been greatly lifted by the meeting with Mr. Singleton. For the first time since her arrest she seemed to have thrown off the shackles of depression and was her old, cheerful self again. When we got home she joked and played with the children just like old times. As much as I loved seeing her this way, I couldn't feel any joy as the weight of eminent financial disaster loomed heavy on my mind. After the kids went to bed Rebekah lay down beside me on the sofa. I put my arm around her and stroked her long black hair.

"I feel much better doing something to prove I'm innocent," Rebekah said. "Just sitting around and waiting for something to happen is hard. You have too much time to think and worry."

"I know what you mean. When things get bad at work, the only way I can get that sick feeling out of my stomach is to start working on solving the problem, one way or another," I replied.

"What can I do to help Ken prove me innocent?"

"Well, you could probably go over all the evidence as it's gathered and help him from a medical standpoint. He probably could use some technical assistance since I doubt he's had any medical training. I'll suggest it to him the next time we meet."

"Good, I just don't want to sit around here all day and worry."

"I know. I'll tell the kids to keep you real busy from now on so you won't have time to think. How about that?"

"You don't need to give them any special instructions on that."

By Friday I hadn't heard from Gena and I was beginning to get panicky. It was less than three weeks to her trial and I had no idea where she was. I decided to call her mother and see if she had heard from her. I called at eight o'clock in the morning hoping to catch her at home.

"Have you heard from Gena lately?" I asked.

"No, after she got out, she called me to thank me for putting up the bond money, but that's the last I heard from her."

"Is everything okay?" Mrs. Lombardi asked.

"Yes, everything's fine, but if you hear from Gena, have her call me okay, I need to get with her to work on her case."

"Okay, I will."

"Oh, . . . one other thing. I've hired a company to try to find your husband."

"What on earth for?"

"I don't know, I just have a feeling we need to find him. Has anyone called you looking for him?"

"No, not that I know of."

"Well, I expect to hear from them any day now, so when I do I'll let you know what I find out."

"Okay, bye."

"Bye."

For several minutes I stared out my window at the busy street below, contemplating my next move trying to locate Gena. A thunderstorm was rolling in from the west and I could see lightning flashing in the distance. The telephone began to ring, but as loud as it was, it couldn't penetrate the depth of my concentration. Rebekah had often complained of this, as she would try unsuccessfully to engage me in conversation when my mind was in this state. Such an attempt was always futile, and she got aggravated when I failed to respond to her.

"Aren't you going to answer that phone?" General Burton yelled from his office.

"Oh yes, I'm sorry," I said, as I picked up the telephone.

"This is Joe over at International Tracers, we've found your man."

"You did, that's great," I said. "Where is he?"

"Mt. Olivet Cemetery in Seattle, Washington," he said.

"He's dead then?"

"Well he doesn't run the place."

"Okay, thank you. Can you get me a death certificate?"

"Sure, but it'll be another eight bucks."

"No, problem, just add it to my bill."

After I hung up the phone I rushed into General Burton's office. "I didn't even hear you come in?" I said.

"You were off in never-never land so I didn't want to interrupt you."

"I'm sorry. I get that way whenever I've got big problems," I said.

"Things aren't going so well?" the general asked.

"Well, they weren't, but I just got a break."

I told him about Gena's father and the insurance.

"That's uncanny, Stan."

"I know. Anyway, now my client's mother can collect her insurance money, and I can get paid."

"That always helps. How much does she owe you?"

"Fifteen hundred for the bankruptcy I did and then whatever we agree upon for the criminal matter. I should get at least half of what I need for Rebekah's defense."

"It has been a good day then," the general said.

"Now if I could only find my client," I replied.

"You lost your client?"

"Well, temporarily. I'm sure she'll show up. She better anyway, otherwise I'm going to have to make good on her bond."

"You're on her bond?"

"Yeah, I'm afraid so."

"How much?"

"Twenty-five thousand."

"Oh no, Stan. Why'd you do that?"

"I felt sorry for her, I guess, sitting there all locked up in the county jail."

"I don't know Stan, you may be too soft to be a lawyer. I'm not sure you're going to make it," the general said.

"What do you mean? I've already made it and nothing can keep me from being successful. I may never be rich, but I'll be a good attorney."

As I was talking to General Burton, the phone rang again. I excused myself, went back to my desk and picked up the phone. It was Debbie at the bank.

"I just wanted to tell you that a wire transfer just came through. The money is in your account."

"Oh, thank God! Thank you for calling."

"No problem."

I went immediately to the bank and had two cashier's checks made out to Worldwide Savings and Loan for the payments and had them delivered over to Mark Pointer immediately. Then I called Rebekah and the investors and gave them the good news. I felt good for a change so I went home to share my relief with Rebekah.

# DEATH CLAIM

ON THE FOLLOWING MONDAY morning I received a registered mail notice. Wondering who would be sending me registered mail, I drove immediately to the post office. I went up to the counter and rang the bell. A man in a gray uniform came over and took my green notice. He walked off and then returned with an envelope. "Okay, here you go. I'll need you to sign this receipt please."

"Sure," I said, as I took the envelope from his hand and jotted my signature on the dotted line.

As I was leaving the building, I opened the envelope and pulled out its contents. It was entitled, "CERTIFICATE OF DEATH." Upon closer inspection I realized it was the death certificate of Michael Roman Lombardi.

I returned to the office and called Mrs. Lombardi. I explained to her what I had done and that now she could claim the hundred thousand dollar face amount of the insurance policy, less the loan she took out on it, of course. She was shocked to hear of her husband's death, but seemed relieved to finally have found him. She agreed to file a claim immediately and send me $6,500 for my legal services on behalf of Gena just as soon as she got the money. Death claims usually are processed pretty fast so I figured within a week or ten days I'd get the money.

When I returned to the office there was a message that Tony had called. I wondered momentarily why he would be calling me, but then I remembered the bankruptcy suit I had filed. I picked up the phone and returned his call.

"Mr. Turner, what is this lawsuit you filed against me?"

"It's a preference suit. Under the Bankruptcy Code, if a creditor gets paid within ninety days of filing bankruptcy, he has to give the money back, otherwise it would be unfair to the other creditors," I replied.

"I've never heard of that before," Tony said.

"Well, whether you heard of it or not it's the law."

"But she owed me that money."

"I know, but it doesn't matter. You've got to give it back. If you don't do it voluntarily, the court will make you give it back, plus court costs and attorney fees."

"Damn it! I can't believe this."

"If you give it back right now, I'll waive attorney's fees and court costs."

Tony was silent for several seconds, then he said, "What if I refuse to give it back?"

"Well, once the court grants me judgment, I'll send over the federal marshal to collect the money. If you refuse to pay it, he'll start taking your property and selling it."

"You son of a bitch!"

"Hey, I didn't make the laws. Write your congressman."

"This stinks."

"It hasn't been fun for Gena either. So, what's it gonna be?"

"Okay, okay. What the hell. Should I bring you a check?"

"That would be fine or I could meet you at your bank."

"Okay, I'll meet you at Republic National Bank in downtown Dallas at one-thirty today," Tony said.

"Fine, I'll be there."

When I hung up the phone my adrenaline was pumping furiously. My strategy was working perfectly. If I could get the money from Tony, I might be able to call the DA and get him to drop the charges immediately. Then it wouldn't matter if I ever found Gena as the bond would be released when the charges were dropped.

I picked up the phone and called Syd Brim. The receptionist gave me the usual runaround about Mr. Brim being in conference, so I told her it was an emergency. She wasn't impressed.

"What sort of an emergency?" she said.

"Listen, if you don't get him on the phone right now, I'm coming over there and kick the damn door down. I've got to talk to him immediately, and it's none of your damn business why."

"You don't need to get hostile. I'll see if I can find him."

"Hello, who is this?"

"Stan Turner."

"Who?"

"Remember, your co-counsel on the Lombardi case."

"What case?"

"Gena Lombardi, do you remember her?"

"Not actually, but what do you want?"

"Would you mind if I talked to the DA? I think I can get him to drop the charges."

"Oh really, sure I don't care. What you got?"

"Restitution and lots of evidence that she didn't intend to defraud anybody," I said.

"Go ahead, what do we have to lose," Syd replied.

"Good, thanks. I'll let you know what happens."

"Great, catch you later."

Feeling like I was on a roll, I called the DA's office. I didn't know who had been assigned to the case so I asked the receptionist to research who was handling the Gena Lombardi case. After waiting on the phone about five minutes, she came back on and advised me Miss Jean Sommers was prosecuting the case and that she would connect me.

"Yes."

"We've never spoken before, but I'm co-counsel on the Gena Lombardi case."

"Oh really, I wasn't aware we had any co-counsel."

"Well, I took the case as a favor, I haven't been paid anything. Miss Lombardi talked me into being co-counsel."

"Okay, so what can I do for you?"

"Drop your case against Gena Lombardi."

"Pardon me?"

"Well, let me put it this way. What would it take for you to drop your case against Gena Lombardi," I replied.

"I don't know what you're driving at."

"Well, if I could provide immediate restitution of all monies lost and show you that you couldn't possibly win the case at trial, would you drop the case?"

"Maybe, but let's not talk fantasy. We know Gena Lombardi doesn't have any money for restitution, and I've got several witnesses all ready to testify that she received their money in the mail and then failed to deliver the merchandise. The statute even contains a presumption of intent to defraud in these circumstances."

"That's true, but it's a rebuttable presumption and I'm going to prove that Gena reasonably believed that she could deliver the merchandise when she took that money from your witnesses. I'm going to show how her boyfriend, Tony, took the money without her knowledge or consent and that's why the goods were not delivered."

"Can you really provide complete restitution?"

"I believe so, I can tell you definitely by the end of the day."

"Well, I'll make a deal with you. If you can deliver the money and get an affidavit from Tony that corroborates what you just told me, then I'll recommend dropping the charges."

"Good, I'll call you this afternoon," I said.

"Okay, good luck," Miss Sommers said.

An ill feeling suddenly overcame me as I mused over the task of getting Tony to sign an affidavit. Getting him to give up twenty grand was a coup in itself, but to ask him to help Gena get out of jail was pushing my luck. There had to be some angle I could use to get him to believe it was in his best interest to sign an affidavit exonerating Gena. Unfortunately, at that moment I couldn't think of what it might be.

At 1:30 I walked into the lobby of Republic National Bank. It was a huge lobby so I was at kind of a loss as to where to find

Tony. I began to wander around searching for someone who looked like an Italian. Tony had said he was wearing blue jeans and a white shirt and he'd have Bridgett with him. Finally, I saw the likely couple in line at one of the teller's cages. I approached them and said, "Tony? . . . Bridgett?"

They looked over at me emotionless. "Mr. Turner?"

"Yes."

"We're getting the money right now," Tony said. Then he pointed over to a sofa and chair and said, "Just wait for us over there, we'll be right over."

I went and took a seat on the sofa and watched them make their way through the teller's line. After a minute they came over to me and handed me a cashier's check.

"I made it out to the United States District Court, like you said. I can't believe I'm doing this," Tony said.

"It's the right thing to do," I replied.

"Now what?" Tony said.

"Now I get the bankruptcy court to approve the restitution, and then I'll deliver it to the DA so the victims can be reimbursed."

"What about this victim?" Tony said.

"Well, I'm glad you mentioned that. You know there is a way you might be able to get what's coming to you," I said.

"How's that?"

"Well, if I could get the DA to drop these charges, you could file a proof of claim in her Chapter 13 and eventually get paid the money that's owed to you."

"What if she doesn't make her payments under the Chapter 13?"

"I can't guarantee that she'll make the payments, but she says she's going to, and she'll have a much better shot at doing it if she's back in her office where she can make some money rather than in jail."

"So what do you have to do to get the DA to drop the charges?" Tony asked.

"Get you to sign an affidavit that you took the money owed to you from Gena's account without her knowledge or consent. You don't have to admit you did anything wrong, and we'll waive any claims against you for taking the money."

Tony looked at me intently like he was actually considering signing the affidavit, then he shook his head and said, "There's no way in hell I'm going to help that bitch."

I looked at Bridgett and immediately realized she was my key. I could see the pain in her eyes, perhaps from guilt, but more likely from a lingering friendship toward Gena. I decided to appeal to her for help. "Bridgett, I don't know you, but you were best friends with Gena, and Gena has told me how close you two used to be. I know things between you two haven't been very good lately, but I can't believe you don't care about her. All I need is a simple affidavit to get Gena off the hook. I'm not asking you to lie, all I want is the simple truth."

Bridgett looked at Tony and then at me, but said nothing. Finally, Tony said, "Come on Bridgett let's go."

As they walked off, I searched for some final argument, a magical phrase or sarcastic comment that might move them . . . but nothing came to mind. I sat down, defeated. I started to rationalize, *well at least I got the money back . . . now all I have to do is try the case and win.* As I got up to leave the bank, I noticed Tony and Bridgett walking toward me. When we met Tony squinted and said, "Give me that fucking affidavit. Maybe that broad can finally get her act together."

I pulled the affidavit from my coat pocket and walked over to the customer service counter. I couldn't help but notice Bridgett was smiling. Tony signed the affidavit and then stomped off. Bridgett turned to me as they were leaving and waived.

I was thrilled with my victory. But unfortunately I didn't have anyone to share my joy with at that moment, plus I still had a date with the DA, so I promised myself that Rebekah and I would crack a bottle of champagne that evening.

Miss Sommers was shocked when I appeared that afternoon with twenty thousand dollars and an affidavit from Tony, but she kept her word and dropped all charges against Gena. When I got back to the office I informed Asshole of my feat and then called Gena's mother.

"Hello," Mrs. Lombardi said.

"Hi, this is Stan again."

"Oh yes, is something wrong?"

"No, I've got good news. The DA has dropped all charges against Gena."

"You're kidding! How did that happen?"

I told her about the deal with the DA.

"That is so wonderful. I just can't believe it. When Gena told me you were her guardian angel I just laughed, but now I know she was right."

"Well. I'm just glad I could help."

"Thank you so much Mr. Turner. I'll always be in your debt."

"You're welcome, should you happen to see Gena sometime soon, have her call me."

"I will. Bless you."

"Good-bye."

"Good-bye, thank you."

Elated by the events of the afternoon, I went immediately home to take the family out to dinner and celebrate. The kids didn't understand why I was so happy, but they didn't mind having a party. Rebekah was somewhat subdued. When I ordered a bottle of champagne Rebekah let me know what was bothering her.

"It's great you got Gena off the hook and got her mother $100,000, but you haven't got a dime yourself, have you?"

"Well no, but they'll send me some money once the insurance check comes," I replied.

"Maybe, but what if they don't?"

"They will, you should have heard Mrs. Lombardi. She couldn't thank me enough. She said I was her daughter's guardian angel."

"What did Gena say?" Rebekah asked.

"Well, actually I don't know where Gena is," I replied.

"What?  How can you settle her case without her?"

"I didn't settle it . . . I got the DA to drop it."

"And she has skipped town?  Why in the hell did you even bother with her if she doesn't care enough to hang around for her trial . . . or at least let you know where she is?"

"I had to get her off.  I didn't have any choice."

"Why?  What do you mean?"

"I guaranteed her bond and when she disappeared I had to get her off or come up with twenty-five thousand dollars."

"Stan Turner you are so stupid sometimes.  Why in the hell did you guarantee her bond?"

"I just felt sorry for her."

"You haven't been screwing around with her have you?"

"No, . . . no way. . . .  She's just someone who has had a tough life.  Her father ran away when she was young and everyone treats her like shit.  I just showed her a little respect."

"Yeah, and see where that got you.  You're damn lucky you didn't lose twenty-five thousand dollars, which we don't even have I might add.  How did you expect to pay the money back if she didn't show up for trial?"

"I took a lien on her Corvette."

"Oh really, well I'm glad you did something halfway intelligent."

"Come on, give me a break.  I did a hell of a job on this case, I want to celebrate.  So if you're through chewing me out, let's party."

Rebekah shook her head in disgust then cracked a smile and said, "Stan Turner . . . how did I ever get hooked up with you?"

"Beats me. . . .  You just got lucky I guess."

# THE BONUS

THE FOLLOWING MONDAY WHEN I got to the office there was a message from Ken Sherlock's office. I was fairly certain what the call was about. I had promised Ken that I would get him an assignment on Parker #3 over a week ago, but obviously that wasn't going to happen. I did receive a final check for $2,200 from Inca Oil, but when we got it we were so desperate for cash we had to use it to pay bills and just keep afloat.

Unfortunately nothing had come in from Gena Lombardi and Kurt Harrison was still in Brazil. Consequently I didn't know what I was going to tell Ken Sherlock when I called his office. While I was fretting over this predicament the phone rang. It was Jane Brown.

"I wondered if you might be free for lunch today?" she asked.

"Sure, that would be great," I replied.

"We'll pick you up at 12:30 then," Mrs. Brown said.

"Okay, fine. See you then."

The papers had been filled with the Taylor Brown and Robert Thorn stories over the past few weeks. With the help of an anonymous tip, the police found the body of the Brown chauffeur, Ronald Sage, in a dump a few miles from Brown's Johnson County ranch. While searching Sage's apartment, authorities found evidence that Sage was trying to blackmail Brown and Robert Thorn over the murder of Melba Thorn. The authorities were not sure if Sage was a co-conspirator or just inadvertently found out about the plot to kill her.

It all seemed to make sense now, Robert and Taylor wanted control of Thorn Enterprises, Inc. so they plotted to have Melba conveniently die in an accident. It might have worked had I not received the telephone calls from Melba Thorn. But there were still three big unanswered questions: who placed the calls, how did they find out about her murder and why did they pick me to call for help?

At 12:30 Mrs. Brown's chauffeur, Ralph, walked in and told me Mrs. Brown was waiting. He was a very imposing figure, tall and muscular, and with that black chauffeur's uniform and those big black boots, he obviously wasn't someone you would want to tangle with. I guess that's the kind of person, however, you'd want to have around to deter any would-be assailants. I got up and followed Ralph out to the limousine. He opened the door and Mrs. Brown smiled and said, "Come on in." I climbed in and Ralph shut the door.

"Do you want to go to the Italian Alps again or would you like some superb Mexican food today?" Jane said.

"The Italian Alps was great, but I like Mexican food too."

"Ah, . . . let's go to Juan Benito's. . . . I feel like Mexican today."

"Fine."

"Ralph, take us to Juan Benito's."

"Yes ma'am," Ralph said, as he turned over the engine and eased out of the parking space.

"Well, did you hear the latest?" Jane said.

"No, what happened?" I said.

"Robert was indicted today."

"You're kidding?"

"No, apparently Ronnie was blackmailing both Robert and Taylor. The police found a letter of instructions to Robert telling him where to deliver money to him. Apparently he was killed before the instructions could be delivered," Jane said.

"I wonder how he found out about the plot to kill your mother?" I asked.

"He probably overheard them talking about it and decided he could use the information to enhance his income," Jane replied.

"So how do you feel about all of this? It must be tough to have your brother and husband arrested for killing your mother."

"Yes, it's horrible. I can't believe Robert and Taylor would do such a thing, but it's sure looking more and more like they did. I just can't believe it."

"I'm really sorry. I guess whoever said money corrupts knew what they were talking about."

The limousine suddenly came to a halt and I looked out and saw an old sign that read, Juan Benito's Cafe & Cantina. We got out and went inside. After a few minutes we were seated and placed our orders.

"So who runs the company if Taylor and Robert are convicted," I asked.

"The board of directors placed me in charge this morning as soon as they got wind of Robert's indictment. I've got complete control now," Jane said. "And that reminds me of one of the reasons I wanted to have lunch with you today."

"What's that?"

"Thorn Enterprises is very appreciative of your investigation of Mom's death. The board of directors feels you should be paid for the time and expenses you've incurred."

"Well, that would be much appreciated since I'm kind of in need of money right now."

"Good, do you have any idea what your time and expenses are to date?"

"Well, I think I calculated about forty-five hours and eight hundred in expenses."

"How much does that all come to exactly," Jane asked.

"I think I figured about $7,500," I said.

"Good," Jane said, as she pulled an envelope out of her purse. "Here, this check ought to cover it then."

I took the envelope and peaked inside. It was a check from Thorn Enterprises for $10,000. "Oh yes! This covers it nicely. Thank you."

"Listen, the board wanted me to convey to you their deepest appreciation for what you've done and also to tell you that in the future they may want to retain you for various projects."

"Oh. Thank you. I'd like that. Let me know if anything comes up that I can help them with."

"I will, definitely."

After lunch I called Rebekah to tell her the good news.

"You're kidding!"

"No. I've got a check in my hand."

"Oh, that's so wonderful, I can't believe it! When did this happen?"

"Ten minutes ago. Jane Brown called and wanted to have lunch. She shocked the hell out of me when she gave me the check. Now I can pay your lawyer."

"Shit, we have to give it to him?"

"Well, I'm going to give him $6,500 and use $3,500 to pay bills."

"Good, at least we'll be able to survive another month."

"That's right. . . . Well, I've got to go, I just wanted to give you the good news."

"Yeah, I'm glad you called, I feel much better now."

After talking to Rebekah, I returned the call to Ken Sherlock's office. Sure enough they were wondering about their assignment on Parker #3. I told them there had been a change of plans and instead of an assignment I could give them half the balance on the retainer immediately with the rest in a week or ten days. They were obviously pleased to get cash rather than the assignment.

Later that afternoon Tom Tower called to see if I had heard from Kurt. Since Kurt hadn't called me I phoned Gwen to see if she knew anything. No one answered at the Harrison mansion so I called Cynthia.

"Stan, I'm so glad you called," Cynthia said. "The FBI agents were just here looking for Kurt again."

"What did you tell them?"

"I told them I didn't know where he was," Cynthia said.

"That's all you told them?" I asked.

"I told them he had been in Brazil, but apparently he left there because I called for him and they said he was gone."

"Was Heloisa with him?" I asked.

"No, she wasn't with him when he left."

"Do you have any idea where he might have gone?"

"He might have gone to California to see Dan Kelley. If he's trying to raise money for the Panhandle Building, Dan's the one who can help him."

"I hope that's what he's doing. Do you have Dan's phone number?"

"Sure, I can get it for you."

"I want to call him and see if Kurt's there or if he knows where he is."

"Okay, good luck. Let me know what you find out."

"I will, bye."

"Bye."

Anxious to talk to Kurt, I immediately called Dan Kelley's number. I knew if I didn't get this mess under control really soon, it was going to be all over for Kurt, the investors and maybe even me. As the phone rang I held my breath.

"Stan, Kurt and I were just talking about you," Dan said.

"Then Kurt's there with you?"

"Yes, he's right here. Do you want to talk to him?"

"Yes, please."

"Hello, Stan."

"Kurt, I've been waiting for you to call. The FBI's still looking for you. They came by Cynthia's office today and scared the shit out of her."

"You made the payments didn't you?"

"Yes."

"I thought they were going to back off once we made the past due note payments."

"That's what I thought too, but apparently they're still worried about the deal."

"Well, I was going to call you tomorrow so I'm glad you called.  Dan's got some investors from mainland China who just signed a contract to buy the Panhandle Building.  They've got more money than God and they're ready to move."

"You're kidding?  Have they seen it?"

"They've got a man looking at it today as a matter of fact. The contract gives them a five-day inspection period.  They can terminate the contract at anytime before the five days expires."

"Are you showing them the entire building?" I asked.

"The manager was instructed to show them every floor," Kurt said.  "They don't care about the condition of the building anyway.  They just need a safe place to put their money," Kurt said.

"Don't tell me anything more about your investors.  I don't care why they want to buy the building, as long as they've got the money and they know exactly what they're buying so they don't come back after you or the owners."

"Okay, do you think Ron Johnson can set up a quick closing on this deal?"

"Oh yes, I know he can."

"What about the FBI?" Kurt said.

"Well, if Worldwide is taken out, what do they have left to investigate?"

"Okay, call everybody and set it up for four o'clock Friday. Come by the house Friday morning at ten with a draft of all the papers.  I'll have the Chinese there and you can go over it with them to make sure everything is in order," Kurt said.

"Okay, but are you sure about this? . . .  I don't want to have Big D, Worldwide and the owners all sitting around a table ready to close this deal and then have the Chinese not show up."

"They'll be there, don't worry.  Just have everything ready."

"You'll need to overnight me a copy of the contract of sale. Dan can't set up a closing without it."

"We'll FedEx it to you today," Kurt said.

"Okay, see you Friday then," I replied.

This was such good news it was scary.  Was Kurt just setting me up to take the fall for him?  I was worried, why would Chinese investors want the Panhandle Building? What if I set up this big closing and Kurt never made it back to Dallas. I'd have Worldwide and the FBI all over me. Unfortunately I couldn't think of any alternative but to go along with Kurt's directions and hope for the best.

After I got off the phone, I called Ron Johnson and alerted him to the fact that we needed a quick closing on the Panhandle deal. I called Cynthia and told her what Kurt had said and asked her to let me know the minute the contract of sale came in. Then I called each of the investors and told them the good news. Tom Tower was particularly elated to hear Kurt had come through.

"I knew Kurt would make this thing work. He's really a genius," Tom said.

"That's not what you were saying about him last week when he was held up in Brazil," I replied.

"Well, I guess I sold him short. I just didn't have enough faith in him."

"Let's wait until Friday before we pat him on the back."

"Oh I'm sure he'll be there, he wouldn't have any reason to lie at this stage of the game."

"I hope you're right, I'll call you when I get the contract of sale so you can decide if you want to sign it."

"Thanks, Stan, for everything."

"No problem, bye."

My next call was the most difficult one of all. It was to Mark Pointer, attorney for Worldwide. He'd not just be glad to hear about a contract on the Panhandle Building, he'd be thrilled. The down side, however, would be that once he and his client got it in their mind that they were being taken out, it would be impossible to work with them if the deal fell through. However, I had no choice but to call and alert them to the strong possibility that the building would be sold. I dialed the number and waited.

"If you're calling about the FBI, I told them Kurt made his first two payments so they're considering dropping the investigation. However, they just wanted to go to Amarillo first and check out the building, you know, just to make sure everything is okay."

"Sure, but that may not be necessary. Kurt's got a contract on the building. I'm supposed to have a contract tomorrow and closing is set for Friday. That is if you guys don't mind getting your loan taken out," I said.

"I doubt if Mr. Wylie would mind much having this loan retired. He's taken a lot of flack from the bank examiners. They still don't understand how Kurt talked him into releasing those CD's," Mark said.

"I wish I could have heard that conversation myself, it must have been some sales job."

"Okay, well that's great news. Send me a copy of the contract when you get it tomorrow, okay?"

"Sure, I'll do it. Thanks."

The next morning the contract arrived via Federal Express around ten. I immediately sent a copy to the owners, Mark Pointer and Ron Johnson. After all of the copies were on their way, I began to examine the contract. The purchase price was more than half a million dollars higher than what Tom, George and Pete had paid for the building. I couldn't believe it, but if the deal went through, they would triple their money in less than ninety days. Before the end of the day Tom, George and Pete dropped by to sign the original contract. Obviously they all loved it and signed it eagerly.

That night I went home feeling pretty good. It seemed my luck was changing and if the closing took place tomorrow, the worst should be over. Then I could concentrate on proving Rebekah innocent of Sheila Logan's murder. The whole family was sitting at the dinner table when the doorbell rang.

"Who could that be?" Rebekah said.

"I'll get it!" Reggie yelled, as he bolted from his chair and ran to the front door. In a minute he came back and said, "Daddy, it's a lady for you."

"I wonder who that could be?" I said, as I got up to go to the door. As I approached the front door, I saw it was Gena

Lombardi. "Gena, where have you been? I thought you skipped the country."

"No, I was just out on the road working. When I called Mom on Monday, she told me you'd got the charges dropped and I was a free woman."

By this time Rebekah and all the three boys were all at the front door listening.

"Come on in," I said.

"Okay, but I can only stay a minute. I just wanted to thank you in person for what you did for me."

"Well, I just did my job."

"No, you did a lot more, co-signing my bond, finding out my father was dead and collecting on the insurance. It's incredible what you've done for me and my family," Gena said.

"I'm glad it all worked out."

"Anyway I just wanted to give you the sixty-five hundred dollars we owed you and a little bonus."

"A bonus? You don't have to give me a bonus."

"Well, I want to. Remember I told you someday you'd be happy you took good care of me."

"Yes, I vaguely remember words to that effect."

"Well there's your bonus," Gena said, as she pointed to the yellow Corvette sitting in the driveway. I was stunned as she handed me a set of keys and an envelope. "Here's the keys and the title. It's all yours. Oh there's still $10,000 owed to the bank, so you can either keep making my payments or sell it and get the five or six thousand dollars equity. I hope you keep it though so you can get rid of that piece of shit Pinto you drive."

"But Gena, you love that Corvette. You'd die for it," I protested.

"I know, it isn't easy for me to do this, but you deserve it Stan," Gena said. "Besides Mom bought me a new Mercedes with that insurance money you got for us, so what do I need with two cars?"

"Oh. I see. Now it all makes sense," I said. "This is so cool! Thank you Gena, this is very nice of you. It's going to be a real pleasure driving a decent car for a change. I'm going to really love it."

I started to approach Gena to give her a hug, but she raised her hand to stop me. "I'd love to hug you Stan, but I've been reading about your wife."

I smiled at Rebekah and said, "You can't believe everything you read. Rebekah wouldn't hurt a flea."

Just then a young man in a brand-new Mercedes drove up.

"Oh, here's my ride. Well, I've got to go. Nice seeing you Rebekah, kids. . . . Good-bye."

"Good-bye, thanks again," I said.

Rebekah and the kids waved good-bye. After Gena left we all went back to the dinner table in a partial state of shock. I frankly had almost given up on even getting paid, let alone getting this incredible bonus. Rebekah seemed a little unsettled about the whole thing.

"You're not going to keep that thing are you?" Rebekah said.

"That thing? It's a 1978 Chevrolet Corvette. It's an awesome machine. You're damn right I'm going to keep it. We could never get a loan on a car like that in a million years. This is an incredible piece of luck."

"But I heard sports cars are gas guzzlers and the insurance premiums are out of sight," Rebekah said.

"Well, just let me worry about that. I've been driving the cheap Pinto for four years and I'm really going to enjoy driving a sports car for a change. Besides, tomorrow for the first time I'm going to drive up in front of Kurt Harrison's mansion and park right next to his Maserati and not feel the least bit humiliated!" I replied.

"Okay, but I'm just worried about the cost of having a car like that."

"Don't worry babe, it won't be that bad. Now, how about a ride!" I said.

The boys jumped up and all ran outside, Rebekah picked up Marcia and she and I joined them in front of the Corvette.

"Can we all fit in there?" Rebekah said.

"Well, this isn't exactly a family car, but I think so," I replied.

Once everyone was in we took off. The sudden burst of power from the big eight-cylinder engine surprised us. The kids screamed with delight and even Rebekah cracked a smile. We drove around town proudly and then took it to Rebekah's mom and dad's to show it off. They were shocked but excited by our good fortune. It was a great evening, one I'll remember for many years to come.

The next morning promptly at ten I drove up in front of Kurt's mansion in the Corvette. I parked between the Rolls and the limo, and when I got out, I looked toward the house, hoping someone had seen me drive up. As I was walking up to the front door, Gwen came out to greet me. "Stan, . . . you got a new car! It's beautiful."

"Thank you. I just got it yesterday," I said.

"Now, that looks more like an attorney's car."

"Yeah, I think I'm going to enjoy driving it."

"You'll have to take me for a spin when you're done with Kurt."

"Sure thing."

"Kurt's inside waiting for you, but before you go in, I wanted to thank you for getting him back here," Gwen said.

"Well, I'm not sure I'm the one who got him back. It seems like he knew what he was doing all along, judging by the numbers on that contract of sale," I replied.

"No, he admitted to me he had planned to stay in Brazil. He had about a half million stashed down there and figured there was no reason to come back. When you called he realized he'd be a fugitive the rest of his life if he didn't clean up the mess he had made and, worst of all, he could never return to the U.S., ever again."

"Thank God he came to his senses. Can you imagine what shit would have come down if he'd never returned?"

Gwen and I walked inside and into the den. Kurt was behind his desk, writing on a yellow pad. "Hi Stan, thanks for coming by this morning. Cynthia's in the backyard showing the Chinese investors around. Did you bring all the papers?"

"Yes, I've got them all here," I replied.

"Good, when they come back in, you can summarize the deal for them and let them look over the paperwork."

"Sure."

"Listen Stan, I want to thank you for knocking some sense into me while I was down in Brazil. I was just so tired and depressed that I temporarily lost my nerve."

"You sure fooled me. From my vantage point you had the world by the tail," I replied.

"It may have looked that way, but I knew everything was going to crater after the Panhandle closing so I decided it was time to run. Then, after you called, I contacted Dan to see if he had come up with any ideas on how to salvage the Panhandle deal. He said he had a couple of good prospects, but he needed me to come to California to work on them."

"I hopped on the next flight to L.A., and Dan and I brainstormed for several days until we came up with the Chinese investor deal. We had heard there were a lot of communist officials in China who had been stealing money from the government and investing it in the U.S. The story was they didn't care much about how good the investment was as long as it was a hard asset like real estate and they could close quickly with little publicity."

"The difficult part was finding them. Dan had some contacts in Hong Kong who finally got us in touch with the right people. From there on it was easy, they loved the idea of buying a building in downtown Amarillo, Texas. The fact that they were going to have to spend a little money fixing the place up didn't bother them in the least."

"Huh, that's interesting. . . . I never knew that kind of activity was going on."

"Oh yeah, billions of dollars are funneled out of China every year," Kurt said.

"Well, at least if they don't like their investment once they buy it, they won't be complaining to the FBI," I replied.

"That's a safe bet," Kurt laughed. "Anyway, when this deal is done I'm going to be square with everyone, thanks to you, Stan."

"Good, I'm glad it all worked out, but I must tell you I was more than disappointed when I learned you'd left the country and abandoned your investors."

"I don't blame you. I don't know why I suddenly panicked. I hope you'll forgive me. I really want you to stay on as my attorney," Kurt said.

"Well, since you're about my only client right now I don't have much choice," I replied.

"Good."

From a distance we began to hear people conversing in Chinese and then suddenly the patio door opened. It was Cynthia and the Chinese delegation. When they all were seated, I passed out copies of all the documents and began explaining them. Luckily several of them spoke English so it went better than I expected.

That afternoon the Panhandle Building sold for the second time in two months. Kurt was forty-five minutes late for the closing, but he finally showed up. He was back on top again and Tom Tower, George Sanders and Pete Hall were as high as Tibetan Monks and just itching to invest in Kurt's next venture. As usual, Kurt paid my bill in cash with thirty-seven one-hundred-dollar bills. I told him for accounting purposes, he ought to always pay by check, but he said he always got better service from people if he paid them in cash.

# LEGAL ETHICS

THAT NIGHT I SLEPT better than I had for months. When I awoke the next morning, however, the harsh reality of Rebekah's predicament finally hit home—I realized we had only two weeks until her trial. We had already made some significant progress proving Rebekah innocent, but time was running out and there was much work to be done.

After I had talked to the witness to the accident, one of Rebekah's friends in the ER was kind enough to get me a census for the day of the murder. What I was looking for was family members of patients who might have been waiting with Bird Logan. After an exhaustive search, I found three people who remembered Bird. They all said that he was in the waiting room the entire time except for about ten minutes when he went to the restroom. None of them could verify exactly what time that was, nor did they remember his condition when he returned.

Rebekah had met earlier in the week with some of her nurse friends and Ken Sherlock. The purpose of the meeting was to brief Ken on hospital procedure, the treatment Sheila Logan was receiving and the manner of her death. The more Ken knew about all of these things the more effective he would be at defending Rebekah.

While all of this was going on, I had hired a private investigator in Corpus Christi to dig up as much information on Bird Logan as he could. The private eye's name was Miguel Valdez. When I got to my office, I put a call in to him to see what he had found out.

"How's the investigation going?" I asked.

"Oh Stan, yes. Let me find your file. One momento, please."

"Okay."

"Stan. Yes, . . . let me see. Mr. Blackbird Logan. Yes, he was born in Midland, Texas, in 1932. He lived with his mama and papa and three sisters in a little house on the south side of town. Ah, his daddy ran a filling station and his mother worked in a general store. Let me see . . . while he attended college he worked part time as a roughneck and learned the oil business. He signed up for the navy in 1949 and . . . let me see . . . he was a medic in Korea. Okay, . . . it was 1955, yeah, . . . 1955 when he was discharged and entered SMU. There he studied geology and got a bachelor's degree in 1959. After he graduated, he got hitched to a Molly Rutherford and they lived together until 1965 when she died in a car wreck."

"A car wreck?"

"Yeah man, is that important?" Miguel said.

"It might be, go on."

"After he graduated, you know, he went to work for Central States Oil Company. He was a geologist there. He worked there for twenty-one years. Can you believe that? Then he unexpectedly quit and went into partnership with a guy named Tomlinson," Miguel said.

"Yes, Brice Tomlinson."

"Right. Inca Oil Company. Ah. . . . Then he married Sheila Morales from Monterrey, Mexico. I'm told they met at a fraternity party at SMU for Bird's fifteenth-year college reunion. Sheila belonged to a sorority, you know, that was helping out with the festivities."

"What else do you know about Sheila?" I asked.

"Her father owned one of the biggest ranches in Mexico. It's supposed to be over 10,000 acres."

"What do you mean *owned?* Did he sell it?"

"No, he died last summer."

"Who inherited the property?"

"It's been tied up in probate, man. Before Sheila died, she and her three brothers were in a big fight with their step-mother for control of the ranch."

"Who was running the ranch during this fight?"

"The executor . . . you know . . . of the estate."

"Was Sheila getting any money from the estate before she died?"

"No way, everything was being kept by the executor . . . you know . . . pending the final outcome of the probate."

"How long is the estate expected to be tied up?"

"Oh man, a probate in Mexico can take three to five years."

"Oh really? Huh."

Up until now I had assumed Bird was the killer. But after talking to Miguel I realized there was no motive. For the life of me I couldn't conceive of a way Bird would gain by Sheila's death. If her money was tied up in Mexico, it was unlikely Bird would ever see any of it for years, if at all. I began to wonder if Bird was really responsible for Sheila's murder. But if he didn't do it, who did? I began to think about probable suspects. It wasn't long before I had constructed a short list of suspects in my mind. Heading the list was Melissa, Bird's secretary. She obviously wanted Bird all for herself, and as long as Sheila was around, the likelihood of that happening was pretty remote. Other possibilities were one or more of Sheila's brothers who may not have wanted to split the ranch with her, her stepmother for the same reason or some other enemy out there I knew nothing about.

"What're you going to do now?" Miguel asked.

"I don't know. I'll have to give all this information to Ken Sherlock and see what he wants to do. Anyway, Miguel you've done an excellent job so far. Keep digging and if you come up with anything else call me, okay? Oh, and send me all the documentation for all this stuff you've been telling me. We may need it for evidence."

"I will, catch you later."

"Bye."

After talking to Miguel, I was anxious to talk to Ken so I called and made an appointment to see him immediately. Several hours later I was sitting in Ken's office, relating to him what I'd found out from Miguel.

"So all along I just knew Bird must be the killer, but now I'm not so sure. There doesn't appear to be any motive," I said.

"Motives aren't always readily apparent," Ken replied, "but you're right, this does bring us back to square one."

"It seems now like Melissa had the best motive for killing Sheila."

"You actually caught them in the act once?"

"Well, I didn't actually see them doing it, but it wasn't hard to figure out what had been going on. Besides, Bird admitted he was having an affair with her."

"What do you know about Melissa?"

"Nothing, absolutely nothing. Well other than she's one hell of a good-looking woman."

"I guess I should go talk to her?" Ken said.

"You think she'll talk to you?"

"If she won't, then I'll take her deposition. I'd rather talk to her alone though."

"I'd like to go with you?"

"I don't know, she's going to be intimidated enough talking to one lawyer. I don't want her to be so scared she won't talk."

"I'll let you do all the talking. I won't say a word. She probably won't even notice me."

"Yeah, right. . . . Okay, but if she seems uncomfortable with you there, I want you to make a hasty departure."

"No problem."

"I'll call her and make an appointment. I'll have my secretary call you to tell you when and where it's at."

"Great, thanks."

After I left Ken's office, I went straight home. It was only 4:45 P.M. so Rebekah wasn't expecting me yet. I slipped in the back door quietly, hoping to sneak up on her. Peter spotted me and started to scream. I quickly grabbed him and covered his mouth so he couldn't be heard.

"Be quiet Peter, I'm trying to surprise your mama."

"Ehhh . . . ehhh . . . ehhh," Peter said.

I put Peter down and said, "Shhh. . . ." Then I crept around the corner and spotted Rebekah. I came up behind her silently and grabbed her shoulders. "Hi babe!"

"Ahhh!" Rebekah screamed. "Oh, you scared me Stan, what do you think you're doing?"

I put my arms around Rebekah and held her tightly.

"I'm sorry. There's been some interesting new developments in your case," I said. "I just wanted to fill you in."

I told her about Miguel, the fact that Bird had no motive to kill Sheila and that Melissa was now a suspect.

"What are you going to do now? We've got less than two weeks to my trial."

"Ken and I are going to see Melissa tomorrow. We're hoping we'll learn enough from her to give us some insight into what really happened. After that I'm sure Ken will put a PI on her to dig up as much info as possible."

"Well, I hope you guys work fast because I'm running out of time."

"I know, babe. Everybody will be working eighteen hours a day from now on. We'll figure out what happened. I promise."

"I hope so, I'm really getting worried."

After our conversation, I headed for the sofa to watch the five o'clock news. I turned on the TV, grabbed a pillow, kicked off my shoes and then lay down on the sofa. It was about 5:05 P.M. so the news was in progress with anchor Sandy Star reporting.

"Now we take you to correspondent Paulette Barclay in Johnson City, Texas, for the latest in the Robert Thorn trial. Paulette are you there?"

"Yes Sandy, Robert Thorn was brought into State District Court today to be arraigned for the murder of his chauffeur, Robert Sage. Sage's body was found in a landfill near Thorn's ranch in Johnson County. Police believe that Sage had been blackmailing Thorn and his partner, Taylor Brown, over information he had about the death of Melba Thorn in a mysterious single-vehicle automobile accident near Florissant, Colorado. Judge Clayton Brooks set bail for Brown at 1.2 million dollars," Sandy said.

"Thank you Sandy," Paulette continued. "Shortly after the bond was set, it was posted and Robert Thorn has now been released. In a brief encounter with reporters Thorn insisted he was innocent and promised he would eventually be vindicated. Asked about whether he thought his mother, Melba Thorn, had really contacted local attorney, Stan Turner, from the dead and asked for his help, Thorn said such claims were just as ridiculous as the charges against him.

"In a related story Taylor Brown was transported to Florissant, Colorado, today to stand trial for the murder of his mother-in-law, Melba Thorn. Brown is set to be arraigned tomorrow, and should be out on bond before the end of the day. Brown too claims his innocence and vows to clear his name. Robert Thorn is also expected to be indicted by the Colorado court in the near future in conjunction with his mother-in-law's death."

That night I fell asleep quickly, drifted into a deep slumber and began to dream. It wasn't long before I woke up Rebekah.

"Wake up Stan. You must be having a dream. You've been moaning like you're in pain," Rebekah said, as she shook my shoulder.

"What? . . . What time is it?" I said.

"It's 3:33 A.M."

"I'm sorry I woke you up sweetheart, but I dreamt I was back at the Holiday Inn in Colorado. I relived the night I was attacked. That big black boot hitting my face seemed so real."

"Go back to sleep, it was just a dream," Rebekah said.

"I've seen that big black boot somewhere before," I said.

"When you got assaulted in the motel?" Rebekah said.

"No, I mean I've seen it somewhere else," I replied.

"Where?"

"I don't know. Somewhere."

"Well, go to sleep, maybe tomorrow you'll remember," Rebekah said.

"I can't sleep. I'm awake now," I said.

"Great. It's 3:30 A.M. and you're wide awake."

"I've got to figure out where I saw it. I remember. It was ah, . . . let me see . . . oh. Now I remember, Jane Brown."

"Jane Brown wore big black boots?" Rebekah said.

"No, but her chauffeur did."

"So what?"

"Her chauffeur is the one who assaulted me. He's the one who kicked me with his boot," I said.

"Do you know his name?" Rebekah asked.

"Ralph. I don't know his last name. That means Jane was behind this whole thing."

"Jane killed her own mother?"

"She must have. They didn't get along too well and Jane was jealous of her brother and even her husband. She wanted to help run the company, but no one took her seriously," I said.

"So you think she killed her mother and then framed her own brother and husband?"

"Yeah, it all makes sense now. Ralph must have taken the Thorn limousine and followed Melba. Then he forced her off the road and she crashed to her death. But getting rid of Mom wasn't enough . . . she had to get rid of her brother and her husband because they controlled Thorn Enterprises after Melba died. So she got Ralph to kill Ronald Sage and planted the evidence needed to be sure both Taylor and Robert were charged and convicted of her mother's murder."

"But who made the phone calls?" Rebekah asked.

"Jane did. She needed someone to start poking around so Sheriff Barnett would figure out Melba was murdered," I replied.

"Why did they pick you?"

"That I don't know."

"Okay, . . . why did Ralph beat you up in the motel?"

"Jane must have been impatient with progress on investigating Melba's death. She needed to give my investigation some credibility so Sheriff Barnett would reopen her mother's case. It was an incredible plan," I said.

"How can you prove it though? No jury will convict Jane just because you think you recognize her chauffeur's boot," Rebekah replied.

"That's true, but all they have to do to prove their case is get his boots and analyze them for my blood. When he kicked my face, my nose was bleeding so he must have got some of my blood on his boot. I'll call the sheriff in the morning and have him check it out."

"Wait a minute. Isn't Jane Brown your client? Didn't she just give you $10,000?"

"Oh shit. You're right. . . . I've got to keep my mouth shut. That's why she paid me the ten grand. She didn't want me to spill the beans if I figured out what happened. Jesus, she is one smart son of a bitch. I can't believe this. I'm going to have to sit back and watch two innocent men be convicted of murder and there's not a damn thing I can do about it."

"You can't let two innocent men go to jail."

"I know, but if I tell the police my suspicions, I'll be violating my duty to my client and I could be disbarred. Not to mention the fact that she could sue me for malpractice."

"Stan, what are you going to do?"

"I don't know. . . . I really don't know."

# RELUCTANT WITNESS

**Tuesday**

THE FOLLOWING DAY KEN'S secretary called me and gave me the time and place of our meeting with Melissa. We were meeting for lunch at Luby's Cafeteria on Alpha Road at noon. I arrived ten minutes early and went inside and waited. Before long Melissa arrived. She walked over to me, smiled and extended her hand.

"Hi, Stan. How's your wife holding up?"

"Pretty well, but she's getting a little nervous as the trial date gets closer."

"I bet."

"How's Bird?" I asked.

"Oh, . . . he's doing a little better. He took Sheila's death pretty bad. At least he's back to work now so his mind will be occupied with other things."

As we were exchanging small talk, Ken walked in and after seeing us, he walked over quickly.

"Hi, I'm sorry I'm late, but the traffic on Central Expressway was murder today."

"That's not unusual," I replied. "Ken, I'd like you to meet Melissa Madigan."

"Hi, Ms. Madigan, thank you for agreeing to talk with us."

"Well, I really doubt if I'm going to be of much help. I didn't know Sheila at all, other than what Bird has told me about her."

"Well, let's get some lunch and then we can talk some more," Ken said.

"Fine," Melissa replied, as she moved to the back of the long lunch line. We followed her and after we had picked out what we wanted, we sat down to eat. Ken ate quickly and when he had eaten about half what he had taken, he pushed away his plate, pulled a cigar out of his pocket and stuck it in his mouth.

"Do you mind?" Ken said.

"No, go right ahead," Melissa said. Everyone smokes back at the office. I've gotten used to it."

Ken lit up his cigar and then leaned back in his chair.

"Melissa, I reckon you know I'm defending Rebekah Turner," Ken said.

"Sure, I read about it in the newspaper."

"Well, I'm pretty damn sure my client is innocent, but the problem is I can't prove it. The DA has a good case, and unless I can flush out the truth here pretty quickly, an innocent young lady may go to Huntsville."

"I don't see how I can help you."

"You may not be able to. Who knows, but I need to find out as much as I can about Sheila and Bird and their friends. This is where you might be able to help. Obviously you know Bird pretty well since he's your boss and boyfriend, and you must know something about Brice Tomlinson."

"What makes you think I'd tell you about either of them?"

Ken took the cigar out of his mouth and laid it on the ashtray while he searched for another match. After he located the match he relit the cigar.

"I can't force you to talk to me, honey. I know that. Sure, I could subpoena you, but if I did, you'd just have a convenient lapse of memory, right?" Ken laughed. "No, I just hoped you'd help me because it's the right thing to do."

"Well, I don't want to do anything to hurt Bird or Mr. Tomlinson, but I don't see any harm in telling you what I know since I really don't think I know anything anyway."

"We're not out to hurt anybody, honey. We just want to find out the truth."

"Fine."

"Okay then. So, let's get started." Ken took out a small notepad and a pen and laid it on the table in front of him. "Did you go to the party out at the well?"

"Yeah, I was there."

"When did Bird leave?"

"Not until Sunday morning. It was very late when the party ended and he was pretty much plastered."

"When did you come back?"

"I left just after they did."

"Were you alone?"

"No, I brought a girlfriend with me."

"Oh, what was her name?"

"Monica Sands, she's a neighbor. I didn't want to go alone."

"It must have been tough for you to see Bird with Sheila?"

Melissa dropped her head for a moment and then flipped her dark brown hair back and looked Ken straight in the eye. "I know how the game works. Bird had to play the role of loving husband, even though he didn't love Sheila anymore. I could have stayed home, but that wouldn't have been any fun. Besides I would have missed Stan and Sheila's little romp in the bunkhouse. God, I would never have forgiven myself if I'd missed that."

Melissa smiled at me and then looked back at Ken who was now taking notes.

"So, what did Sheila and Bird do after Stan and Rebekah left Saturday night?"

"Sheila locked herself in the motorhome and wouldn't talk to anyone. Bird mixed with the crowd, trying to act like nothing had happened. After the party was over, he crashed in the bunkhouse."

"Where did you all sleep?"

"We had a station wagon so we put the seats down and slept in it."

"Did you see Bird at all that night after the fire in the bunkhouse?"

"I wanted to, so I went to the bunkhouse hoping to be able to sneak in and be with Bird, but there were a couple of other guys in there passed out so I went back to the car."

"Did you see Bird and Sheila take off in the morning?"

"Yeah, I was awakened by their arguing."

"About what?"

"Bird wanted to go back to Dallas since the well had come in. He had lots of work to do to get the well into production. Sheila wanted to go home to Corpus."

"So, who won the argument?"

"I thought I heard Bird say he would take Sheila to Love Field so she could catch a flight home."

"What was Mr. Tomlinson doing while all this was going on?"

"I didn't see much of him. I think he was pretty busy on the rig, supervising the men working there. I don't think he was planning to go home until Sunday night."

"When did you and your friend leave?"

"Right after they left, we packed up and headed home too."

"When did you get back to Dallas?"

"It was nearly noon before we got home."

"What did you do all day Sunday?"

"I crashed. I didn't sleep too well in the station wagon, plus the drive home tired me out."

"When did you get up?"

"It was dark when I finally woke up, after seven."

"Okay, honey, just a couple more questions then I'll let you go. I really appreciate you talking to us. This is a personal question, but it's something I'm really curious about."

"What?"

"Was Bird planning to divorce Sheila?"

"No, he made it clear he wouldn't divorce her."

"Why? Didn't he love you?"

"Yes, but there are things more important than love as far is Bird is concerned."

"Like what?"

Melissa took a deep breath, smiled and replied, "I think I've said enough. I've got to get back to work."

Melissa got up and slipped her purse over her shoulder. Ken and I got up and put on our jackets.

"Sure thing, Miss Madigan, I understand. You've been mighty helpful already," Ken said.

Melissa turned to me and said, "Stan, I really hope Rebekah gets off. I know she's not a killer."

"Thank you," I replied. "I'll tell her you said that."

"Oh. One last question," Ken said. "What are your plans now that Sheila is gone? Are you and Bird gonna get hitched?"

Melissa turned and gave Ken a dirty look. "Good day, gentlemen," she said and then left.

After our meeting, we went back to my office to digest what we had learned. General Burton was there so I introduced him to Ken and then we went into my office.

"Well, Melissa seemed pretty calm," I said.

"She's a slick little lady, that's for sure," Ken replied.

"So what do you think, Ken? Is she a murderer?"

"She had a motive and she sure doesn't have an alibi. All we need to do is put her at the hospital around the time of the murder."

"How do we do that?"

"I don't know. We just have to keep digging and if she was at the hospital, hopefully we'll find that out before it's too late."

"I wonder why Bird wouldn't divorce Sheila if he didn't love her anymore? She wasn't going to get her inheritance any time soon. I can't imagine him waiting four or five years just to become a minority partner with Sheila's family."

"It doesn't make a lot of sense does it, Stan. There's obviously more going on here than meets the eye. Unfortunately, we're running out of time."

"So, now what?" I asked.

"Why don't you keep digging into Bird's life. Check back with Miguel and see if he's found out anything new. I'll do some more checking into Melissa's story. Someone may have seen her leave her apartment on Sunday or maybe someone saw her at the hospital."

That night I worked late trying to put some of the pieces together in the Sheila Logan puzzle. When I got home the house was dark and Rebekah was sitting on the sofa sobbing.

"Honey, what's wrong?"

As she looked up at me, I could see her bloodshot eyes in the dim light.

"Why are you crying, babe?"

"I'm going to miss you Stan."

"What are you talking about?"

"We've had a good life, haven't we?"

"Of course, but don't talk like this. We're going to get you off, don't worry."

"I can't imagine not seeing my babies grow up. I love them so much, Stan. Please take good care of them."

"Rebekah, come on now. You've got to be optimistic. We met with Melissa Madigan today, you know, Bird's secretary. Remember she was having an affair with Bird? Well, she had a motive to kill Sheila and she has no alibi. I bet you she did it."

"Was she at the hospital?"

"We don't know for sure, but Ken's going to find out. It's just a matter of time."

"But the trial is less than two weeks away. What if you can't find out by then?"

"We will, you've got to have faith."

Rebekah put her arms around me and laid her head on my shoulder. "I went to mass this morning and prayed to God to help us. Do you think he was listening?"

"Of course he was, he's always pulled us through in the past, and he'll be there this time."

Rebekah squeezed me tightly and said, "I hope so. I couldn't bear to live without you."

"You won't have to, I'm afraid you're stuck with me for life."

"I hope so."

# THE MOTIVE

**Friday**

By week's end I was exhausted. All week I had been digging into Blackbird Logan's life. I'd talked to dozens of his friends and co-workers, college buddies, past employers, neighbors and anyone else who might know something about him. I'd done the same thing for Sheila. I felt I knew both of them intimately, but I still couldn't find the motive for Bird to have killed her. Then it hit me. Tex had referred me to Inca Oil and he wouldn't have been working there unless someone was buying insurance. I put a call into Tex immediately.

"Hey, Stan the man, what's going on. Oh, shit! I'm sorry, I almost forgot about the murder trial. How's Rebekah?"

"Not too well, she's convinced she's going to get convicted."

"What about your attorney who has never lost a case?"

"He's never lost a DWI case, I don't think he's done too many murder trials."

"You think she's going to get convicted?"

"No, I won't let that happen. That's the reason I called. I need to ask you a question."

"Sure."

"You wrote some insurance at Inca, didn't you?"

"Yes I did, some pretty healthy premiums, if you know what I mean."

"What did you write?"

"Five million on Brice Tomlinson and Bird Logan. Do you know what the annual premium is on a policy that size?"

"No, but I can imagine it must be a bunch. What about the wives?"

"No, nothing on the wives."

"Damn! . . . Hmm. . . . You must have done an insurance portfolio analysis, right?"

"Of course."

"How much insurance did Bird have on Sheila?"

"None. Isn't it funny how no one ever buys insurance on a wife. Do you know how much it would cost to replace the average wife with children?"

"No, not really?"

"Well, considering the typical wife is a housekeeper, laundry maid, baby-sitter, cook and sex partner, studies show it would cost about $56,000 a year to replace her."

"I can believe that."

"So every man ought to have about a quarter million of coverage on his wife just to replace the economic loss he'd suffer should she die."

"Huh. . . . Very interesting."

"So that's why I almost always attach the family rider to every policy I write."

"The family rider?"

"Uh huh. It's a nifty little attachment to the man's policy that provides coverage for the wife and kids."

"How much coverage?"

"The wife gets twenty percent of the face amount of the husband's policy and the children get five percent."

"You mean Sheila was insured for one-fifth of Bird's five million dollar policy?"

"Exactly, one million dollars if my math is correct."

"Thank you, Tex! You may have saved Rebekah's life."

"Really? How's that?"

"I'll explain later. I've got to run, talk to you later."

"Bye."

It all made sense now. Bird had married Sheila for the money he expected her to inherit. He never really loved her. When it became apparent she wasn't going to inherit anything anytime soon, he had to come up with an alternate plan. It was pretty clever buying a big policy on himself and sneaking in a rider on Sheila. It almost looked like he didn't plan it. Then all he had to do was set someone else up to take the fall for Sheila's death, and he's one million dollars richer.

# THE PLAN

**Monday**

OVER THE WEEKEND I advised Ken of the insurance on Sheila's life and how cleverly Bird had purchased it. He was excited with this development, but warned me that having bought an insurance policy on Sheila did not prove anything. His only hope was that he could plant some reasonable doubt into the juror's minds by telling them about Melissa and Bird and pointing out to them how each of them would gain by Sheila's death.

Over the very depressing weekend, I had spent most of my time trying to convince Rebekah she was not doomed. In the process of brainstorming about the case, we came up with a plan to try to trick Bird into confessing. I called Ken and told him about it, and he said he would check with the DA and see if they'd go along with it.

On Monday I got a phone call from Ken's office, letting me know that we had a meeting with the DA at his office at eleven. I figured the DA must have liked my idea and agreed to participate in the plan. I arrived at the Dallas courthouse at 10:55 A.M. and took the elevator to the seventh floor. Ken was sitting in the waiting room reading a magazine when I arrived.

"So the DA must have liked my idea, huh?"

"Apparently."

"Good. I think it just might work."

Ken got up and told the receptionist we were ready to see Paul Snyder. After a minute a tall, skinny man with curly blond hair walked out into the reception room and greeted us.

"Hello Ken. How are you?" Mr. Snyder said, as he shook Ken's hand. Then he turned to me, smiled, extended his hand and said, "You must be Stan Turner, free-lance detective *extraordinaire*."

"What?" I replied, puzzled by his remark.

"I'm just joking with you, Stan. That was pretty nice work on the Melba Thorn murder."

"Oh, thanks," I said. "But I'm not so sure I did anything extraordinary. It seems someone has been manipulating me."

"Really? So you think there's more to this story than what the press have been reporting," Snyder said.

"Oh yeah, definitely."

"Well that's all very interesting, but luckily I don't have to prosecute those cases so let's talk about your wife," Snyder said. "Anyway, your idea about blackmailing Bird Logan is intriguing."

"Nobody knows you hired Miguel, right?" Snyder said.

"True."

"If he contacted Bird and said you had hired him and that he was about to report back to you with lots of incriminating evidence, that might get Bird's attention . . . if he's the murderer."

"That was my thinking," I said.

"Do you think Miguel would be willing to do it?" Snyder asked.

"Miguel will do just about anything if you pay his price. He's got a big family so he needs the work."

"The question I have to ask myself is: Why should I do this? I've got a suspect with motive, opportunity and plenty of witnesses who saw her at the scene of the crime. Why should I bust my ass on the eve of trial to try to prove someone else did it?"

"Because you're not absolutely sure Rebekah did it, and you couldn't sleep at night if you thought an innocent woman might have gone to prison," Ken replied.

"You give me too much credit, Ken. I'll sleep just fine whether we do this or not. If I do it, it will be because it can't hurt. I have nothing to lose. If Bird falls for the trap, then I've got my killer. If he doesn't, I've strengthened by case against Rebekah."

"I don't care why you're doing it," I said. "Let's just get on with it. We're running out of time."

"Okay, but understand you'll have to foot the bill on this since it's for your wife's benefit."

"No problem, I'll cover it."

"Good, then I'll talk to the local police and you get with Miguel."

"I will, thank you Mr. Snyder, I really appreciate you doing this."

When I got back to the office, I called Miguel and asked him if he would participate in our plan. He agreed if I gave him another two thousand dollars now and five thousand if Bird incriminated himself. I didn't have much choice so I agreed. We decided Miguel would contact Bird at his home in Corpus. The phones would be tapped and if they met, Miguel would be wearing a wire. It was agreed the ploy would begin on Wednesday as it would take a couple days to set up.

# MONICA SANDS

**Tuesday**

MY ADRENALINE WAS PUMPING in anticipation of Wednesday's escapade. I went over the details of the plan in my mind. If it were going to work, there couldn't be any last minute glitches. There wasn't time for a postponement; Wednesday was it. After a while I realized I had been staring out the window for some time. Looking at my watch I saw it was ten-fifteen. I gazed at the pile of work stacked up on my credenza, but I had no motivation to work on it. Suddenly the phone rang and jerked me from my trance. It was Ken.

"I'm meeting Melissa Madigan's friend, Monica Sands, at the Golden Eagle restaurant in Richardson. Wanna come?"

"Absolutely, what time?"

"Eleven-thirty. I thought we'd beat the crowd."

"Good, I'll be there."

My thoughts shifted from Bird to Melissa. In my heart I didn't think Melissa was the murderer. She was so sweet and was concerned about Rebekah, but she did say she knew Rebekah wasn't a murderer. How would she know that? I wondered. At eleven o'clock I grabbed my coat and took off for the meeting. No one was there yet so I got a booth and waited. At eleven twenty-five a young redhead walked in and looked around nervously. I surmised it must be Monica Sands. Ken walked in right after her and they exchanged greetings. I got up and waved to Ken and he escorted Monica over to where I had been sitting.

"Thanks a lot for meeting with us, Ms. Sands. I know you're probably pretty busy, but this is important."

"Yes, Melissa told me that you might call."

"That's good. We won't take much of your time, I just have a few questions. We can eat first if you want."

"No, I'm a little nervous so let's get the questions over with first."

"Fine, I understand you went to the comin'-in party for Parker #3?"

"Right, Melissa asked me to go with her. It sounded exciting so I agreed."

"Did you meet Sheila and Bird Logan?"

"Just a quick introduction, I really didn't get to talk to them. It was pretty crowded and they were busy entertaining all the investors."

"Did you witness the confrontation between Sheila Logan and Rebekah Turner?"

Miss Sands put her hand over her mouth to hide her expression. "Oh yes," I thought it funny at the time, but obviously it's not so funny now." Miss Sands looked at me and said, "I'm sorry Mr. Turner about your wife. I hope she didn't do it."

"Thank you, she didn't."

"You know, Mr. Logan probably set you up, don't you?"

"What do you mean?"

"He wanted Sheila to have a boyfriend just in case he got caught with Melissa."

"Now how would you know that, honey?" Ken asked.

"Well, Melissa told me one time that Bird was hoping Sheila would have an affair so he would have a little insurance."

"So you think Bird encouraged Stan and Sheila to have an affair?" Ken asked.

"You should have seen the hostesses pumping both of them with champagne all night. It wouldn't have surprised me if Bird hadn't instructed them to do that."

"Why were you watching Stan and Sheila?"

"Well, Melissa asked me to. You know, she was very interested in both of them."

"I see. Did you see anything else unusual?"

"Mr. Logan had a conversation with both Stan and Sheila just before they met at the bunkhouse."

"Oh really?"

"Could you hear what they said?"

"No, it was too noisy to even think, let alone hear someone talking twenty yards away."

"Did you see Stan and Sheila go into the bunkhouse?"

"Yes, I sure did. I was following Stan, Mr. Turner, and when they were both inside I went and told Melissa what was going on."

"What did she do then?"

"She hightailed it over to the bunkhouse to see for herself."

"Okay, the next day when you went home, did you see anything unusual?"

"No, nothing other than Sheila and Bird arguing. Oh, and of course the wreck."

"The wreck?" Ken said."

"Yeah, you know, when Bird stopped for the dog."

"You and Melissa saw the wreck?"

"Sure, we didn't stop because the police and ambulance were already there, and Melissa saw Bird climb into the ambulance so she knew he was okay."

"What did you do after that?"

"Melissa dropped me off at my place and I crashed on the sofa and watched TV."

"Did you go out at all Sunday?"

"No, my boyfriend came over and we just messed around and then went out to dinner."

"Well, honey, thank you for the information. How about some lunch now?"

"That's all?"

"That's it, you've been a great help."

After lunch Miss Sands left, and Ken and I had another cup of coffee while we analyzed the information Miss Sands had provided us.

"That was certainly an enlightening interview," I said.

"That it was, son. This case is getting more intriguing every day. Unfortunately, I'm not sure we're any closer to determining the killer's identity than we were an hour ago."

"True, I guess there's no doubt now that Bird was setting me up to be Sheila's lover, but we don't know for sure if he was also setting Rebekah up to take the fall for Sheila's murder."

"Exactly, and now we know that Melissa was aware that Sheila was in the hospital. I'd lay you odds she went to the hospital to see what was going on."

"I think you're right."

"Well, this afternoon I'm going to the hospital and pass Melissa's picture around to see if anyone saw her."

"Where did you get a picture of her?"

"I had someone catch her coming out of work yesterday."

"Huh. Well let me know what you find out."

"I will."

We got up and left the restaurant. I decided not to go back to the office and opted to go home and check on Rebekah and the kids. As I drove home, I began to ponder what life would be like without Rebekah. How would I bring up four children under age ten without her? I began to feel angry that this was happening to us. After all, what had we done to deserve this? We had worked so hard to get where we were in life, and now, for no good reason, our life was about to be shattered. It wasn't fair. It just wasn't fair.

Rebekah and the kids were happy to see me. It seemed like the right moment to talk to the kids about what was happening and prepare them for the worst. Rebekah was sitting on the sofa and the kids were sitting around me on the floor.

"Do you kids understand what's going to happen next week?"

"Yeah, Mom's going on trial for murder," Reggie said. "But she'll be found innocent, won't she?"

"Probably, but you know sometimes innocent people are convicted."

"That won't happen will it, Daddy," Mark said, as he began to cry.

"It might, so you kids are going to have to be strong. If Mom is convicted, we'll appeal it. We'll do everything we can to keep her out of jail."

"Mark, why are you crying?" Peter said.

"Mom's going to jail, they're going to take her away from us."

"Mommie, they won't take you away, will they?" Peter asked, as his eyes began to swell up.

"No, I hope not, but just in case they do, you need to be prepared." Peter crawled over to Rebekah and latched on to her leg. Rebekah gently stroked his hair and then pulled him up into her lap.

"We knew you kids would hear about what was going on so we wanted to discuss it together to be sure you understood what was happening," I said. "If you have any questions, just come to me or Mom and we'll talk about it, okay?"

"I love you Mommie, I won't let them take you away," Mark said.

"I know, honey . . . I know."

# THE RUSE

**Wednesday**

WHEN THE APPOINTED HOUR arrived, Ken, Snyder, Miguel and some local detectives had gathered at Miguel's office. The phone was being monitored and taped. Miguel picked up the phone and made the call.

"Hello," a male voice said.

"Hello, Mr. Bird Logan please."

"This is he."

"Yes, Mr. Logan . . . this is Miguel Valdez . . . you don't know me, but I know a lot about you."

"What do you want?" Bird asked.

"I'm a private investigator and I've been hired to search into your past and find out all of your hidden secrets," Miguel chuckled.

"Well if you think I'm going to tell you anything, you're fucking crazy!" Bird replied.

"No, . . . no, you don't understand, I've already learned everything about you there is to know."

"Oh yeah, like what?"

"I know you killed your wife and I know why you did it," Miguel said.

Bird was silent for a moment and then he responded.

"You're fucking crazy, good-bye!" he said and hung up.

"Damn it!" Ken said. "I thought we had him."

"No, actually I thought that went quite well," Snyder said. "He's not stupid. He's not going to say anything incriminating over the telephone. I'm sure he knows his phone is tapped."

"So what now?" I said.

"If he's interested, he'll probably go to a phone booth and call back to set up a meeting," Snyder said.

"But, how's he going to do that, Miguel didn't even give him a phone number," I said.

"I looked in the Yellow Pages, there is only one private investigator named Miguel. If he wants to find him, he'll do it and it won't take him long."

"So what do we do now?" Ken said.

"Order pizza," Miguel replied.

Miguel got on the phone and order a pizza and we all sat around hoping for a phone call. After about an hour our patience paid off.

"Hello, Miguel Valdez."

"Hello, this is Bird Logan, is this the Miguel I was talking with earlier today?" Bird asked.

"Yeah man, I tried to talk to you this morning and you hung up on me," Miguel said.

"What do you expect. This kind of thing isn't something you talk about over the phone. We need to meet."

"Okay, I'll be happy to meet you Mr. Bird, just tell me the time and the place."

"The bait shop off Ocean Boulevard at the end of the pier . . . 5:30 P.M. sharp."

"Okay man, I'll be there," Miguel said.

"Good."

Miguel put down the phone and smiled gleefully. "The Bird has taken the bait."

"All right!" I screamed.

Ken smiled and extended his hand to congratulate me. Snyder looked pleased, I guess he won either way. It didn't matter to him whether Rebekah or Bird killed Sheila as long as he got credit for convicting the real murderer. During the next several hours Miguel and Snyder worked on his script for his meeting with Logan. When the appointed hour approached, Miguel was fitted for his wire and all the electronic equipment was tested.

At five o'clock Miguel got in his Jeep and drove to the pier off Ocean Boulevard. We all followed him in a gold Chevy van driven by two undercover police officers dressed for a day on the beach. Miguel got to the appointed meeting place at 5:20 P.M. and waited. We all huddled inside the van and listened. At 5:35 P.M. Bird made his move.

"Sir, you wouldn't be Miguel would you?" Bird said.

"Yes, you must be Bird," Miguel replied.

"Let's take a walk down the beach."

"Sure."

There was about a minute of silence as the two strolled down to the beach. We could hear the wind blowing, the sea gulls screaming and the waves pounding on the sand, as well as Miguel's heart beating rapidly.

"Now what's all this about information you've dug up?" Bird said.

"I was hired to gather evidence against you for use in the Rebekah Turner trial. I've been checking into your background and all of your activities for the past few years," Miguel said.

"Who's your client?" Bird asked.

"Well, I'm not at liberty to say, but he's not a rich man and can only pay me a pittance for my work. On the other hand I know you are about to become a very wealthy man, and this information is much more valuable to you."

"So, it's safe to say you haven't told anyone about what you've turned up."

"No, absolutely not. No one knows yet, but my client is pressing me for the information so I'll have to tell him soon. Unless, of course, someone else wants to buy the information for a higher, much higher, price."

"I don't know what you think you've got on me. I had nothing to do with my wife's death, but I don't want you spreading lies about me that might get Rebekah Turner acquitted."

"Of course, I understand, you had nothing to do with your wife's murder, and Jesus was never a Jew, right?" Miguel laughed.

"You think you're a real comedian, don't you?"

"I'm sorry man, but you crack me up."

"Let's cut the bullshit, okay? How much do you want?"

"Well, for a man who's about to get a million dollars does it matter?"

"You're damn right it matters. What's your price?"

"One hundred thousand dollars would be satisfactory."

"You're fucking crazy! I'm not paying you a hundred grand," Bird said.

"Well, okay, . . . just forget it then. It doesn't make any difference to me whether you die in the gas chamber or not."

"Why you dirty prick! How do you know I won't just kill you and dump your body in the bay?"

"Do I look stupid? My cousin has all the information in a manila envelope addressed to the district attorney in Dallas. If I don't come home tonight by seven o'clock, he's going to put it in the mail."

"If I give you the $100,000, how do I know you won't come back for more later?"

"You have my word, of course, but I know you have killed two, maybe three people already so if I tried to press my luck with you, I'd most likely end up dead, right?"

"You're full of shit. I haven't killed anybody, but you're damn right. I will kill you if you double-cross me!"

"Good then. We have a deal?"

"I'll give you twenty-five thousand and not one penny more?"

"Isn't your freedom worth a hundred grand?"

"Twenty-five thousand, take it or leave it!"

"Okay, I'll take it."

"How do you want me to deliver the money to you?"

"In anticipation of us doing business, I took the liberty of getting a locker in the dressing room over by the bait shop. Here is the key. Put the money in a beach bag, nothing larger than twenty-dollar bills, and leave it in the locker. Then have the key returned to me by messenger by five. I'll give the messenger the manila envelope when I get the key."

"Fine, but remember, if you double-cross me, you're a dead man."

"Don't worry man, I want to stay healthy so I can spend all the money."

"Okay, one last thing, what are you going to tell your client?"

"I'm going to say I didn't find anything very interesting. You're just a model citizen, right?"

"Okay, get the fuck out of here! I don't want to ever see your face again."

"No problem, man. It was a pleasure doing business with you."

Later that evening, Ken, Snyder and I took a Southwest flight back to Dallas. Before we left I called Rebekah and told her the good news. She was excited and told me to hurry home so we could celebrate. On the plane I was excited and relieved that Rebekah was off the hook so I was buying cocktails for everybody on the plane and no one was turning them down. When the plane arrived, Rebekah was waiting for me at the gate. After I called, she had gotten a baby-sitter and was ready to celebrate. I asked Ken and Snyder to join us but they politely declined.

Thirty minutes later we were sitting on the top of the Southland Life Building in downtown Dallas enjoying a delicious steak dinner and a bottle of champagne. From this posh little restaurant you could see the entire city and at night the lights were magnificent. "I bet you never thought your life would be so exciting, did you?" I said.

"Somehow being on trial for murder isn't the kind of excitement I relish," Rebekah replied.

"Do you realize I've been practicing law six months now?" I said.

"Yes and do you realize after we eat these steaks, we won't have enough money to buy breakfast tomorrow?" Rebekah replied.

"Well, if it hadn't been for all your legal expenses, we'd be sitting pretty."

"Well, if you'd kept your eyes off Sheila Logan, I wouldn't have had any legal expenses."

"Yeah, . . . maybe . . . but anyway, it was a pretty good six months overall, don't you think?"

Rebekah laughed. "We're both still alive if that's what you mean. Neither one of us is in jail! . . . Hey, that's a plus."

"Okay, okay, . . . but aren't you happy?" I said.

Rebekah looked up at me with her big brown eyes, smiled and replied, "Yes, Stan Turner, I'm happy. Then she broke out in laughter. "I don't think I'll live past thirty, but it's going to be a hell of a ride getting there."

"You're a real clown," I said. "I'll try to make the next six months less exciting."

"Good."

The next day there was a prominent story in the newspaper about the arrest of Bird Logan for his wife's murder and the dismissal of all charges against Rebekah. The story intimated that Bird might have been responsible for his first wife's death as well. For the first time since Sheila's death, I began to think of her. She was a wonderful woman, and it was so outrageous that her life had been suddenly snatched away from her. I felt anger and sadness at her loss, so much so I couldn't hold back my tears. When Rebekah walked in and saw my distress she questioned me.

"What's wrong, Stan?"

"Oh, . . . nothing, I'm just glad all this mess is over."

"Me too. You sure you don't want to go back to selling insurance?"

"Are you kidding . . . no way."

# REVELATION

SEVERAL DAYS LATER I was at the office pondering what to do about Jane Thorn when General Burton came in, nodded and went into his office. It was a beautiful day and he had obviously been to the golf course. I got up, followed him to his office and stood in the doorway.

"So, how'd you shoot?"

"Horrible, I couldn't putt worth a damn."

"Oh really. That's too bad," I said. "Oh, guess what?"

"What?" the general said, as he looked up at me.

"I'm having lunch today with Jane Brown."

"What's the occasion?"

"We're going to talk about the work I'm going to be doing for Thorn Enterprises in the future."

"Well, that's great, Stan, I'm happy for you."

"I'd invite you along, but Jane might want to talk in private."

"Well, that's okay. I understand. I've got a lot of work to do anyway."

"I'll see you later then."

"Okay."

At twelve o'clock Ralph walked in the door and advised me Jane was waiting in the car. I followed him to the limousine, joined Jane in the back seat and we drove off. Ralph took us to a very chic French Restaurant near Northpark. We went inside and were seated quickly. Jane obviously had frequented this establishment many times as they treated her like a queen. The waiter brought us drinks and French bread and then took our orders. We sat and engaged in casual conversation with soft music playing in the background.

"So Stan I heard about your wife. It's so wonderful they dropped the charges," Jane said.

"Oh, I know. I've never been so happy," I replied. "The last few months have been hell, but I guess you, more than anyone, can appreciate what it's like to have a family member charged with murder."

"Oh yes, it's been very difficult for me with Taylor and Robert under indictment. The stress is something awful," Jane said.

"Jane, something's been bothering me about your mother's death?"

"What's that?"

"How in the hell did I get involved?" I said.

"You were just lucky I guess. Someone just picked you out of the blue to start the ball rolling," Jane replied.

"I don't think so. I think I was carefully picked and manipulated as part of an intricate plan to gain control of Thorn Enterprises."

"What are you saying, Stan?"

"I want to know why you picked me for your grand scheme?"

"What are you talking about, what grand scheme?"

"Don't play innocent with me, you called me pretending to be your mother, didn't you?"

"No, you're crazy. . . . What's got into you?"

"I know Ralph killed your mother."

"What? That's ridiculous."

"Come on, quit the charade. I know Ralph took Robert's limo and followed your mother on Highway 24 and ran her off the road near Wilkerson Pass. Ralph's more than your driver, isn't he Jane?"

"Stan you've really got a lot of nerve. I'm leaving," Jane said, as she started to get up.

"Sit down, Jane!" I haven't finished. I'm not quite sure why you had to kill Ronald Sage. Did he find out about your scheme by accident or was he in on it from the beginning?"

Jane stared at me silently as I continued. "It was pretty clever though, planting all that evidence to make the police think Taylor and Robert were the murderers. Is money and power all that important to you that you would kill your own mother and send your brother and husband to the gas chamber?"

"You don't know what it's like to be treated like a piece of furniture all you life. Mom never cared about me, all she wanted me to do was to look pretty and keep quiet. I asked her to let me help in the business after Dad died, but it was like talking to a rock, and Robert just laughed at the idea. I hated them. I felt like a zombie. Was I alive or was I dead? I wasn't sure."

"What about Taylor, didn't you love him?"

"Get serious, he was Mom's idea. I was part of the merger between Thorn Enterprises and Brown Properties."

"So you decided to have it all, huh? It was certainly an ingenious plan, setting up your brother and husband to take the fall for your mother's death, and then having to take over control of Thorn Enterprises in the midst of such tragedy. I think your family greatly misjudged your business acumen."

"They never gave me a chance. I know I can run Thorn Enterprises ten times better than any of them and I'm going to show them."

"But the most incredible part of the scheme was getting me involved. You figured you'd get some kid right out of law school, who didn't know his ass from an earlobe, to stumble onto your mother's murder. You figured handling me would be easy, didn't you?"

"That's right, and if you mention one word of this garbage you've been spouting off here today, I'll have you disbarred. Everybody knows what a person tells their attorney is privileged, and you can't tell a soul anything you know that might incriminate me," Jane said.

"You're absolutely right, but do you remember that check you gave me for ten thousand dollars?"

"Yes, your retainer check."

"It was from Thorn Enterprises, Jane; I'm not your attorney. I work for Thorn Enterprises and I called the sheriff a day or two ago and told him to check Ralph's boot for blood . . . my blood. Was that you who lured me into opening my door so Ralph could beat the shit out of me?"

Jane glared at me without a sound. "You're out of your mind."

"I don't think so. The sheriff called me this morning and said they indeed found my blood on Ralph's boot. It's over Jane. The police are on their way over right now to arrest you."

I looked up and noticed two uniformed policemen and a detective talking to a waiter. He pointed toward Jane and the men approached us.

"One more thing Jane. I'm curious, how did you find me anyway?"

"Gena Lombardi told me all about you. She's my travel agent. When she told me you were renting an office from General Burton, I couldn't believe it, it was perfect."

"Jane Brown," the detective said.

"Yes."

"You'll have to come with us. We've got a warrant for your arrest." The two uniformed officers grabbed Jane by both arms and pulled her up out of her chair.

"I'm coming, you don't have to manhandle me."

"I'm sorry Jane, I always liked you, I never thought it would end this way."

The next day I got a phone call from Gena. Apparently she forgot she had promised to drive Miss Texas Wine Country in her Corvette in the Fourth of July parade. They had just called her to confirm that she would be there, and she wanted me to cover for her. Since Gena had been so nice to give me the car I could hardly refuse.

I met Miss Texas Wine Country at the staging area. She climbed into the Corvette and sat on the back of the rear seat. She was beautiful in her white swimsuit and I was proud to be driving her in the parade. As we took our place in line, the bands began playing and the crowd roared with delight over the magnificent floats on display.

When the parade was over, I was tempted to get better acquainted with my passenger, but luckily Rebekah and the kids showed up before I had a chance. After the parade we took the kids to the midway at Fair Park, which was open for the Fourth of July. Then we watched a spectacular fireworks show. It was a fitting end to the first six months of my legal career.

That night there was a full moon, the stars were radiant and Rebekah and I were in an amorous mood. We put the kids to bed early and retired to the bedroom. Rebekah had made a miraculous recovery in the few days since her case was dismissed. The tension in her face was gone, her bloodshot eyes had cleared up and the color had returned to her face. As I gazed into her eyes, I silently thanked God for delivering us through the horrors of the past few months. She smiled at me as if she could read my mind, then reached up and gently pulled my lips down to hers.

We made love that night more passionately than we'd ever done it before. When our energy was spent we lay in each other's arms in a peaceful bliss.

"That was wonderful," Rebekah said. "I guess I need to go on trial for murder more often."

"Well, I almost lost you, babe. I've been worried sick about you. I don't know what I would have done if you'd been convicted."

"You probably would have found some cute blond to take my place."

"No way, no one could ever replace you."

"She wouldn't have been as good a mother as me though. Our kids would have suffered had they hauled me off to prison."

"That's for sure."

Rebekah laughed. "Bird was such a fool to fall for our little scheme."

"Huh?"

"He was so paranoid he paid twenty-five thousand dollars to shut up Miguel. . . . What a fool; Miguel didn't have shit."

"What?"

"You know what I love about you, Stan. You're so positive. Everything you see glitters. You never see the evil in people. You always look for something good and when you find it, you're blinded by it."

"You're talking in circles, Rebekah. I don't understand what you're talking about."

Rebekah laughed and shook her head. "You're so naive. Do you think I'd let another woman have you? Sheila was after you from the minute she laid eyes on you. I could see that the first time we met."

"What?"

"I've got ten years and four children invested in you Stanley Turner, and no little bitch is going to take that away from me! Trust me!"

I sat up in the bed and looked at Rebekah in disbelief.

"Rebekah, cut it out! You're scaring me."

"I'm sorry, I can't keep this inside me. I've got to tell someone. I couldn't believe my good fortune when I saw Bird and he told me what had happened. God, what luck!"

"I don't want to hear this. You told me you were innocent. I believed you! I trusted you!"

Rebekah sat up, smiled and laughed, "Like I said, that's what I love about you, Stan. You're so gullible. . . . Okay. . . . Okay. . . . Relax, I'm just fooling with you."

*Brash Endeavor* is author William L. Manchee's third novel, he also penned *Twice Tempted* and *Undaunted.* In addition to writing, Manchee practices law in Dallas, Texas, where he lives with his wife and four children.

# What people are saying about Brash Endeavor

## Review, Dallas Observer, Thursday, July 30, 1998

William Manchee could be Dallas' answer to John Grisham. Manchee, an author who has maintained a private law firm in Dallas since 1975, recently published Brash Endeavor, a page-turning tale of a small-time lawyer in over his head with some big time clients. Just like Grisham's books, the protagonist appears to be a thinly veiled version of Manchee. The novel follows Stan Turner--the character that Manchee introduced in the well-received Undaunted—as he moves to Dallas to open up his own law practice and becomes involved with an insurance scam that ends up with his wife being falsely accused of murder. It sounds like just the kind of potboiler that Grisham is known for. Let's just hope Manchee doesn't option any of his books to movie producers.

*Allison Robson*, a newscaster for *CBS Affiliate, KLBK TV, Ch 13* in Lubbock, Texas recently wrote, *"Brash Endeavor"* was fabulous-a real page turner-I didn't want it to end!

Manchee spins a good yarn, and Stan Turner is a believable and likeable character that I plan to read again and again. *Chris Rogers, author of Bitch Factor and Rage Factor.*